## *"What kind of car do you drive?"*

"What?" Emily laughed a little. "My car? A Mazda. Why?"

Adam shrugged. "Just curious. It suddenly seemed very strange to me that you've worked for me for—what? ten years?—and I don't even know what kind of car you drive."

She took a sip of her drink and smiled. The taut lines around her eyes and mouth were loosening, and her cheeks had taken on a bit of color. "I know what you drive. A BMW. Beige."

"See? That's what I mean. You know a lot more about me than I know about you. You must be secretive."

"I'm not!" Emily protested. "There's just not anything to know about me."

"We'll see about that." He paused and thoughtfully sipped his drink, studying her. Emily shifted a little under his gaze. "Ah-hah." He pointed a forefinger at her. "The first signs of nervousness. You have something to hide."

Dear Reader,

When two people fall in love, the world is suddenly new and exciting, and it's that same excitement we bring to you in Silhouette Intimate Moments. These are stories with scope, with grandeur. These characters lead the lives we all dream of, and everything they do reflects the wonder of being in love.

Longer and more sensuous than most romances, Silhouette Intimate Moments novels take you away from everyday life and let you share the magic of love. Adventure, glamour, drama, even suspense— these are the passwords that let you into a world where love has a power beyond the ordinary, where the best authors in the field today create stories of love and commitment that will stay with you always.

In coming months look for novels by your favorite authors: Maura Seger, Parris Afton Bonds, Elizabeth Lowell and Erin St. Claire, to name just a few. And whenever you buy books, look for all the Silhouette Intimate Moments, love stories *for* today's women *by* today's women.

Leslie J. Wainger
Senior Editor
Silhouette Books

# A Very Special Favor

## Kristin James

Silhouette Intimate Moments

Published by Silhouette Books New York

**America's Publisher of Contemporary Romance**

SILHOUETTE BOOKS
300 E. 42nd St., New York, N.Y. 10017

ISBN: 0-373-07136-1

First Silhouette Books printing March 1986

America's Publisher of Contemporary Romance

Printed in the U.S.A.

**Silhouette Books by Kristin James**

Silhouette Intimate Moments

*Dreams of Evening* #1
*The Amber Sky* #17
*Morning Star* #45
*Secret Fires* #69
*Worlds Apart* #89
*Cutter's Lady* #125
*A Very Special Favor* #136

## KRISTIN JAMES

a former attorney, is married to a family counselor, and they have a young daughter. Her family and her writing keep her busy, but when she does have free time, she loves to read. In addition to her contemporary romances, she has written several historicals under another name.

# Chapter 1

It was the most miserable birthday of her life.

Emily couldn't think of many that had been especially happy, but this one was the bottom of the barrel. She hadn't wanted to turn thirty; somehow she had always assumed she would manage to avoid it. But there it was, as real as anything: April 14, and she was thirty years old.

She wiped away the fog on the bathroom mirror, put there by her long, steamy shower, and leaned closer until her nose was almost touching the glass. There was the faintest crinkling of skin around her eyes, a softening at the edge of her lids that presaged lines and wrinkles. And there, between her brows—wasn't that a line? Emily fumbled for her glasses on the counter beside the sink and put them on. Yes, that was definitely a thin line right above the bridge of her nose.

Emily sighed. She felt like crying. The steam fogged up her glasses, and she removed them. Glumly she plugged in the blow dryer and began to dry her hair. It was a long operation, as her hair hung halfway down her back. She stared sightlessly into the mirror as she wafted the black gunlike dryer over her head; without her glasses, her reflection was a blur unless she stuck her face right up against the mirror. But it didn't matter. She didn't do anything special to her hair as she dried it; it simply hung long and straight. And she had no desire to stare at her image for fifteen or twenty minutes; she knew all too well what she looked like.

She was plain. Her fine hair was dark ash-blond, the color often called "dishwater blond." It was an apt term, she thought, at least in the tone it conveyed; her hair had the colorless quality of blond hair, with none of its golden brightness. Her face wasn't ugly, but it was ordinary in the extreme; there were no high cheekbones, nothing unusual about her mouth or nose, no vivid color in her cheeks. Her eyes were large, but of a soft gray color that did nothing to capture anyone's attention, and they were surrounded by lashes as pale as her hair. Besides, the large glasses she wore successfully hid her eyes. All in all, hers was a face that faded into the background, the kind that was hard to recall minutes after seeing her.

Emily flicked off the dryer and set it down, flexing her stiff arm. She glanced down at her body. It was as unimpressive as her face. She was taller than average, and slender, with rather nice legs, but her breasts were too small to say that she had a nice shape. It didn't seem fair. You'd think that women who weren't attractive shouldn't worry about aging. After all, if you had never had the looks to begin with, why should you be scared of losing them? But that wasn't the way it worked at all. Instead, she found herself bitterly regretting the loss of one of the few assets she had had: youth.

Emily's lips twitched in irritation, and she forced herself to return to the job of getting ready for work. She didn't often indulge in feeling sorry for herself. Usually she was quick to point out that she had a wonderful boss and an interesting job, no illnesses or handicaps, enough money to buy the things she wanted, and even a nice amount in savings. Her life was a vast improvement over her mother's or aunt's. She had a great deal more than a lot of people, and it was pointless to cry because she didn't have everything she wanted. But today she couldn't seem to shake the bluesy feeling.

She dressed quickly, pulling on underwear, hose and a slip, then a plain, light-brown suit with an eggshell-white blouse beneath. She stepped into low-heeled, comfortable flats. The outfit did little for her skin or hair, but it was quiet, comfortable and inconspicuous, which suited Emily. All her life she had tried to draw as little attention to herself as possible. She would have felt foolish in something bright or eye-catching. It would be like a plain old cow dressing up in silks and satins—beautiful clothes, she thought, would only serve to point up her own plainness. The thing that horrified her the most was someone staring or laughing at her.

She pulled her hair back and fastened it in a wide barrette. While Emily preferred to wear her hair long, she hated it hanging down beside her face and getting in her way while she worked, so she typically caught it at the nape of her neck with a barrette or ribbon and let it lie in a long tail down her back. She applied a light lipstick, the only makeup she wore, and left her room.

As she drew near the kitchen, the sound of women's voices raised in a quarrel assaulted her ears, and she grimaced. They were at it again. Couldn't they ever get along?

"...can't even make a simple piece of toast," Aunt Rosemary was saying bitingly as Emily stepped into the room. Her aunt stood beside the stove, holding a blackened piece of bread out in front of her accusingly, glaring across the room at Emily's mother. Rosemary's graying hair was twisted into a tight bun, and she wore a long, dark-gray, corduroy robe. Her face was devoid of makeup and stern as a judge's.

Nancy, Emily's mother, was braced against the kitchen counter, her arms crossed in front of her and her chin thrust out defiantly. As always, she was in vivid contrast to her sister, with her large hoop earrings, her hair an unnaturally bright shade of gold, and a flimsy, hot-pink robe barely concealing the black slip beneath it. She had not yet put on her makeup for the day, but her lashes were still sticky and black with mascara from the night before. Emily felt the usual twist of pain and embarrassment. Why did her mother try to look like someone straight off the streets?

"If you didn't go out drinking all night, things like this wouldn't happen," Aunt Rosemary continued primly, her mouth a thin, censorious line. Emily disliked her aunt's attitude as much as her mother's. Nancy embarrassed her, but Rosemary invariably raised her hackles.

"Good morning," she said, to interrupt the fight, and both women swung her way.

"Hello, Angel." A broad smile lit Nancy's face, and Emily had to smile back. Nancy had never been a particularly good mother; she had usually been more interested in parties, men and fun than in raising a young daughter. But there had never been any doubt in Emily's mind that Nancy loved her, even during those years after Emily's father deserted them and Nancy had left Emily with Rosemary for long stretches of time.

"Good morning, Emily." Her aunt's smile was tight and perfunctory, but she threw an approving glance over Emily's outfit. Rosemary wasn't the kind to express her love for her niece, but Emily knew that she, too, cared for Emily in her own way. She had raised her sister's child much of the time and had done it without complaint, and she took a great deal of pride in the way Emily had turned out—far more than she did in her own daughter, Jeanette.

"We were getting breakfast ready," Nancy explained, and Emily had to hide a smile.

Rosemary glared at Nancy. "*I* was getting breakfast ready. *You* were letting the toast burn."

"Why do you keep harping on that?" Nancy shot back, her hands on her hips. "It was just a little mistake."

"Everything you ever do is 'just a little mistake.'"

Emily sighed. "Mother. Aunt Rosemary. Please." For the umpteenth time she wondered why the two sisters, so unable to get along together, insisted on living with each other. Even more, she wondered why she remained here with them.

Emily had continued living with her mother after she was grown both out of habit and to help her mother financially. Nancy's job as a clerk in a department store was anything but highly paid, and the modest rent Emily gave her had enabled her to keep up the mortgage payments. Two years ago Rosemary and Nancy had decided to pool their resources, and Rosemary had moved in with them. That had made it financially unnecessary for Emily to remain, but still she had stayed. Rosemary had looked at her disapprovingly the time or two she had mentioned getting her own apartment; and Nancy, coming close to tears, had reminded her how little time they had spent together when Emily was a child. Emily had felt like retorting that that had been Nancy's fault, not hers, but she had bitten back the words. And she had stayed. It had seemed like a small enough thing to do, and she had no particular reason to leave. Certainly she didn't have enough of a social life for the two women's presence to interfere. Most of the time Emily was content. She could retreat to her bedroom when she needed solitude. But today their bickering was more than she could bear.

"Couldn't we forget it? There's no harm done. I'll put in another slice of toast."

Nancy beamed at her and tossed a look of triumph at her sister. Rosemary's mouth tightened even further, and she turned back to the stove to prepare the scrambled eggs. Nancy sat down at the table and began to gossip about the next-door neighbor's granddaughter, who had taken up with a struggling rock musician. At the stove, Rosemary's back grew stiffer and stiffer.

Finally, as Rosemary set down the bowl of eggs on the table, she intoned, "That girl is going to the Devil."

Emily dished out a small amount of eggs, grabbed a slice of toast and ate hurriedly. If there was anything worse than her mother's gossip, it was a lecture from her aunt on the wages of sin. She took a final gulp of orange juice and stood up. "I have to run. Thanks for breakfast, Aunt Rosemary."

"You work too hard," her mother scolded. "It's not even seven-thirty."

"I know. But I have a pile of work on my desk." It wasn't a lie, exactly. There was always a pile of work on her desk to be done; there was just no special reason for her to go in early today to see to it.

She smiled and waved to the two women, grabbed her purse from the counter, and hurried out the side door. She went lightly down the two cement steps and along the narrow driveway to the street. Rosemary's car was parked under the single carport, her mother's in the driveway, and Emily's in front of the house on the street.

Her car was a blue Mazda RX-7 sports car, so low slung that she practically had to crawl into it. It was the kind of car no one expected Emily to own, and Emily loved it.

Though she tried her best to appear inconspicuous in her dress and makeup, the car was different. Inside it, she felt hidden from the world and unafraid of its opinion; it didn't matter that the RX-7 was a vivid blue or took off with a roar. She drove with speed and skill, loving the freedom and excitement of darting in and out of traffic, of hearing the engine vibrate with power. It was the one outward expression in her life of her inner yearning for excitement.

Emily took Reynolda Road downtown. Japanese cherry trees arched across it, heavily laden with pale-pink flowers, like a delicate, fluffy roof. The trees that lined Reynolda were beautiful any time of year, but they were especially lovely in April, when the cherry trees bloomed, and in the fall, when the leaves blazed golden. In those seasons Emily always took that route downtown, despite the fact that it was slower.

The familiar skyline came into sight after she passed Reynolds High and climbed the hill. There was the pint-sized replica of the Empire State Building that was the Reynolds Building, the white solidity of the Wachovia Building, the distinctive Hyatt Hotel tower, Integon, and the glittering blue glass box of Allied Central Bank, where she worked. She turned into the parking garage where she rented space by the month and parked her car in its assigned slot, then walked the four blocks to the bank. She passed through the glass doors into the spacious lobby, where a large fountain flowed peacefully, and took an elevator to the sixteenth floor, where she stepped out into a small lobby of hushed elegance.

*Marshall, Pierson, Tidrell, and Sommers*, stated conservative brass letters on the wall across from the elevators. A plush, muted-rust carpet softened the floor, and the walls were lined with paneling and pale, textured wall covering. Here and there dark-framed prints of the hunt, horses and the English countryside adorned the walls. The receptionist's desk was impressively large and dark, and the lobby couch and chairs were brown leather. Everything about the law offices bespoke age, money and competence.

It was not yet eight o'clock, and the receptionist, like most of the employees, wasn't there yet. The lobby and hall lights had been turned on, but most of the offices on both sides of the hall remained dark. Emily walked down the hall and turned the corner. Her office was three doors down, and she saw that it was ablaze with light, as was Adam Marshall's office across the hall. Adam must already be here. Even as she had the thought, Adam stepped out of her office, frowning, his head bent in thought.

After all these years, Emily was still struck anew by the crisp, masculine beauty of Adam Marshall's face and form. He was tall without being gangly, strong without being hulking. His shoulders were wide, his waist and hips slim, and his legs long. His hands were long and well-formed, sensitive, yet made unmistakably virile by the sprinkling of black hairs across the backs. Just to look at his hands made a woman imagine them on her skin, they were such a compelling mixture of tenderness and strength.

Adam's hair was black, thick and lustrous, but neatly trimmed. His eyebrows and lashes were as dark as his hair, the eyebrows straight slashes across his face, the lashes indecently thick and long. His eyes were a clear, piercing blue, in vivid contrast to the dark hair and lashes. The lines of his face were strong and clean, almost too handsome, but saved from perfection by a small scar near his lips that gave his mouth an amused quirk.

He was dressed in a pearl-gray, perfectly fitted, three-piece suit, and a silk shirt so pale a gray it was almost white, accented by a charcoal-gray silk tie. A discreet, oval, silver tie tack was nestled against the dark silk. Like the law office, he was the picture of wealth, breeding and competence. But there was more to him—a quality of rock-hard solidity, a sense of strength and determination. The combination of qualities made him a presence to be reckoned with in the courtroom. Out of court, it brought him any woman he wanted and more than a few he didn't.

Emily had loved him for years.

Adam glanced up and saw Emily, and he smiled with relief. "There you are. Good."

"Did you need something?"

"I was looking for the Raynor file."

Emily stepped past him into her office, unlocked her desk and pulled out the bottom drawer. "I was typing interrogatories on it yesterday, so I had it in here." She handed him the thick manila folder.

"Great. I don't know what I'd do without you." His mouth quirked up in the grin that always made Emily a litle weak in the knees. "Come into my office. I was dictating some notes for you, but you might as well take them down."

Emily grabbed a pen and pad from her desk and followed him across the hall. Adam's office was large, and furnished with the same heavy, walnut pieces found throughout the firm. His desk, a credenza and one chair were piled high with manila file folders, blue-backed documents and brown manuscript covers. His briefcase lay open on his desk, half filled, and he stuffed more folders into it as he talked to Emily. He reeled off a list of things for her to do that would take at least three days to accomplish, and Emily jotted them down rapidly, unconcerned by the impossibility of doing them all. In this office it wasn't normal if they weren't at least a week behind. Emily was accustomed to working well into the evenings or on the weekends.

Adam picked up a folder and flipped through it, pausing in his conversation to read a paragraph. Emily watched him, taking the chance to look at him unobserved. The sun fell through the wide, plate-glass window onto his hair, bringing out the faintly red highlights. Emily wondered how it would feel beneath her fingertips. She imagined sliding her fingers down his hair and onto the warm flesh of his neck. She swallowed and glanced away. It would never do for Adam to glance up and catch her gazing at him with her heart in her eyes.

"Okay." Adam closed the folder and tossed it into the briefcase. "Let's see—where was I?"

Emily glanced down at her yellow legal pad. "You wanted me to call Phil Barrett and move your appointment with him to Friday at eight."

"Yeah. My case starts Thursday, so I'll have to see him before court."

"The Parkins case?"

He nodded. "That's why I'm running over to Raleigh today." He closed the lid of the briefcase and snapped it shut. "I'll be gone all day. Oh, I almost forgot. Make a plane reservation for the engineer in Arizona. I'll put him on the stand Tuesday. So get him here Monday at a decent hour."

"Dr. Alexander?"

"Right. After you make the reservation, call and tell him. Better yet, tell his secretary. He's forgetful as hell unless you're talking about downdrafts and wind speeds."

"All right." Emily dutifully jotted a note to herself on the pad.

"I guess that does it. Take messages for me all day. If you have to get in touch with me, I'll be at Hinton and Barnes. Jerry Fullmer's office." He lifted the heavy case from his desk and started out the door as he spoke.

Emily followed him into the hall. "Have a good day."

"Thanks, but I doubt I will. See you tomorrow." He started off briskly down the hall, and Emily looked after him wistfully.

He hadn't even mentioned her birthday. Of course, there was no reason why someone like Adam Marshall should remember something as insignificant as his secretary's birthday. The other secretaries in the office had probably given him a birthday card to sign for her and solicited a contribution from him for the surprise birthday cake and present that were traditional in the firm. But busy as Adam was, he would have noticed it with only a small portion of his mind and forgotten the matter immediately after. She shouldn't expect him to remember; it was silly. Yet she couldn't still the pang of hurt.

She had loved Adam from the moment she'd met him. He had been fresh out of law school, hiring his first secretary. She had just graduated from a two-year secretarial program at Forsyth Tech and had been scared to death coming into the interview. Adam's sheer masculine handsomeness had thrown her into an even greater panic. But he had been calm and kind and led her easily through the questions until her nerves had subsided to a faint tingling in the pit of her stomach. By the end of the interview she'd had a hopeless crush on him.

It was the kind of thing that should have gone away over the course of time. He had, after all, been married to a beautiful former debutante and never exhibited the slightest interest in Emily, except in regard to her work for him. Under the pressure of working closely with him, he should have lost all mystery and charm; she should have come to know his bad habits and weaknesses. But it hadn't worked that way. His indifference didn't quench her feelings, and working with him only made her like him more. His weaknesses were excusable and rather endearing, and his

strengths blazed forth brighter than ever. Her crush had
changed over the years into a deep love. Even his bitter,
black moods two years before when his wife left him hadn't
changed her feelings. His pain had pierced her to the quick.

It was an utterly unrequited, totally impossible love, and
Emily knew it. She wasn't foolish enough to hope that
Adam Marshall would ever even think of her as a woman,
let alone fall in love with her. She was merely an efficient,
not-too-attractive legal secretary, whereas he...well, he was
Adam Marshall, the golden son of a golden family.

The Marshalls were one of the oldest, wealthiest and most
respected families in the state of North Carolina. They had
settled in the central portion of the state in the early 1800s,
and ever since had been leaders in banking and law. Adam's
great-grandfather had been a federal judge; his grandfather had founded his law firm. Another ancestor had estab-
lished Allied Central Bank, and the family still owned a
large percentage of stock in it. One of Adam's uncles was
president and CEO there. As if prestige and old wealth
weren't enough, Adam's father, Leith, had married Joyce
Taggart, heiress to the Taggart Textile Mills fortune. The
Marshalls were social leaders, civic leaders and business
leaders, the cream of Winston-Salem society.

And Adam was the bright, shining star of the family—
handsome, brilliant, a charismatic attorney and a model
son. Women wanted him; men admired him. Parents praised
him to their children, and the younger attorneys in town
emulated him. Emily knew he was as far away from her as
the sun from the cold moon. He could have his choice of any
woman in town, and his pick would be only the most beautiful, the most sparkling society woman, a woman who
made all other women pale in comparison. A woman like
Cassie Marshall.

It filled her with churning emotions to even think of Cassie—anger, sympathy, pain, depression. Adam still loved Cassie. Since she had left him, there had been a certain weariness on Adam's face that hadn't been there before, lines of pain and disillusionment that would never leave. Emily had always envied Cassie for having Adam's love. For the past two years she had despised her, too, for causing him such anguish.

"Hi, Emily." Anna, Parke Wilson's secretary, greeted her with a smile as she walked past down the hall, startling Emily from her reverie.

Emily straightened, pulling her thoughts back to the present, and forced a smile. "Hello. How are you?"

"Fine."

Emily went back to her cubbyhole of an office and switched on the word processor. It looked as if it was going to be a long, bleak day. She might as well get started on Adam's list of jobs.

Slowly the office filled up. Secretaries strolled past Emily's office on the way to their own cubicles or to the less-prestigious open desks in the secretarial pool area. Most smiled or tossed her a wave. A partner or two of the firm passed by without a word. Three young associates stuck their heads in to say good morning. They were smart enough to have figured out that the fastest way to the ear of the future leader of the firm was through his guardian secretary. A few minutes later Leith Marshall, Adam's father and the most senior partner, strode by, head erect, impeccably dressed, gold cuff links winking at his wrists. He never glanced toward either side as he made his imposing way to his corner office. Physically he was an older version of Adam, but he lacked the warmth and charm that gave

Adam his charisma. There was something about him that was too cool, too sober to inspire affection.

By noon Emily had finished the most pressing items on Adam's list and about a third of the things left in her desk from yesterday. As usual she decided she would eat a carton of yogurt from the refrigerator in the coffee room and spend her lunch hour at her desk, trying to catch up. However, just as she was about to leave her office, her cousin Jeanette whipped around the corner. "Emily! I was afraid I wouldn't catch you. I'm taking you to lunch."

"I was just about to get some yogurt and—"

"And spend your lunch hour working," Jeanette finished for her disgustedly. "Honestly! Sometimes you boggle my mind. Don't you realize it's your birthday?"

"Did you have to remind me?" Emily countered ruefully.

Jeanette grimaced. "Don't be silly. You can have just as much fun after you turn thirty as before."

Emily smiled. It would probably be true for Jeanette; she had fun no matter where she was, what she was doing or how old she was. But then, her cousin was everything that Emily was not. Jeanette was vibrant and worldly. Her blond hair was a captivating gold; her gray eyes had a sparkling, silver tone. She dressed in soft, stylish clothes in pastel colors that enhanced her delicate, blond coloring. She had had several lovers, yet had remained unattached and heart-whole. Emily could think of no one less like Jeanette's mother, Rosemary—or less like herself. Yet the two of them were the best of friends and always had been. Jeanette was the only person to whom Emily had revealed her feelings for Adam Marshall.

"Now, come on." Jeanette linked her arm through Emily's and steered her down the hall toward the elevators. "You are going out for a birthday celebration."

"But my purse is back in my office," Emily protested.

"You won't need it. I'm not about to let you back in there. I figure once you got inside, the bars would slam down."

"Okay. Okay." Laughingly, Emily gave up.

They ate in the gardenlike restaurant in the atrium of the Hyatt and chattered away, catching up on the events in each other's lives over the past few weeks. Emily noticed without rancor that the events were largely on Jeanette's side, not hers.

"How's Len?" Emily asked, and Jeanette laughed and shook her head.

"He was ages ago. We must not have talked in a month. How about you? Have you met anyone interesting?"

Emily looked down at her plate. "You never give up, do you?"

"No," Jeanette admitted readily. "Not when your happiness is the issue."

"I'm happy."

"Uh huh." Her cousin's voice dripped sarcasm.

"Well, I am. I love my work."

"You love your boss."

"I love my work, too. It's fascinating."

"Dear girl, there's a lot more to life than typing up legal briefs or fetching coffee for Adam Marshall."

Emily's eyes darkened with sadness. Jeanette was right. Life was passing her by. She had never been so keenly aware of that fact as she was today. She hadn't really tasted anything of life. She didn't have the slightest knowledge of the things most women knew. At thirty, she was still a virgin. No man had ever made love to her. She hadn't known love or passion, except for the impossible, unfulfilled feeling she had for Adam. She was drying up, she thought, her femininity eroding more and more with each passing year. She didn't know. Didn't share. Didn't belong. She felt beyond the pale, and worse. The years had slipped away, and now she realized how empty they had been. She had missed something vital.

"Oh, Em, I'm sorry." Jeanette saw the flare of pain in her cousin's eyes and immediately regretted her words. "I didn't mean to upset you. It's just that when I see the way you hide yourself and hold yourself down, it makes me so angry! I wish you'd let go, be what you could be, and let the male half of this town see what they're missing. I want you to have fun and be happy."

Emily managed a smile. "It's okay. I'm fine. Really."

Jeanette looked at her doubtfully. She was sure that Emily wasn't okay, but she didn't know what she could do or say to make it better. Emily would be happier if she just dropped the subject, and Jeanette knew, after years of nagging, that her urgings did nothing to change Emily. No doubt the best thing to do was simply change the subject. She took a sip of sweet iced tea and began brightly. "So, how are Mother and Aunt Nancy?"

Emily returned from lunch a trifle late, but there was no one to notice or complain. The messages had stacked up on the receptionist's desk in the lobby, but only two were for her, the majority for Adam. The ones that were hers were business calls, nothing personal. It seemed a fresh reminder of how empty and lonely her life was.

The ache inside her grew throughout the afternoon, though she kept steadily at her work, refusing to let the sorrow overcome her. But she couldn't shake the gnawing certainty that her young adult life was over without her ever having really experienced it. What must it feel like to step into a room and have a man stand up to meet you, his eyes glowing with desire and love? What would it be like to lie next to a man, his body filling the bed with masculine warmth and strength? She tried to picture a man in her bed, turned on his side to face her, smiling and satiated, his large hand reaching out to slide along the curve of her body. But she could envisage no man's face except Adam Marshall's.

Her stomach quivered. It wasn't just any man she wanted. It was him. Only him. Yet wanting him was like crying for the moon. There was no way she could ever have Adam in her bed. Wouldn't it be better to settle for another, lesser man, someone she might be able to attract? She tried to imagine who such a man could be, but she couldn't think of one. There were bars where she could go, of course, and perhaps if she sat there long enough someone would pick her up. But that idea frightened and repulsed her. There was an officer downstairs in the bank who always smiled at her. And there was an attorney in the firm who flirted with everyone and had a reputation for sleeping around. But her soul shied away from either one of them. The truth of the matter was that she wanted only Adam, and the idea of sleeping with someone else seemed sordid. But if she did not, she would never have a chance to experience a man's touch or feel the force of his passion—and such a future seemed horribly bleak.

In the middle of the afternoon Jill Chester, the secretary next door to her, invited her down to the coffee room for the afternoon break. Emily knew she was about to receive the obligatory surprise birthday party, which further dampened her spirits. It seemed the height of irony to be celebrating something that distressed her so. However, she knew that the other secretaries had put in a great deal of effort on it, as she herself had done for others in the past, so she pasted on a smile and tried to act both surprised and pleased.

Nearly all the secretaries were jammed into the small lounge area, as well as a couple of attorneys whose offices were nearby. They sang "Happy Birthday" when she appeared, and Emily blushed, self-conscious, as always, about being the center of even such a small gathering. She blew out the candles and opened her card and the present, an elegant glass paperweight. She cut the cake and passed it out, and even managed to force down half a piece herself, despite the heavy lump of unhappiness in her chest and stomach.

Fortunately the afternoon break was short, so the small party broke up soon after everyone had a bit of cake and coffee. Emily, clutching her gift and card and murmuring profuse thanks, was able to escape to her office. There she sat down and opened the card again and ran her eyes over the signatures, pausing when she came to Adam's familiar bold writing. No doubt one of the other secretaries had slipped into his office and stuck the card out, opened, for him to sign, and he had quickly, carelessly scrawled his name across it. Emily could picture him doing it; she had often brought in papers and waited for him to sign them. He'd hardly glance up, his concentration still on what was before him, and reach out to sign it. Or at times he'd lean back with a weary sigh and push his horn-rimmed glasses up onto his head and rub his eyes before he leaned forward and wrote.

Tears stung her eyes. Emily swallowed hard and set the card down on her desk. What a case she was today—ready to cry at a birthday card, without even knowing why! Determinedly she put on the Dictaphone headset, turned the machine on and began to type.

The rest of the afternoon dragged by as Emily worked on doggedly. Around five the rest of the firm's employees began to straggle out, and within an hour the other offices along the hall were quiet and unlit. Emily continued until almost seven, when the ache in her back from long hours of typing made her quit. The work didn't improve her spirits, but the prospect of going home to her mother and aunt was even more unappealing. Finally she switched off the word processor and removed the diskettes. She stood and stretched and cleaned her desk, shoving all the files on which she was currently working into the capacious bottom drawer. She locked the desk, the tall metal file cabinet and the small plastic diskette holder, than gave her office one final encompassing glance to make sure everything was in order.

The phone rang. The night system had switched on at five-thirty, when the receptionist left, so the main line rang in every office. Emily had ignored the calls, and they had gradually grown fewer and fewer. This was the first ring in almost thirty minutes. She started to leave without answering it, then hesitated. She was probably the only one in the office now; perhaps she ought to pick it up. Usually she did.

With a little grimace she reached over and lifted the receiver. "Marshall, Pierson, Tidrell, and Sommers."

"I figured you were still there," her mother's voice said disapprovingly. "I was hoping maybe you'd gone out for a drink for your birthday after work. *Hoping*, not expecting."

"Hello, Mother."

"Hello, yourself. Do you realize it's seven o'clock?"

"Yes. I'm just finishing up."

"Uh huh. Well, I'm running out for the evening, so I figured I better call, since I wouldn't get a chance to see you."

"That's nice."

"Rosemary baked you a beautiful chocolate cake, which I could eat if I still had a figure like yours." Nancy sighed. "But I can't stick around here much longer. That woman's about to drive me out of my mind."

"That woman" Emily understood to be her aunt. "Still arguing?"

"When aren't we? But that's not what I called about. Did you see the newspaper today?"

"No."

"Well, look at the society section. You'll never guess who's getting married."

"Who?" Emily asked with little interest.

"You'll never believe it. Sherry Pike."

"Sherry Pike!" Emily sat down. "You're joking." She thought of the rotund little girl she'd gone to elementary school with, then the rotund teenager with braces and bad skin in high school. She'd had little in the way of looks and even less personality. Even Emily had acknowledged herself superior to Sherry Pike. She was the last person Emily would have dreamed of getting married.

"I'm not joking. I saw it right there in the newspaper. Now I ask you, if Sherry Pike is marrying—an engineer, no less—what are you doing still single?"

"Oh, Mother."

"Don't you 'oh, Mother' me. You know I'm telling the truth. Sherry Pike is a zero, and she's getting married next month, and you're sitting in a law office at seven o'clock in the evening, typing! Now, if that doesn't shake you out of it, I don't know what will. You ought to get right up and put on some lipstick and go down to O'Grady's and—"

"Mother!"

"Emily!" Nancy retorted. "I'm telling you this for your own good."

"Please don't." Emily's eyes were suddenly swimming with tears, and her words sounded suspiciously quavery. "Look, I can't talk now. I've got to go. Bye." Without waiting for an answer, she set the receiver back on the hook.

It was rude, she knew, but at the moment she was beyond caring.

Her mother's news put the perfect finish on a miserable day. It seemed as if everyone in the world had found love except her. Every other woman—even Sherry Pike!—had been initiated into the mysteries of men and lovemaking by the time they were thirty. She was fast on her way to becoming a dried-up, old spinster, with no hope in sight. She thought of Adam. She thought of her lonely room, her virginal bed. She put her head down on her desk and cried.

## Chapter 2

Adam Marshall turned into the underground parking lot of Allied Central Bank and stopped. The security guard gave him a slight wave, and the black bar across the entrance lifted. Adam raised his hand in acknowledgment and drove through, turning to the right and circling down to the third level, where he pulled into the parking slot marked "Marshall, A." He stepped out of his beige BMW and pulled the heavy briefcase out of the back seat, then walked across to the elevators, inserted his key and pushed the button. He shrugged his shoulders and massaged the back of his neck with one hand as he waited for the elevator to arrive. He was tired from a long day of conferences and the ride to and from Raleigh.

But there were still a few things he needed to catch up on, and he figured he'd better check his messages. If he knew Emily, they'd be sitting in a neat pile on his desk, arranged in order of urgency. There'd be another neat pile of opened mail, also arranged in order of importance. Thank God for

Emily. He had never guessed when he hired her how valuable a secretary she would turn out to be. To replace her he'd need a full-time secretary and a part-time one.

He was sorry he'd forgotten to wish her a happy birthday this morning before he left. He should have remembered; it was only yesterday that Mary Sinclair had given him the card to sign. But with the sudden trip to Raleigh it had slipped his mind, and he hadn't recalled it until the middle of lunch. He wondered what Mary had bought Emily with the money he'd given her. He also wondered if there might be any of the cake still sitting in the coffee room. He hadn't stopped for supper on the way home.

The elevator arrived, and he stepped inside, again using his key before he punched the law firm's floor number. When the doors opened onto Marshall, Pierson's lobby, he started around the back way to his office. It was a longer walk, but it went past the coffee room. The halls were lit, but the offices were dark. At the far end of the hall behind him, he could hear the whine of the cleaning crew's vacuum. He switched on the light in the coffee room. The coffee pot was empty and clean, and he debated whether to make himself some coffee. It didn't seem worth the effort, with only him in the office. But then, if he got caught up in his work, he might be there for another three hours. He'd stayed that late lots of times. Or, at least, he had in the past couple of years. Since Cassie had left, there hadn't been much to go home for.

He pushed the somber thought out of his mind and glanced around the room. Everything was tidy. He opened the refrigerator and peered in. There was the cake, or, rather, a fourth of it, creamy-white and decorated with sugary, pink roses. It had been neatly sliced into squares. Adam smiled. Typical. Emily was nothing if not efficient. He took a couple of pieces and ate one standing up as he pulled out the coffee can and paper filters. What was cake without coffee?

He had just stuck the filter into its holder when he became aware of a faint, strange noise. He stopped and listened. It came again, but he couldn't identify it. For some reason it bothered him. He set down the piece of cake and went to the door, where he looked each way down the hall, but saw nothing. He heard the sound again, faintly. It sounded like ... crying.

He frowned. Surely not. There wouldn't be a woman crying up here at seven in the evening. He took a few steps down the hall and rounded the corner. He stopped. Light slanted out of one office among all the dark ones. Emily's office. His frown deepened, and he strode forward much more quickly. Emily? Crying?

There was an audible sniff, and the sound of someone blowing her nose. Adam reached the doorway and halted. Emily sat in her typist's chair, turned away from the door.

"Emily?" he asked tentatively, concerned, yet suddenly uncertain whether he should barge in on her.

Emily swung around, startled, her mouth dropping open. Her eyes were red, the lids puffy, and the flesh around her eyes had the pasty look of someone who'd been crying. Her nose was a little pink, too, and there was a soft, tremulous quality to her mouth. She had definitely been crying.

"Adam!" Her voice was hoarse. Her hands flew up to her face, and she wiped at the wetness on her cheeks. "Oh, no. Oh, I'm so sorry."

"Sorry! What are you talking about?" He stepped into the room. His blue eyes were soft with concern, and Emily's stomach knotted helplessly.

Why did he have to return now? If ever there was a day when the fates were against her, it must be this one! Emily knew she looked awful. She rarely cried, and when she did, it wasn't done prettily. No doubt her face looked splotched and swollen, and during her bout of tears much of her hair had slipped out of its barrette at the nape of her neck, and now it straggled damply around her face. Clumsily she shoved her hair back and tried to tuck it behind her ears.

"I, uh, nothing. I'm—oh, I must look like an idiot."

A faint smile touched his lips. "Don't be silly. What's the matter? What happened?"

"Nothing. Really. It was silly. Just nerves, I guess." Then, much to her horror, two fat tears slid out of her eyes and rolled down her cheeks to plop onto her suit. One hand flew to her mouth and pressed against it. That didn't do anything except hide the helpless trembling of her lips. The tears seemed to have a mind of their own.

"Emily!" Adam squatted down beside her, one hand resting on the back of her chair, only inches from her body. His nearness further unnerved her, and Emily could only shake her head silently. Nothing would come out of her mouth—or at least nothing coherent or sane.

"I'm sorry."

"Would you stop saying that? There's no reason to be sorry. Just tell me what's going on." He tried a teasing smile. "Didn't you know you aren't supposed to cry on your birthday?"

He'd remembered! Even through her misery and embarrassment, that registered. Emily felt a little bit lighter. She tried a smile, but the tears still came, and she swiveled away to grab another tissue and blow her nose again.

How humiliating! Emily wished she didn't have to face him again. She shook her head. It was easier to speak, she thought, if she didn't have to look at him, didn't have to see the kindness in those blue eyes. "It's nothing. Really." Her voice shook and stumbled, but at least she got the words out. She blew her nose again. "Just blues, I guess, from turning thirty."

He'd had no idea how old she was. There had never been any reason to wonder. It came as something of a surprise to Adam, though he couldn't have said whether he had thought she was older or younger. "Ahhh," he said knowingly, teasing her. "Thirty. Well, that explains it. You know what you need?"

He turned her chair back around so that she faced him. Emily shook her head.

"A drink," he answered his own question. "Come on. I'm taking you down to The Pub."

Emily stared. "Oh, no. Really. That's not necessary."

"Of course it is. It's part of every good attorney's job description: Take your secretary for a drink on her thirtieth birthday. Come on." He picked up her handbag from her desk and held it out to her. She took it numbly, but still didn't stand, and he put his hands on her arms and pulled her up. Heat flashed through her arms and straight into her head at his touch. She thought her cheeks must have flushed and wondered if he'd noticed it.

"Adam, please. I ought to go home. I can't go out in public like this."

"Like what?"

Mutely she gestured toward her tearstained face and swollen eyes. Adam grimaced. "It's dark inside The Pub. Let's go. I'm not accepting a negative reply."

She gave in. She couldn't deny Adam anything, and, besides, no matter how humiliating it was, she couldn't pass up a chance to be alone with him for a few minutes.

Emily tucked her purse under her arm and left her office. Adam followed, flipping off the lights as they went. They were silent as they walked to the elevator and waited for it to come. Emily was pale and still, just the opposite of the whirling, clashing emotions inside her. She was scared, awkward, embarrassed—and excited. Except for the office Christmas party every year, she couldn't remember ever being in a relaxed, social atmosphere with Adam. She wished she could think of something to say. She wished she hadn't just cried all over the place like an idiot.

The streets outside were nearly deserted. They walked the two blocks to The Pub at Adam's usual quick pace. When they reached the bar he held open the door for her and put his hand lightly against the small of her back to guide her in. It was nothing but a small, polite gesture, but Emily felt his touch all through her.

It was dim inside, and the post-business day crowd was already thinning out. Adam easily found a small table at the rear of the room. It was a quiet bar, without the loud, pulsing noise of a sound system blaring out rock 'n' roll; even the conversations around the room seemed muted.

They sat down, and Emily folded her hands in her lap, feeling tongue-tied and awkward. Adam was being very kind, but he must think her all kinds of a fool. She glanced at him. He was leaning back in his chair and loosening his tie. He smiled at her. "Feel any better?"

She nodded. "Yes, thank you." This was crazy, she thought. She talked to him easily enough in the office. But this seemed almost like a date, and she was clamming up, as she did in any social situation.

"What would you like to drink?"

Emily hesitated. She rarely drank anything alcoholic. "I guess, uh…" Her eye fell on a colorful card in the center of the table that depicted a cool, pink drink, topped with a strawberry. "A strawbery daiquiri." That seemed safe enough. It was pretty, and she'd had daiquiries before and had hardly been able to taste the liquor.

The waitress in a short skirt came by, and Adam ordered Emily's drink and a Jack Daniels on the rocks for himself. After she left, Adam asked a casual question about work, and Emily was glad to have a subject she could speak on without feeling awkward. She relayed as many messages as she could remember and told him which of his tasks she had been able to finish. By the time she was through with business talk, the waitress had reappeared with their drinks and a small bowl of popcorn.

Emily took a quick sip of her drink. It was both sweet and tangy, and so cold it made her throat hurt. She took another sip, then swished the straw around in the drink, grateful that she had something to do with her hands. She wondered what to say now that the office had been disposed of. "How was Raleigh?"

He shrugged. "Same as ever. At least we should be able to go to trial this week. For a while I was afraid we'd have to ask for another delay."

"Good." Emily took another gulp of the icy drink. At least it gave her something to do during the awkward pauses. But at the rate she was going she'd be through before Adam drank half his bourbon.

Adam took a swallow of his drink, and it slipped like liquid fire down his throat. He'd had nothing to eat since lunch, so the alcohol spread quickly through his veins, soothing away the day's tension. He watched Emily nervously sipping at her daiquiri and wondered what to say. He'd pulled her out of the office and down to the bar on impulse, thinking only that a long drink in a quiet bar would calm her and maybe lighten her spirits. But now that they were here, he didn't know what to do.

His first impulse was to find out what had made her so unhappy; in his personal life as well as in his business, Adam's first reaction was to go straight to the problem and get rid of it. But now, with Emily sitting there so stiffly, fiddling with the straw and the garnish, and avoiding his eyes, he wondered if questioning her would be an unwelcome intrusion. Emily was a closed-up person. It occurred to him that he knew very little about her, not even what kind of car she drove or where she lived. He wondered if she ever wore jeans and a T-shirt.

"What kind of car do you drive?" he asked suddenly.

"What?" Emily blinked, then laughed a little. Without her even realizing it, the drink was relaxing her. "My car? A Mazda. Why?"

He shrugged. "Just curious. It suddenly seemed very strange to me that you'd worked for me for—what? ten years?—and I didn't even know what kind of car you drove."

She took another sip of her drink and smiled. The taut lines around her eyes and mouth were loosening now, and her cheeks had taken on a bit of color. "I know what kind of car you drive. A BMW. Beige."

"See? That's what I mean. You know a lot more about me than I know about you. I think you must be secretive."

"I'm not!" Emily protested, not even noticing that her awkwardness had slipped away. "There's just not anything to know about."

He chuckled. "I find that hard to believe."

"It's true."

"There must be *something* to know about you. Lots of facts. Like where you live."

"In an old house off Silas Creek Parkway." She lifted her hands, palms up. "See? I told you. Nothing interesting."

"Ah, but we're only beginning."

"It'll be over very quickly, I'm afraid."

He grinned, the slightest bit of challenge glinting in his eyes. "We'll see about that." He paused and sipped thoughtfully at his drink, studying her. Emily shifted a little under his gaze. "Ah hah." He pointed a forefinger at her. "The first signs of nervousness. You have something to hide."

Emily blushed, thinking of all the things she had to hide. Her love for him. The embarrassment of being unwanted, of being thirty and still a virgin. The loneliness, the awful crush of future loneliness. The hunger of her thoughts.

It was strange how something that you wanted so much to hide would fill your mind until you could think of almost nothing else. Until it would be easy to slip and say it.

Emily took another long sip of her drink. It was almost gone now, and she was aware of a certain fuzzy warmth inside her. She turned her head to look at Adam, and the movement seemed peculiarly removed from her, as if she watched herself do it—and watched it in slow motion, too. "I wonder if I'm getting drunk."

"Don't be silly." Adam signaled the waitress to bring another round. "You've only had one drink."

She gazed at him gravely. "I don't think I hold my liquor very well."

Her wide-eyed gravity amused him, and he smiled. "Good. Then I'll have no trouble getting the information I want."

"You're going to be sadly disappointed."

"I'll be the judge of that."

The waitress set down the second set of drinks and removed the empty glasses. Adam took a sip. The straight liquor on an empty stomach was beginning to make him quite mellow, and Emily's blushes piqued his curiosity. He wondered what someone like her would have to feel guilty or secretive about. She seemed the model of propriety to him. Hell, he'd never even seen her flirt with his brother, Taggart, who usually brought out the sin in anyone. "Any roommates?" he asked.

Emily looked startled. "What? Oh. Questions-and-answers again?"

"Yeah." The corners of his mouth lifted without quite forming a grin. Emily thought she would have answered a million questions to see that movement again.

"Sort of. I live with my mother and aunt."

"Your mother and aunt?" His eyebrows rose.

"I told you my life was dull."

"Men?"

"Men?"

"I know you aren't married, but there must be some guy lurking around. Friend. Fiancé. Lover."

It sent a quiver of desire through her abdomen even to hear Adam's voice say the word. It made her think of beds and tangled sheets and bodies intertwined. Of a man's hard hand drifting over her. Adam's hand. Her nipples tightened at the thought. She looked away, afraid he'd see her thought. Good heavens! Talk about a sex-starved spinster—going hot and liquid inside at the mere mention of the word "lover."

Adam saw her glance quickly away, and he realized he'd touched a sore spot. Her tears tonight must have been about a man. He should have known. Wasn't it always love that hurt you the worst? He felt a wave of empathy and reached out to cover one of her hands with his. "I'm sorry. Is that why you were crying?"

Emily's head snapped up, and she turned scarlet. "How did you know?" She bit her lower lip and looked away. Her voice was so low he could barely hear it. "But, no, I guess it's obvious, isn't it?"

"Obvious?" he repeated, a little puzzled.

Her chin came up, and she stared back at him with something like defiance in her face. "That I—you know—don't have—" She stopped, unable to force out the words.

Adam leaned forward, his brow furrowed, thoroughly confused now. "Don't have what?"

"A man!" Her face felt like fire.

His brows shot up. "You mean your boyfriend left you?" What a strange way to put it!

"I mean I don't have one!" Emily snapped. "I never had one. Never will have! That's my problem. I'm thirty years old and I've never even slept with a man!" For a moment they stared at each other in silence. Then Emily realized what she had revealed—and to whom—and she blushed to the roots of her hair. "Oh, God!" She grabbed her drink and took a huge gulp, finishing it. Two drinks on an empty stomach—no wonder she was blurting out crazy things! She must be drunk. She pressed her hands to her blazing cheeks. "I'm sorry. I'm making a perfect fool of myself."

"No, don't think that." Adam frowned. He didn't know what to say. Her words had stunned him. He'd never really thought about Emily's love life before, but he would have figured that she had one. Why hadn't Emily ever gone to bed with a man? Surely it wasn't that she was too prudish, or she wouldn't be crying over it. On the other hand, he didn't see how it could be lack of opportunity. Emily wasn't beautiful, of course, at least not in the breathtaking way Cassie was, but she certainly wasn't bad looking. She was rather shy and subdued, but once you got to know her, she had a pleasant personality. She was intelligent and kind, and sometimes that quiet shell cracked open to reveal a quick sense of humor. He would have thought there had been men who wanted her.

Adam tried to remember whether he had ever seen her talking to a man, but he could think of no time that hadn't been purely business. He couldn't even recall her flirting in the hall with Jimmy Swale or Cap Wilson, both of whom were inveterate skirt-chasers. He closed his eyes, trying to envision Emily as he had seen her around the office. She always stood a little apart from him, he thought, even when she was showing him something on a paper. Often she crossed her arms over her chest. And that was with him, whom she'd known for ten years. Imagine how she must be with a stranger. He had seen her on the street a couple of times, and she walked with her head down, not meeting anyone's eyes. He had practically had to run right into her to say hello. The clothes she wore were always like the ones she had on now: plain in style and color, without a hint of sexuality to them. Obviously she closed herself off from men long before anything could get to a romantic stage. Adam frowned, wondering why. Emily Townsend, up till now as familiar and ordinary to him as his favorite old jacket or the comfortable leather couch in his parents' den, had suddenly become a puzzle. And puzzles intrigued him.

Tears welled in Emily's eyes and spilled over, and she averted her head, fumbling in her purse for a tissue. Oh, Lord, here she went again! Adam must be extremely sorry he'd brought her here.

It surprised her that he hadn't pulled his hand away from hers yet. Instead his fingers had slipped around and into her palm, so that he was holding her hand instead of just covering it with his own. His hand was warm and strong. Comforting. She couldn't stop herself from gripping it back.

"You want to talk about it?" he asked softly.

She shook her head, but her tongue had a mind of its own. The words were pushing up out of her throat, her pain struggling to be expressed. Suddenly she was talking, her voice jerky and shaky with tears. "It's so awful. I feel like a...a dinosaur."

"A dinosaur!" A small smile flickered across Adam's mouth, amused but not hurtful, warm and close. "Surely not."

"I think I'm the only woman left in America who's so naive."

"It's not a crime to be a virgin, you know."

Emily's other hand clenched around the tissue, wadding it into a tiny ball. "I've missed out on so much of life! I feel so empty and useless. Life has passed me by. I've never known—oh, I can't explain it." She couldn't, simply couldn't, tell Adam how she ached for love and passion. She was sure her face would betray her, that he would see that it was his love and passion she longed for.

"Your life's not over yet."

Emily's eyes flashed, and she pulled her hand out of his grasp. "You think if it hasn't happened by the time I'm thirty that it will after? I won't get any more attractive as I get older."

"Emily..."

"No!" She gave a decisive shake of her head. "Let's not embarrass us both by pretending that I'm anything but plain. I faced up to that fact years ago." She paused and continued wistfully, "Still, even plain people would like to experience something that's so essential, so basic to life."

"There's no reason why you shouldn't." He felt helpless, an uncommon emotion for him. He was used to taking on people's problems and solving them, fighting their battles for them. But here he didn't know what to do.

Emily circled the rim of her empty glass with one forefinger, her eyes fixed to the movement of her finger. She gave a dry, humorless little laugh. "Sometimes I feel so desperate, so walled-in, that I've thought about going to a singles bar and trying to pick somebody up. Only I'm afraid no one would be interested in me, and that would be the final humiliation." She wrinkled her nose. "Besides, I don't have the nerve."

"No!" The idea horrified Adam. "That wouldn't—well, it would be all wrong."

"I don't have that many possibilities," Emily pointed out wryly and gave him a small, embarrassed grin. "I thought about asking Jimmy Swale if he'd sleep with me, just for the experience. You know, no strings attached."

"Jimmy Swale!" Adam's voice boomed out, and several other patrons of the bar turned to stare. He lowered his voice, but the tone was still full of indignation. "Jimmy Swale! Good God, Emily, why him? Swale's an inconsiderate pig. A thorough male chauvinist."

"Because everyone knows that Jimmy will sleep with anybody."

"What a recommendation."

"It is, if you're afraid of being turned down," she retorted, looking carefully away from him. "Besides, I didn't want a long-term affair. I just wanted someone who would do it, and afterward there wouldn't be anything messy or embarrassing."

"Well, if you want it quick and without commitment, you certainly picked the right person." Adam shook his head, his face still flooded with something close to anger. "That's absolutely insane. Believe me, going to bed with Jimmy Swale wouldn't give you the experience you wish you had. It'd be an exercise in cold, mechanical sex, which isn't at all the lovemaking you think you've missed out on. I don't understand you. If you wanted to experiment like that, why didn't you ask someone you knew and liked? Someone who'd treat you well. Why in the hell didn't you ask me?"

Emily's head snapped up, and she stared at Adam, her mouth dropping open. She was drunk, she thought. She had to have heard him wrong. Adam couldn't have just offered himself as her partner in sexual experimentation. He returned her gaze, scowling. She cleared her throat. "You?" Her voice came out a squeak.

His scowl deepened. "Yeah. Me. You needn't look so astonished. I am a functioning male."

Emily's mouth opened and closed, and no sound came out. She reached for her glass, but it was empty. She picked up Adam's and took a healthy swallow. The bourbon roared down her throat to her stomach, and she grimaced at the taste. But at least it had unstuck her voice. "But why?"

"Because I can't stand the idea of you throwing yourself away on someone like Jim Swale. It would be an absolutely awful experience, the worst way, short of rape, to introduce you to sex." He sighed and rubbed the back of his neck. "Frankly, I think you ought to wait for a man you love. It's by far the best. But if you're going to insist on this...education, you should at least have someone who likes and respects you. Who'll treat you as you should be treated. So you'll have a nice memory, not something you want to forget."

He was serious. He wasn't joking; she hadn't heard him wrong. Adam Marshall was offering to make love to her. It scared her to death.

When Emily continued to stare at him silently, Adam shifted a little in his seat. "Come on, now, if you choose Jimmy Swale over me, I'll be completely humiliated." He quirked an eyebrow. "Would you like references?"

Numbly she groped for something to say. "But our jobs— what about afterward?"

He shrugged. "That's no problem. We agree that it will be only for the one time. We're both mature; we'll go into it without any false expectations. When it's over, we'll simply continue as we always have. I promise, it will be without commitments or entanglements, just like with Jimmy Swale. Does that allay your fears?''

''I guess so.'' It was hardly the romantic invitation into Adam's heart and bed that she had always daydreamed about. And Emily knew that while it would involve no commitment or entanglement for Adam, she would be even more hopelessly in love with him after it was over. The whole thing had heartbreak written all over it. Her icy, formless fear began to emerge into specifics: what if Adam was repelled by her inexperience and unattractive body? What if it was so beautiful and wonderful that her love for him would become too painful to bear? What if afterward she wanted him so much that she chased him and made a fool of herself and disgusted him?

But despite the coldness of the arrangement, despite the possible disastrous consequences, Emily knew she couldn't turn him down. It was like having a little bit of heaven dropped in her lap, and nothing could prevent her from grabbing it and holding it close, however briefly.

She swallowed. ''All right. I agree.''

# Chapter 3

Emily's glance skittered toward Adam and then away. She was tight as a bowstring, her heart racing with a combination of fear and excitement. Had he meant tonight? Were they going to get up and walk out of here and go to a motel? Her hands were ice cold, and she was certain she couldn't move from her chair. It was too sudden, too swift, too glorious.

"Uh, Adam, when—I mean—tonight?"

He glanced at her, startled, then grinned. "You've got to get rid of this prosaic tendency. Not tonight; that's too hurried. It's got to be something special. I want to think about it. The next couple of weeks are too rushed because of the trial starting Thursday. Tell you what. As soon as this case is over. How does that sound?"

She nodded, relieved. It would give her time to anticipate, to savor the idea, to get ready.

"Right now, I think we both need something to eat. Let's go over to the Twin Cities Club."

"Oh, no," Emily demurred hastily, thinking of how her tear-blotched face and plain business suit would go over in such an exclusive private club. Adam was being polite, but she knew she would be an embarrassment to him there. "I really need to get home. I, ah, my aunt probably kept my supper warm for me."

"All right." He signaled the waitress for the bill, then asked the waitress to call a taxi.

"A taxi?" Emily repeated, puzzled, as the woman walked off. "It's only a couple of blocks to the garage."

"I'm sending you home in it," he replied. "You're in no condition to drive."

"I'm not drunk!" Emily protested.

He shot her a telling look. "Perhaps. But I think you're too woozy to drive. Your car will be fine, and you can catch a ride in tomorrow, can't you? I could come by and pick you—"

"Oh, no, no, that's fine," Emily interrupted hastily. "My mother can drive me in."

Adam paid the bill, and they left the pub, his hand firmly gripping her elbow. Emily would have liked the feel of it much better if she hadn't suspected that he did it only because he was afraid she might stagger and fall.

"I only had two drinks, you know," she pointed out.

His eyes lit up in amusement. "I know. But I'm wondering if it isn't enough that you'll regret it tomorrow. That you'll wish you hadn't told me what you did, hadn't agreed to..."

Emily lifted her chin stubbornly. "*I'm* not backing out. I meant what I said." Then her courage crumbled, and she glanced away. She continued in a slightly muffled voice, "But I can see why you would regret it after you thought about it a little. I'll understand; I won't be hurt. You don't have to go through with it."

The cab pulled up to the curb, but Adam didn't move toward it. Instead he took Emily's chin in his hand and forcibly tilted her head up so that she looked into his eyes. "I'm going through with it. I won't regret it or change my mind. You ought to know me well enough to know that once I set my mind on something, I won't let go. I wanted to give you a chance to back out if you want."

"I won't."

A faint smile flickered across Adam's face. "Okay. Then I'll see you tomorrow morning." He released her chin and turned toward the cab.

The driver had hopped out and stood holding the door open for Emily. As she got in, Adam handed the driver a crisp bill. "She'll give you the address." He leaned down to look in the window. Emily looked a little forlorn and lost in the big back seat. "Good night."

"Good night."

The driver took off, and Adam crossed the deserted street. Hands shoved into his pockets, he strolled the few blocks to the Twin Cities Club. But once inside, he glanced into the elegant, hushed dining room and decided that he really didn't want to eat there by himself. He knew practically everyone seated at the tables, and he was sure he would be invited to eat with someone, but tonight he didn't feel like listening to anybody's chatter. He turned on his heel and left, stopping by a small cafe on his way back to the office and grabbing a hamburger to go. Eating out of a sack while he worked was something he was accustomed to. He'd done a lot of it the past couple of years.

He entered the dark, silent building and rode up to the firm's office. The buzz of the cleaning crew's vacuum had circled the building and was now near his office. Adam walked down the hall to the coffee room and retrieved the briefcase he'd abandoned there when he heard Emily crying.

He shook his head in silent amusement. What a night. He certainly hadn't expected it to turn out like this when he'd been driving back from Raleigh.

He went on to his office, nodding to the man running the vacuum sweeper through the hall, and closed the door behind him to cut out some of the noise. A faint sense of sadness and loneliness drifted over him. It didn't gut him as it had right after Cassie split, but it was still there. He was beginning to wonder if he'd ever get over it. When Cassie had left him, he'd spent more than one night here, working until his eyes wouldn't stay open any longer and he'd finally fallen asleep at his desk. He hadn't been able to face the empty house, the wide, cold bed. Usually he had awakened long before anyone came to work and had gone home to shower and change, then returned to the office, but once or twice Emily had come in to find him slumped in his chair, sound asleep.

Adam set down the briefcase and the hamburger sack on his desk, but didn't flip on the lights. The curtains were open, and there was enough light from outside for him to pick his way across the familiar room. He strolled to the window and stood looking out for a moment. The lights of the city glittered before him; he loved this view. A full moon brightened the night sky. He wondered if it was really true that a full moon made people behave crazily. A smile touched his lips. He'd certainly strayed way off the beaten path tonight.

He could hardly believe that he and his very efficient, proper secretary had spent the evening discussing her lack of a love life. It was even harder to believe that he'd offered to introduce her to the delights of sex. Adam shook his head, smiling faintly, and leaned against the window, crossing his arms. It didn't sound like him at all. It was much more the sort of thing his brother Tag would do. Tag was the one who was wild, the playboy for whom all women seemed to fall. He could well imagine him agreeing to initiate a distraught virgin into the rites of womanhood.

But not himself. Not Adam Mashall. He was too staid— too dull, Cassie would have said. He was the sort who always walked the narrow, proper path, who did and said all the right things. He was the son who'd followed the family tradition and entered the family firm. He'd married a girl of whom everyone had approved and whom he had adored, and he'd never been unfaithful to her in the eight years they were married. He did his best on every case and didn't shirk his responsibilities. He dressed well, spoke well, looked good, and was one of the best attorneys in the state. He was, in fact, a perfect pattern of the first son of a well-to-do legal family. He definitely was not the kind who did something as crazy as this.

But then, since the divorce he'd done a lot of crazy things. A few years ago he would have been appalled at the idea of sleeping with a woman for whom he felt no desire or love, only a mild liking. But when Cassie had told him that she'd been having an affair for six months and was divorcing him to marry her lover, Adam's sexual confidence had been shaken to the core. At first he had holed up like a wounded animal, burying himself in his work and hardly seeing anyone, even friends and family. Then, when the shock had subsided a little, he had begun a frantic, joyless sexual marathon, engaging in countless, meaningless one-night stands. Emily had said that Jimmy Swale had the reputation of sleeping with anyone. Frankly, he knew he hadn't been much better.

He had finally slowed down the unhappy, sterile bed-hopping, and for the past few months his sex life had been much calmer and more infrequent. But it still had no meaning for him. Sex had become for him, not making love, but an animal instinct that had to be satisfied, with no more real meaning than eating when he was hungry or sleeping when he was exhausted. Since Cassie left, it had ceased to be special. One woman meant no more to him than any other. It might as well be Emily in his bed. At least, after ten years of working together, he had more real liking for her than he did for most of the women who had been there. It wouldn't be a difficult favor; he'd become adept at performing in bed despite a lack of real, driving desire. And Emily wasn't quite the plain Jane she thought she was.

It meant a great deal to Emily. Adam could tell it was tearing her up to think that she was too unattractive for a man, that she had missed out on the greatest secret of life. He owed her whatever help he could give her. She'd helped him through the worst times after Cassie's departure. She had wakened him the time or two she'd found him asleep in his office in the morning when she came in, and had told him gently to go home and shave. She had ignored his sudden, unreasonable bursts of temper, and had covered up the mistakes he'd made in his exhausted, shell-shocked state. She had warded off phone calls and made excuses for him to friends and family, until his mother had taken to calling Emily "the dragon that guards your office."

Most of all, one evening when they had been working late, long after everyone else had gone, she had stepped into his office to ask him a question and found him with his face in his hands, awash in pain and self-pity. She hadn't left, hadn't snapped at him, but had simply come quickly to his side and bent over him, asking if she could help. He had poured it all out to her: the betrayal, the anguish, the emptiness, the grief. And she had listened—without comment, without question, without fussing or hovering as his mother did. She had let him talk it all out until at last he'd reached the end, drained and almost peaceful.

For that night, even this intimate favor was hardly an adequate return.

Adam sat down in his broad, leather desk chair and swiveled around to gaze out the window. He would need to plan this thing carefully. It was important that it be just right. There mustn't be anything sordid or cold about Emily's introduction to lovemaking. Of course, there wouldn't be any hint of love between them, but he could nevertheless do his best to make sure that it was special and lovely for her. He'd done it all with love once, and he knew how to make it sweet and gentle, how to wrap it with beauty.

The first problem was where. A motel was too sterile, yet his apartment or her house seemed too intimate and at the same time too mundane. Besides, her aunt and mother lived with her, which made her house completely out of the question. He formed a triangle with his hands, resting his chin on it, thinking. Then he smiled. Of course. It was the perfect place—his cabin in the Smoky Mountains. It was remote and romantic, set in the midst of a wilderness of trees and flowering vegetation, with a breathtaking view of the mountains. It would be hard to find anything more beautiful. The spring evenings would still be cool enough for a fire in the fireplace, and they could sit in front of its blazing warmth, sipping wine and melting into lovemaking.

Just the thought of it brought a certain heat to his abdomen. He'd never brought a woman there—Cassie hadn't liked it, and later he hadn't wanted the intrusion of his casual lovers—but now it seemed a perfect place for a love affair. They could spend the weekend there and make love more than once, not just have a single brief encounter.

Adam leaned his head back against his chair, making plans, thinking that he would call the caretaker who lived in the small town nearby and tell her to get the cabin cleaned and ready, deciding what wine he would take with them.

Funny, he found he enjoyed whipping up the romantic scheme; he hadn't planned something like this in years. Strange as the whole thing was, he was actually beginning to look forward to it.

Emily arrived at the office the next morning with a slight headache and a very nervous stomach. She had awakened late and feeling less than her best. The quick shower she took had improved her state only a little. She had dressed and fastened her hair back in the usual way, then stood for a moment staring at her image in the mirror. She was, she decided, unrelievedly plain and dull. How could Adam even consider making love to her? Last night Adam's offer had been astonishing, but she'd been too stunned and fuzzy-headed to really think it through. This morning, in the cold light of day, it seemed impossible.

At breakfast her mother had been excited and curious about Emily's visit to a bar the evening before, while Aunt Rosemary had still been bristling with disapproval over Emily's coming home in a cab, smelling of liquor. Emily had sighed inwardly. She was going to have to make Rosemary realize that she was a grown woman now and making her own decisions, no longer answerable to her aunt. If Aunt Rosemary got this forbidding over a couple of drinks, she could just imagine what she'd say when she found out Emily was going to spend the night with a man!

But then, Emily didn't know if she would spend the night with Adam; perhaps he only intended a brief sexual encounter. Perhaps he intended nothing at all this morning—after he'd woken up and realized he'd been suffering from temporary insanity the night before.

He wouldn't go through with it, she told herself. Last night he had been a little bit tipsy and had felt sorry for her. He'd offered out of sympathy, but this morning he was bound to realize he couldn't be that generous. He would back out. She mustn't get her hopes up. She must not let herself believe that her fantasy was going to come true.

Her mother had driven her to the office, and with each passing mile Emily had been more and more filled with dread. She couldn't face Adam this morning. It would be embarrassing even to see him and know she'd poured out her secrets that way. And it would be absolutely humiliating when he called her into his office and explained to her—very gently, of course—that the wild scheme he'd suggested to her last night simply wouldn't work. She would have to smile somehow and be very nonchalant about it, act as if she had never taken it seriously, as if she weren't cut to the bone by his rejection. She didn't know if she could do it.

By the time Emily reached the office her knees were trembling and her stomach was roiling with fear. It was a vast relief to turn the corner to her office and see that Adam's office was still dark. It was even more of a relief when she looked over his daily schedule and saw that he had an early appointment at another lawyer's office, then had to file a petition and see a judge at the courthouse. With luck she wouldn't see him all morning.

The nerves in her stomach subsided enough that she was able to fix a cup of coffee and immerse herself in her work. Two hours later she was seated in front of her word processor, her fingers flying, a Dictaphone headset on her ears, when a sharp rap on the wall just inside her door broke her concentration. She glanced up and saw Adam standing in her doorway.

"Adam!" She flushed, then paled. Her stomach curled into a tiny ball. She snatched the headset from her ears. "I'm sorry. I was concentrating so hard I didn't see you."

"I know. That's why everyone keeps trying to steal you from me."

"What?"

"Half the guys in this firm have suggested trading secretaries with them, or at least loaning you out to them every once in a while."

"Oh."

"I just got back from the courthouse." He tossed a manila folder onto her desk. "You can file that." He paused awkwardly. "Uh, why don't you come into my office for a second? I have something I want to talk to you about."

"Of course." She managed a smile. Her hands had turned as cold as ice. He was going to say it now. He would call her into his office and tell her that the scheme he'd suggested last night would never work out.

It took an effort of will to push back her chair and stand. She didn't want to go. She didn't want to hear it. But Adam was standing, politely waiting for her to walk past him out of the door, and she had to make herself move. She walked mechanically through the door and across the hall into his office. He followed her, shutting the door behind him. Emily crossed her arms and looked at one of the pictures on his wall, staring with great intensity at the pen-and-ink sketch she'd seen a thousand times before.

Adam cleared his throat and moved around to the side of his desk. He didn't quite know how to broach the subject. All the way over from the courthouse, he'd been nervous about seeing Emily again. He'd wondered how she would react. He imagined she might be horrified at what she had revealed last night and would tell him she had no intention of going through with it. It would be a relief, of course, because it really was a crazy idea. He'd felt a few reservations about it himself this morning. Still, it would be disappointing if she did cancel it after all the planning he'd done last night—and he'd already called the caretaker of the cabin before he left his house this morning.

He had gone by Emily's office to tell her his plans and to see if she had changed her mind, but when he'd stopped at her door and seen her typing away, looking so much as she always had, he'd felt terribly awkward. To buy time he had asked her over to his office, but now he was even less sure of what to do. Usually, when Emily came into his office, he was seated behind his desk and she either stood or sat in front of the desk. But now, considering the subject, that seemed much too formal, too boss-to-secretary. On the other hand, it would be weird for them to sit down side by side in the chairs facing his desk. So he remained standing, hovering at the edge of his desk. Emily stayed on her feet, too, turned partially away from him and staring fixedly at the sketch on his wall.

Adam glanced at the picture but could see nothing remarkable about it. He looked back at Emily, and his gaze flickered down her body. He suspected she had a good figure hidden under the plain, chocolate-brown suit. Slender. Long legs. He couldn't tell about her breasts; the jacket effectively negated them. Nor could he see the curve of her derriere. He wondered what she looked like without clothes. Why had he never noticed her figure before? He cleared his throat. "Ah, I did some thinking last night after I came back to the office."

Emily pressed her lips together tightly. Here it came.

"And, uh..." Adam paused. He was strangely tongue-tied, and he couldn't keep his eyes from wandering over her. He thought he'd never really looked at her before, never really seen the contours of her face or the line of her throat. He felt like an idiot, staring at someone he'd known so long as if he'd just met her. Thank God she wasn't looking at him, or she'd think he'd gone crazy. He moved a step closer, his eyes narrowing. What color were her eyes, anyway? It was hard to see them behind those glasses. He fished in his coat pocket for the horn-rimmed glasses he used for reading, then stopped. He could hardly put on his glasses and lean forward to inspect her eyes. He tried to remember what he'd just said.

Emily was rooted to the spot, her nerves on edge during his fumbling words and long silence. Finally she could stand it no more and blurted out, "It's all right. You don't have to think of a polite way to phrase it." Adam's eyebrows rose, but she was talking too rapidly for him to speak. "I understand. You've probably realized that it was a—a—that it wasn't feasible. I'm sure you want to call it off, and, of course, I don't blame you. It's—well, we both probably had a little too much to drink last night."

Adam started toward her, then stopped and crossed his arms against his chest. He sat down on the edge of his desk. "What are you saying?"

"That I won't be surprised or upset with you if you want to call it off."

"I didn't say I'm calling it off." Adam watched her carefully for her reaction.

His words startled her so that Emily turned and looked straight at him. "You aren't?"

He shook his head. "Not unless you want to. Did you have regrets about agreeing to it?"

"No." She still stared at him wide-eyed, as if she couldn't believe her ears.

"Neither do I."

Emily had to press her lips together to keep from bursting into a sunny grin. She mustn't let him see how overjoyed she was at his words or he'd know how she felt about him. It was best to keep things on as cool and friendly a plane as he did. "Well, then. I guess we're still—" How did one express what they were planning?

Adam chuckled, his blue eyes warm with amusement. "Yeah. Hard to find the words for it, isn't it? That's why I was mumbling around so."

Emily smiled back. "Oh. I see. I thought you were trying to find a nice way to get out of it."

"No, I was just trying to tell you what I'd planned. I thought we could go up to my cabin in the mountains. Spend the weekend. How does that sound?"

It sounded heavenly to her. A whole weekend in the mountains with Adam! It was more than she could have dreamed of. "Uh. Very nice. That sounds lovely."

He wished she'd shown a little more pleasure. A little sparkle. He wondered if she was looking forward to it with anticipation, or if she regarded it as something to be gotten through in order to have the same knowledge that other women had. But, when he looked closer, he saw a pink tinge to her cheeks and an unusual brightness in her eyes. Her mouth curved softly into a smile. Emily was so restrained, perhaps that was as much as she expressed excitement. On the other hand, maybe he was making up the signs, wanting it to be something more than a clinical experiment for her. Because if that's all it was, it made him nothing but the instrument—and he didn't like the way that felt.

"I figured the weekend after the trial," he went on, to cover his sudden twinge of discomfort. "It starts tomorrow and will probably last next week, then be over the next."

Emily nodded. "That's fine."

He found he didn't want to tell her the rest of his plan. In the face of her cool collectedness it would sound foolish. He'd just let it happen as they went along. They stood for a moment in silence; then Adam moved away from the desk, breaking the awkward pause. "Well, I guess that's all I had to say." He moved around the desk to his usual place in the deep, leather chair. "Any messages?"

"Of course." Emily pointed to a spindle sporting a myriad of pink slips of paper. He groaned comically, and she smiled, then turned and slipped out of the room. She went straight into her office and sat down, swiveling around so that her back was to the door. Her knees were shaking so much that she didn't think she could have stayed on her feet another second. Nor could she stop the huge smile spreading across her face. Her heart was beating like a jackhammer. The day had turned overwhelmingly bright and exciting. He hadn't backed out! He'd meant it. He'd really meant it! She was going to have her moment of love with Adam.

Emily left work that afternoon earlier than she had in years. She was home before five-thirty, and raced up the stairs to her room. She opened the closet door and leafed through her clothes. Once she had allowed herself to believe that the weekend with Adam was going to take place, she'd realized that she had to have a wardrobe for it. It was that knowledge that had sent her rushing home early to search her closet.

It didn't take long to establish that, just as she had feared, she had no clothes suitable for a weekend in the mountains with Adam Marshall. She needed something casual, but most of her clothes were suits and dresses for work. The clothes she wore around the house would never do. Old, faded jeans and sloppy sweatshirts. A couple of dark, well-worn, turtleneck sweaters. She couldn't go to a romantic assignation looking like a slob! Of course, there wasn't really any romance to it, but that didn't mean she shouldn't make an effort. Just the opposite, in fact. Adam didn't love her and—face it—would probably have a difficult time working up the requisite passion. He was, after all, doing this solely out of kindness. So it was her obligation to look as attractive as she possibly could, so that he would have less trouble creating a spark of desire for her.

She wouldn't want anything that was an obvious, and miserable, attempt at looking sexy, of course. Nothing flashy or garish. Just something stylish and appealing to the eye. Something that would enhance her features, make her look as good as she was capable of looking. Emily frowned. There was nothing in her closet that fit the bill.

Then it came to her: Jeanette! She and her cousin were the same size and almost the same height, with very similar coloring. She could wear Jeanette's clothes. Jeanette wouldn't mind. She was always trying to push some of her outfits onto Emily, pointing out how they would enhance Emily's figure or suit her coloring. And Jeanette would have just the sort of things Emily would need for this weekend. She was an attractive career woman who always dressed very smartly. Many of her clothes were too revealing or too attention-getting for Emily, but she was sure that Jeanette would have some outfits that would do. Emily grabbed her purse from the floor, where she had dropped it in her haste to get to her closet, and dashed back down the stairs. She hurried through the house and out to her car, thankful that neither of the older women was there to ask questions. She backed her little blue car out of the driveway and with a roar took off for Jeanette's apartment.

Jeanette was surprised to find her cousin on her doorstep only minutes after she herself had come home from work. "Emily!" she cried, and stepped back for her to enter. "Come on in." She was dressed in a stylish, pink, silk suit with a long, baggy jacket that had full sleeves. On her it looked both classy and alluring; Emily thought that if she had worn it, she would have looked like a clown. Jeanette had always had a certain panache that enabled her to carry off even the strangest new fashions.

With the familiarity of a longtime friend, Emily walked into Jeanette's living room and sat down on the sofa. Jeanette followed her. "You want something to drink? I'm having a glass of white wine."

"No, thank you."

Hostess duties over, Jeanette sank into an easy chair and propped her shoeless feet up on the coffee table. "What brings you here? And so early!" She glanced teasingly at her watch and made an expression of shock. "Why, it's not quite five-thirty."

"All right. All right. I get the point. But I have something I wanted to ask you." Emily couldn't wait for a few minutes of chitchat to get to the object of her visit.

"Sure. What?"

"Could I borrow some of your clothes?"

Jeanette stared. "You're joking." Emily shook her head. "Of course you can! I've tried to get you to a million times." She jumped to her feet. "Come on. Let's check out my closet."

With Emily right behind her, Jeanette strode into her bedroom and flung open the door of the large, walk-in closet. It was filled with clothes. Jeanette had always loved clothes, and her job as a fashion buyer for a large, department-store chain enabled her to indulge her passion. The sheer size of her wardrobe overwhelmed Emily.

"Now, what sort of thing are you looking for?"

Emily smiled. "Your saleslady training is showing. Although I have to say, you have more clothes here than a lot of small stores."

"I love my work," Jeanette replied airily. "No more stalling. Let's get down to business."

Emily drew a breath. "I want something casual. Slacks and a blouse. Or maybe jeans, but not like mine. Something more . . . you know."

"Yeah, I know. Attractive."

"Yeah."

Jeanette began to go through the hangers on a low rod of slacks and skirts. "What's the occasion?"

"I'm going to a cabin in the mountains."

"Oh, really?" Jeanette's curiosity was thoroughly aroused now. "Then why the need for something nicer than old jeans?" She stopped suddenly and turned her head to look at Emily, her eyes sparkling with interest. "Are you going with a man?"

Emily nodded. She should have known Jeanette would guess why she needed attractive clothes.

"Who? Anyone I know?"

Emily hesitated. If anyone knew her secrets, it was Jeanette. But she hated to say it was Adam, because Jeanette would be bound to misinterpret her.

"Come on. Give," Jeanette prodded. "This is old Jeanette, remember, who knows all about you."

"Don't get excited, because it's not what you'll think, but . . . it's Adam Marshall."

"Adam Marshall!" Jeanette's hand fell away from the hangers, and she turned her whole body around to face Emily. "How can it not be what I think? Don't try to tell me you two are going to a cabin in the mountains to work on a case."

She reached out and seized Emily's wrists and pulled her out of the closet, towing her over to the bed and firmly seating her on it. Then she hopped onto the bed herself and sat facing her, skirt hiked up inelegantly so she could sit cross-legged, leaning forward, elbows on her knees. "Now. Divulge."

Emily smiled. "This is just like when we were teenagers."

"Yeah. Except now we're talking about something a lot more interesting than we ever did then. Come on. Tell Jeanette all about it."

"It's not—we aren't—well, it's something very strange."

"So tell me! I want to know what miracle happened. Yesterday you were down in the dumps about turning thirty and being alone, and today you're talking about spending a weekend with Mr. Wonderful."

"I started crying yesterday after work. It was really stupid. Mother called me and told me about Sherry Pike getting married, and I hung up and started crying."

Jeanette's face softened. "Oh, Emmy..."

"Then Adam came back to the office and found me sobbing like an idiot at my desk. He was so nice, like he always is, and he took me down to The Pub for a drink to cheer me up."

"This is getting good."

"I had a couple of drinks and—well, I made a fool of myself." A blush crept up her face. How could she tell Jeanette about the loveless arrangement she and Adam had made? "Adam wanted to know what was wrong, and I told him that I was unhappy about being thirty and a virgin and all."

Emily sneaked a glance at her cousin. Jeanette nodded encouragingly. "And?"

"And, well, he offered to...uh..."

"Initiate you?"

"Yeah, sort of. And that's why we're going to his cabin in the mountains."

"Then how can you say it's not what I'm thinking! It's exactly what I was thinking."

"But it's not romantic or anything."

"Not romantic! Sweetheart, what else would you call a rendezvous with the man of your dreams at a secluded cabin?"

"I mean, he's not interested in me."

"A guy wants to take you to his cabin and make love to you, and you say he's not interested? How do you figure that!"

"He's doing it as a favor! It's just that he's so kind."

Jeanette rolled her eyes. "Uh huh. I know lots of men who are kind and generous like that. They just love to do women favors."

"No, I mean it! I'm sure he's never thought of me sexually. He felt sorry for me, and he likes me. So he offered to—"

"To be the sacrificial lamb." Jeanette finished for her, a Cheshire-cat grin spreading across her face. "I never realized what a paragon Adam Marshall was."

"Jenny!"

"Now don't start sticking out your chin at me. I'm not criticizing Adam Marshall. I'm simply pointing out that you're looking at this in a screwy way. No man is going to make love to you out of pity. Somewhere, somehow, he's got to feel a certain amount of attraction to you." Emily started to speak, but Jeanette stopped her with an admonitory finger. "Even—*even*—though he may not realize that fact himself."

Emily shot her a skeptical look. "You're saying Adam really wants me deep down and doesn't know it?"

"I'm saying maybe he has feelings for you that he hasn't realized because he's spent the last couple of years so hung up on his ex-wife. At the very least he likes you and feels enough chemistry with you that he's willing to make an offer like that. The guy isn't going to jump into bed with you if you don't somehow attract him, no matter how sorry he feels for you."

"Jenny, I'm not going to get my hopes built up about this."

"You never get your hopes built up about anything! And, damn it, you ought to! I tell you what, Adam Marshall doesn't feel half as sorry for you as you do for yourself."

Emily's eyes flashed. "That's not true!"

"Isn't it? Then why don't you make an effort? Why don't you try? You've had the greatest opportunity you'll ever get dropped in your lap, and you're sitting there talking about how little it means. You could make it mean a lot. Even if Adam does have as little feeling for you as you say, you could change that during the weekend. You'll be together, entirely alone, for a whole weekend, and you'll be making love. Sharing something like that can change your relationship. You've got a chance to create something with him. Show him how attractive you can be. Make him sit up and take notice."

"How am I supposed to do that?"

"Well, you've made a start on it. You've come over here to get some decent clothes. Next you can get rid of those glasses. Your eyes are your best feature; show them off. Wear makeup. I'll lend you some of that, too."

"But—"

"But what? You aren't a teenager anymore, with my mother telling you what you can and can't do. You're an adult now, and fully capable of getting contacts. Remember how much you wanted them when you were a teenager?"

"Yeah." Emily remembered very well. She had spent many nights crying over the fact that Aunt Rosemary had decreed that contact lenses were too expensive and frivolous. "But somehow, as I got older, it didn't seem so important anymore. I'm used to my glasses. I'd feel almost naked without them on now.''

"You mean you got to where you hid behind them, just like you do behind those plain clothes, so nobody can really see you."

Emily frowned. "I don't know."

"I do. And don't say they're too expensive. I know you. You never spend money on clothes or going out or anything except books. You're bound to have a healthy amount of cash stashed away somewhere."

"Yeah, I could afford to buy them."

"Then do."

Emily stared thoughtfully down at her hands. She would look more appealing to Adam without her glasses, even though the idea of not wearing them was somehow frightening. When he kissed her—a flash of heat ran through her body at the thought—her glasses would be in the way. They would be awkward, an impediment; even removing them would be a distraction. And she hated to appear in any way klutzy or fumbling or inappropriate. "Maybe you're right. I'll make an appointment with an eye doctor tomorrow."

"Hallelujah!" Jeanette threw up her hands ecstatically. "Next item, your hair. It'd look much better if you'd cut it off about shoulder length. Your face is long and thin; you need some fullness and softness around it, not long straight hair that just pulls your face down. Have it streaked. That'd really brighten it up."

Emily shook her head decisively. "No. I couldn't."

"And why not, may I ask?"

"I like my hair long."

"Why? Because it always drove Mother crazy?" Emily shot her a startled look, and Jeanette chuckled. "I realize that was your one form of rebellion, but there's no reason for holding on to it just because Mother didn't like it."

"That's not it."

"Then what is?"

"I don't want to do anything . . . conspicuous."

"It'll be conspicuously pretty, that's all."

"Streaking my hair, cutting it off, perming it—it'd be like trying to be something I'm not. Calling attention to myself. It would only emphasize how plain I am. It would look incongruous."

"Don't be an idiot. It would not."

"Dyed blond hair is flashy."

"You think my hair is flashy?"

"No, but you're naturally blond."

"Not this pretty a blond. I have my hair frosted. And I'm not talking about even doing that much to yours. Just have it streaked a little."

"No. Really, Jeanette, I couldn't. I'd feel like a fool."

"Honestly! You are the most exasperating person!" Jeanette glared at her for a minute, then sighed and shrugged. "Okay, I give up. On that topic, at least." She gave a sudden, gamine grin. "But, oh boy, am I going to fix you up with clothes."

She jumped off the bed, pulling Emily with her. "Come on, girl, let's hit that closet. We're going to make one celebrated trial lawyer sit up and take notice."

# Chapter 4

Jeanette raided her closet with glee, pulling out several pairs of slacks and designer jeans and tossing them onto the bed, then following them with light sweaters in creamy, pastel colors that almost made Emily's mouth water.

"Oh, Jeanette, these are beautiful." Emily picked up a Carolina-blue, short-sleeved, cashmere sweater. "But do you really think this color..."

She trailed off wistfully, and her cousin grimaced and pounced on the sweater, turning Emily to face the mirror and holding up the sweater in front of her. "The color is perfect on you. I don't know why you insist on wearing tans and browns; they do nothing for you. Wearing things with color does not make you look like a neon sign, you know. Pastels are gorgeous on you. Look."

She exchanged the light-blue sweater for a bulkier one in a pale, pinkish mauve. Emily smiled. It was a beautiful sweater, and it did seem to add color to her face, yet it wasn't flashy or conspicuous.

"You're taking both of those," Jeanette pronounced. "Here, try on these jeans and slacks. And I think I'll get you a lighter top, just in case it's not as cool as usual in the mountains."

They wound up with two blouses, two sweaters, a pair of mauve slacks, a pair of tan slacks, and a pair of jeans before Emily called a halt to the search. "Jeanette, please. I'll only be gone two days. I can't take an entire wardrobe!"

Jeanette wrinkled her nose. "I guess that's enough. Now let's look at dresses."

"Dresses! I don't need any dresses. We're going to a cabin in the mountains, remember?"

"Sure. But you've got two weeks before then." Jeanette removed a turquoise suit with white trim from the closet and held it up. "How about this? Wouldn't that look great in the office?"

"No! Absolutely not. I am not borrowing your clothes to wear to the office the next couple of weeks. I want to look nice that weekend, so Adam won't be revolted by me, but I will not start dressing up every day, as if I'm trying to attract him. After what he's been kind enough to offer, I don't want him to think I'm chasing him, trying to turn his offer into something much more."

"Really, Emily! A man like Adam Marshall is not going to get scared because you start dressing nicer. I suspect he'd be pleased to see you doing something with yourself."

"No."

Jeanette pulled out a soft, black skirt and a black jacket with a flirty little ruffle below the waistline. The top was collarless and the neckline cut in a low V. A fragile piece of black net dotted with a few large, black sequins filled in the V. It was simple, classic and utterly beautiful. Jeanette dangled it tantalizingly. "You can't pass this up, can you?"

"It's gorgeous," Emily breathed, and she reached out to touch the material; then she drew her hand back and shook her head reluctantly. "There's no reason to take it, though. I'd never wear an evening suit at Adam's cabin. I couldn't even wear it to the office."

Jeanette sighed and hung it back on the rod. "Oh, all right. If you're going to be that stubborn..."

Emily began to gather up the clothes. "Thank you for all this. You don't know how much I appreciate it."

"Just a minute. You're not through yet. You have to have shoes." Jeanette began digging through the neat line of shoes that ran along the shelf above the clothes.

"I have shoes."

"They won't look as good with these clothes as mine." She selected a pair of tan flats and a pair of sandals and put them down on the bed beside the stack of clothes. "And jewelry."

"Jewelry? With jeans and slacks?"

"Sure." She crossed the room and opened a large jewelry box. She pulled out a pair of pale-blue, translucent earrings shaped like seashells and held them up against the sweater. "Perfect. And the pearls are just right with that pinky outfit."

Emily had to admit that they did look attractive against her skin, as did the simple, gold chain Jeanette pressed upon her. They added the jewelry and shoes to the growing stack of clothes. Jeanette studied the pile for a moment, making sure that she had included everything. Then she turned to her cousin earnestly. "Promise me one thing."

"What?"

"You'll buy yourself some sexy lingerie."

Emily blinked. She hadn't really thought about it, but in this situation, that was as important as her outer clothes, probably more so. "All right."

"Silk and lace. Feminine. Sheer," Jeanette pressed.

Emily laughed. "Okay, okay. I understand what you're talking about, and I promise I'll buy some."

"Good." Jeanette broke into a grin and stepped forward to hug her. "I'm so happy for you."

"Thank you." Emily burst into a smile, "Me, too."

The next day Emily went to be fitted for soft contact lenses. She was told that the lenses would be ready in less than a week, giving her ample time to become accustomed to them before her weekend with Adam. She returned to the office excited and eager, yet nervous at the changes she was suddenly making in her life.

The next two and a half weeks crawled by. Adam, immersed in his trial, was gone all day, and Emily saw him only late in the afternoon, or in the evening if he asked her to stay and help him prepare for court the next day. Wrapped up as he was in the trial, Adam spoke of little else, never alluding to their upcoming trip. He seemed to have no qualms about the weekend, as Emily did. But then, she pointed out to herself, it wasn't important enough for him to get nervous. In fact, his attitude was so much the same that Emily sometimes wondered if he had forgotten about it, and there were moments when she wondered darkly if he had meant what he said.

Emily couldn't maintain a tenth of the indifference Adam exhibited. She was on an emotional roller-coaster ride, shooting up to ecstatic eagerness one minute, then plunging down to gloom and fear the next. She daydreamed about being alone with Adam, imagined sitting beside him in his car on the way to the cabin, walking with him through the trees, sitting across from him at the table. Lying in bed with him... Such pictures made her shiver, half afraid, half trembling with yearning.

She couldn't stop thinking about making love with him.
She saw him bare-chested, arms hard and muscled, reaching for her. She wondered if the same dark hair that was on
his head curled on his chest. She wondered how his lips
would feel. Would he caress her? Would his fingers roam
her body sweetly? Would his lips and tongue seek out her
flesh? Night after night she had trouble going to asleep, and
during the days she couldn't concentrate on her work. Her
mind was always on Adam.

Somehow the time passed. She got her contacts and began wearing them over the weekend. She wore them most of
the day at work, building up until by the end of the next
week she could leave them in almost full time. She had resisted the vanity of having the lenses colored blue or green
to make her eyes appear a prettier color than gray, but even
so they made her eyes seem suddenly huge and soft and
pretty. She wondered if that was real or merely her imagination. Adam hadn't even noticed that she was wearing
them.

She went to a department store to buy new underwear and
a sexy nightgown one evening after work. Emily had always hated shopping for lingerie, perhaps even more than
shopping for other clothes. She was certain that the salesclerks looked upon her with disdain because she was plain,
and that seemed especially true for lingerie, where all the
garments were so feminine and sensual. She felt like an alien
in the lingerie department, as if she had no right to be there.
But this time she was buoyed by the inner knowledge that
she was buying garments for a man to see her in, that she,
too, could pass the test of being a woman, and she bought
the dainty pieces of silk and lace with assurance and enjoyment.

That left only one thing she had to get before the next
weekend, the thing Emily dreaded most—a contraceptive.

Every evening after work she drove to the drugstore on her way home. The first night she didn't even get out of her car, but simply turned for home, promising herself that she would do it the next night. The next evening she managed to forget to stop altogether. The third day she once again drove to the drugstore and forced herself to go inside, where she wandered through the aisles, refusing help from the salesclerks. Finally she found the contraceptive section. It seemed distressingly near the center of activity, directly in front of the raised pharmacy area and right beside a cash register. She stopped a few feet away and glanced at the line of four people waiting at the cash register. She retreated to the toothpastes.

The line at the cash register diminished to two, then to one person, but it never completely disappeared. Emily loitered around the toothpastes until she felt embarrassed, then went on to the cold medicines, which were nearer to her target. She edged closer. This was ridiculous, she told herself. She was thirty years old, a grown woman. Nobody here knew her, and no one would care what she bought. Women bought such things all the time now; this wasn't the forties, for heaven's sake. There was absolutely no reason to be embarrassed.

But she couldn't help wishing she had a wedding ring on her finger. And she couldn't help thinking that the clerk behind the register would look at her and the product and wonder what a woman who looked like her would need with a product like that. Surely in just a weekend she wouldn't get pregnant....

Emily gave herself a firm mental shake. Thinking that way could lead to disaster. She had to buy something. She had to pluck up the courage somehow. There was really no other choice.

She sidled a little closer, her eyes scanning the amazing array of boxes. She'd never dreamed there would be so many different things to choose from. Closing her mind to the rest of the store, she made herself pick up a box and read the instructions. Ugh. She set it down and picked up another. They all sounded so messy and so . . . so jarringly interruptive. She couldn't imagine stopping Adam as he kissed and caressed her and saying, "Excuse me, I have to slip into the bathroom. . . ." It was a relief to finally come upon one that could be put in place in the morning and then forgotten about for the rest of the day.

Now all she had to do was buy it. Her fingers tightened around the box, and she stole a sidelong glance at the cash register. Still two people there. She wandered back through the store. Perhaps if she bought something else it would sort of cover it, as if that weren't *all* she had come in for. She trailed along the aisles and finally wound up with a paperback book and a bottle of shampoo that she didn't need. She went to the cosmetics checkout counter, where there was no line, and set her purchases down on the counter. She pulled out her billfold, determined not to look directly at the salesclerk. To add to her embarrassment, she could feel the color rising in her cheeks.

She paid the total, the clerk sacked the purchases with gum-chewing indifference, and Emily grabbed the brown bag. Through! She sailed out the front door, feeling suddenly lighthearted and rather proud of herself. Once again she'd gotten through a situation that earlier would have frozen her with embarrassment.

The final arguments for the trial were presented on Tuesday, and Adam returned to the office looking worn and tired. There was a seemingly perpetual frown between his eyes. Emily knew that he wouldn't be able to rest until the jury came in with a decision. He spent the evening catching up on the work that had been accumulating while he was in court, but he didn't ask for her help, and Emily went home.

He was in and out of the office the next day, frowning, his gaze abstracted. Still he said nothing about their weekend, now only three days away. He spent most of the day at the courthouse, waiting for the verdict. Emily had to admit to herself that her major interest in the verdict was that it come in quickly, so it wouldn't interfere with their weekend.

As she sat at her desk late in the afternoon, drafting a letter that Adam had left for her to do and waiting for him to return, a tall man with shaggy black hair and vivid blue eyes stuck his head inside her office and grinned. "Hey, sweetheart. How you doing?"

"Tag!" Emily couldn't help but beam. Taggart Marshall always had that effect on everyone. "I'm okay. How about you?"

He shrugged and ambled inside to fold his long frame into the straight-backed chair beside Emily's desk. "I take it the counselor's not in his office?"

Emily shook her head, swiveling her chair to face him. It was impossible to work with Tag in the office. "He's in court, waiting for a verdict."

"Oh." Tag grimaced and stretched out his legs in front of him, hands crossed behind his head. "Any point in hanging around waiting for him?"

"No telling. He's been in and out a lot today. He'll be back, but I'm not sure if it will be in ten minutes or a couple of hours."

Tag grinned. "I'll stick around for a while. It'll be more fun talking to you, anyway. Adam will probably lecture me."

"Are you in trouble again?"

He assumed an expression of mock hurt. "You wound me."

Emily chuckled. If Adam Marshall was the perfect son of the family, then his youngest brother, Tag, was the perfect black sheep. The middle brother, James, had shocked and dismayed the family by not joining the family firm when he graduated from law school, but going instead into criminal law in the local Federal Attorney General's office. It was even rumored that James had so far forgotten himself as to have political aspirations. But at least he was incisive, stable and aware of his responsibilities as a Marshall.

Taggart was none of those things. He enjoyed partying more than working. He had dropped out of law school halfway through the first semester. He preferred sailing the Intercoastal Waterway to the banking or executive positions offered him by his Marshall and Taggart uncles. He had no ambitions that anyone could determine, except to enjoy himself. He was wild and feckless—and thoroughly charming. Emily couldn't imagine loving him as she loved Adam, but he was always fun to talk to.

Taggart's eyes narrowed, and he studied her intently for a moment. Then his face cleared. "You don't have on your glasses, do you?"

Emily shook her head. She hadn't worn them all week, and Adam still hadn't noticed. "I got contacts last week."

"They look nice. You've been hiding awfully pretty eyes."

"Thank you."

There was the sound of hurrying footsteps in the hall, as if someone was almost running. Tag and Emily exchanged a questioning glance just as Adam burst into the room. His color was high, and his blue eyes sparkled. A grin spread across his face. "Emily!" He glanced at his brother. "Why, hey, Tag." He turned back to Emily, who had risen to her feet, pulled up by the force of Adam's excitement. "We won it! Four hundred thousand in damages—every cent I asked for."

"Adam, that's wonderful!"

He laughed, and, much to her surprise, he lifted her up into his arms and whirled her around. "Wonderful? It's unbelievable! I didn't think we had a chance with that jury." He set her back down on the floor and planted a firm kiss on her mouth before he let her go. "Let's celebrate!"

He turned to his brother. "What do you say, Tag? Want to go get a drink and some dinner?"

"Sure," Tag agreed lazily.

Emily stood stock still behind Adam, her eyes dazed. She could still feel the warm imprint of his mouth on her lips and the pressure of his arms around her body; his distinctive scent lingered in her nostrils. A hot surge of emotion rushed through her body, a mingling of longing, excitement and love far out of proportion to the exuberant, celebratory hug Adam had given her.

"You'll come, too, won't you, Emily?" Adam swung back around to face her. "My client and his wife are coming by in a few minutes, and we're going out for steaks."

Normally Emily would have refused such an offer, feeling that Adam was merely being polite, and that she would be out of place with him and his clients. But now, so intense and sudden were the feelings brought about by Adam's hug, she quickly answered, "Yes. I'd love to. Thank you."

"Great. Cut off your machine and get your stuff, and let's go. We can meet Doug and Susan in the lobby."

Emily cleared her desk in record time and turned off her word processor while Adam went over to his office, Tag ambling along after him. Emily ran a fast brush through her hair and put on lipstick, then picked up her purse and turned out the light in her office. She waited just outside her door in the hallway, wanting to give Tag time alone with Adam to discuss whatever he had come up here for. It was only a little after four. Emily wondered if she had ever left the office that early before. She didn't think so. But today she didn't feel the slightest guilt. She was too excited.

After a few minutes Adam and Tag emerged, and they started down the hall to the reception area. Doug and his wife, a beaming, middle-aged couple, were waiting for them. Susan threw her arms around Adam and hugged him. "I'm sorry," she said as she stepped away. "But I just had to do that. I'm so happy!"

Adam smiled. "Don't apologize. I never mind being hugged by an attractive woman." he introduced his brother and Emily to the couple, and they started on their way.

Adam was in a charged-up, recklessly happy mood. Emily couldn't remember seeing him quite this carefree and elated since his divorce. He and Tag vied with each other making quips, and he told several funny stories about his trial experiences. He grinned and joked and laughed, and Emily felt warmed and breathless just watching him.

They visited Schober's, a bar on West Fourth, then went on to the Tavern in Old Salem, the well-preserved, original, Moravian settlement. The restaurant there was colonial in appearance, and the waiters and waitresses dressed in colonial-style clothes. The food was delicious, but Emily hardly noticed. She was aware of little except Adam's presence beside her. His arm touched hers casually now and then; his fingers grazed hers when he handed her the butter dish or the salt; he smiled and glanced at her as he talked. It was, of course, perfectly meaningless, but still the sight and sound and feel of him filled Emily's senses.

She was sorry when the group broke up around eight. Doug and Susan left them at the restaurant, and Emily rode with Adam and Tag back downtown. The meal had ne-

gated whatever effect Emily's drinks had had on her tonight, so Adam dropped her off at the parking lot to get her
car.

"Where's your car?" he asked, turning into the lot and
cruising along the rows of cars.

"It's all right. You can let me off here."

"Nonsense. I might as well take you right to it. Where is
it?"

"Second level."

Adam took the up ramp. He was curious to see her car.
Ever since he'd realized how little he knew about her, he'd
wanted to pick up information about her. The fact of the
matter was that he'd had Emily on the brain far too much
during this trial. He rarely had trouble concentrating on his
case; usually a trial completely filled his life. This time,
however, thoughts about the weekend with Emily had sifted
into his mind at the most inappropriate times and places.
Thoughts of how he would please her, how he would touch
her or kiss her, kept creeping into his mind and wrecking his
concentration. It had been silly, as he'd told himself often;
it wasn't as if the weekend with Emily was important to him.
But he supposed the importance of it to her made him anxious to make the experience exactly right. That was what
added the pressure right at the time when he needed it least.
It had been an effort to keep his attention fully on the trial,
which had made this trial more stressful than any he'd done
in a long time. And that was why it had been such a relief to
get it over, why he had felt so giddy and excited when he'd
heard the winning verdict. Now he could relax and go ahead
with his plans for the weekend.

"There it is."

Adam braked and looked at the car Emily had pointed to.
"That's your car?" It was a sports car, not at all the model
of Mazda he had pictured when Emily told him what she

drove. It didn't satisfy his curiosity; it made him wonder about her all the more.

"Yes." Emily opened her door and slid out. "Thank you very much for dinner." She turned toward the back seat, where Taggart sat. "It was nice to see you, Tag." She started toward her car.

"Wait a minute." Adam scrambled out of his seat and followed her, reaching her door just as she did and opening it for her.

"Thank you." Emily glanced at him, startled, and started to get in.

"Wait." Adam caught her arm, and she stopped. Her clear gray eyes gazed up at him, puzzled. He frowned. "There's something different about you. I've noticed it all evening. What is it? Your hair?"

"I'm wearing contacts."

"Of course!" It was obvious now that she'd said it, and he felt like a fool for not realizing earlier. Her eyes were larger and clearer than he'd ever seen them. He could see that they were gray. He hadn't known their color before. "You look nice without your glasses. Why didn't you get contacts earlier?"

Emily shrugged "I guess I'd become used to my glasses." It occurred to her that Adam would realize she had purchased them for him, and the idea embarrassed her. She added hastily, "My cousin's been bugging me to do it for a long time, and she finally talked me into it."

"I'm glad." He smiled, and Emily's stomach started its usual acrobatics. "Uh, Emily, I wanted to talk to you... I'd like to take you to dinner Friday night. To Ryan's."

Emily stared. "What?"

"I want to take you out Friday. Say, seven. Can you come? We'll head up to the cabin the next morning."

"But you don't need to—I mean—that's like a date."

He grinned "It *is* a date. You didn't think we were just going to hop into bed right off, did you?"

Emily blushed. "Well, I . . ."

"I think a romantic date would be in order. A little wooing, to set the stage." Adam raised his hand and brushed a knuckle down her cheek; she felt it clear down to her bones. His eyes gazed down into hers, kind and smiling and too entrancing for any degree of comfort.

"It's okay," she replied nervously. "You don't have to."

"I want to. Think of it as part of the whole 'experience.' Okay?"

"Okay."

"Then it's a date? Seven?"

Emily nodded, unable to speak. On impulse Adam leaned over and kissed her lightly on the forehead. He stepped back. "See you tomorrow."

"Good night." It came out soft and breathless.

"Good night." He walked away to his car and turned. "Oh. I won't be in until late tomorrow morning. I plan to catch up on my sleep."

Again Emily nodded, and he gave her a wave, then stepped into his car and drove off. Emily remained standing beside her open door, gazing after his car until it turned and went down the ramp, out of sight. Delight and panic warred within her. She'd never dreamed Adam might take her out, might treat her as if theirs were a normal relationship leading up to sex. It sounded wonderful. But how would she act? What was she to say? And what could she possibly wear! She had to see Jeanette. Emily jumped into her car and backed out, tires squealing.

Ten minutes later Emily was at Jeanette's apartment. "I'm back. I need something dressy. Adam's taking me out to Ryan's Friday night."

"Terrific!" Jeanette was all smiles. "Are you sure there's not something more going on here than you say?"

"I'm positive. It's just that he's so nice. He wants to give me the 'whole experience.' So he's going to take me out Friday and then drive up to the mountains the next day."

"That black suit is exactly what you need."

Emily thought of the dress Jeanette had offered her last time. The neckline was a little low, but it was a beautiful dress, and it didn't really reveal anything—she didn't have that much to reveal. And she wanted desperately to wear it. "Yeah. That's the one I want."

"Good. You can have it. On one condition."

"What?"

"You come here before you go out Friday night and let me fix your hair and makeup."

Emily gave her a suspicious glance.

Jeanette grimaced. "I promise I won't make you look like a clown—or a lady of the evening or whatever it is you're scared of. Just a little makeup."

"Okay. I promise."

On Friday afternoon Emily left work a little before five and drove to Jeanette's apartment. It was the third time in two weeks that she'd left work early, and she felt a little guilty, especially since she didn't need that much time to dress. But she'd been too nervous to remain seated at her desk a minute longer.

Jeanette plonked Emily down on a small stool in the brightly lit bathroom and handed her a bottle of pale foundation. Emily applied it sparingly under Jeanette's eagle eye. Jeanette herself applied the soft eyeshadow and blusher, then let Emily finish with lipstick and mascara. Jeanette inspected Emily's face carefully and beamed. "There. Now look at yourself." She turned to face the mirror. "Isn't that beautiful? And it doesn't look garish or conspicuous."

Emily wasn't so sure. The pink blusher was a little too much, she thought, and she looked so—different. Still, her face was softer and prettier than usual; she couldn't deny that. And she'd never realized how attractive plain, gray eyes could be. "Adam won't recognize me."

"He'll be bowled over."

Next Jeanette went to work on Emily's hair. First she curled it on hot rollers to give it body, then brushed it out and pulled it up on top of Emily's head in a soft pompadour. It took forever, it seemed, but when it was finished Emily had to admit that it looked lovely.

She was ready for the final touch: the elegant, black evening suit. Emily slipped it on and gazed at her image in the full length mirror hanging on Jeanette's closet door. She didn't look flat-chested or gawky or skinny—all the adjectives she usually applied to her figure. Rather she appeared elegantly slim and far prettier than she could ever remember. Maybe she wouldn't have to worry about Adam's feeling embarrassed to be seen with her. On the other hand, maybe she was seeing herself through rose-colored glasses, thinking that she was pretty just because the dress was. Emily turned uncertainly toward her cousin.

"You look lovely," Jeanette said firmly, obviously aware of Emily's thoughts. "Just wait. Adam will think so, too."

Emily thanked Jeanette and left, turning down Jeanette's offer of a relaxing glass of wine. She drove the short distance home and went into the house to find Aunt Rosemary and her mother sitting on the living-room sofa like a pair of mismatched bookends. Emily groaned inwardly. She had told them last night that she was going out on a date tonight, hoping that they might treat the occasion normally if they had a little time to adjust to it. Her hopes had obviously been futile.

Each of the women had dressed up in her own way, Rosemary in a somber, charcoal-gray dress that would have done a Puritan proud, and Nancy in a bright, pink dress that was too short for a woman her age, and extra rings, chains and bangles. "Hi," Emily greeted them weakly. "What are you all doing?"

"Waiting for your date, of course," Aunt Rosemary informed her sternly. "You don't think we're going to let you go out with some young man we've never met, do you?"

"Let me!" Emily echoed in astonishment. Did her aunt think that because she lived with them, they still retained control over life?

"Oh, Ro, don't be so Victorian," Nancy complained before Emily could gather her wits enough to contradict her aunt's assumption. Nancy winked at her daughter. "I'm just here to see this handsome young man. I'm so excited for you to be going out and having fun at last—and with someone like Adam Marshall! A mother couldn't ask for more."

"I don't want you two sitting here like vultures when he comes!"

"Don't worry. I won't let Rosemary ask any embarrassing questions," Nancy replied.

Rosemary shot a glare at her overly made-up sister. "I won't let *her* make a fool of herself."

Wonderful. Now the two of them were going to start arguing. Emily dropped into the armchair across from the couch and wracked her brain for a way to get rid of them. Nothing came.

"You look pretty, Emily," her mother remarked. "Not quite enough color, really, but still very pretty."

Rosemary frowned. "That neckline's awfully low. Couldn't you wear a scarf there?"

"Good God!" Nancy retorted in horror. "I know nobody thinks I have much taste, but even I know that would look awful."

"At least it would look decent."

"Decent! 'Decent' is not your major goal when you're going out on a date."

"It ought to be. Especially when you're going out with your boss. The way Emily looks, he'll think she's out to catch him, that she's advertising that she's willing to get involved in one of those 'office romances.' "

Emily felt a flush creeping up her neck. She hadn't been able to work up the courage to tell Nancy and Rosemary that she was spending the weekend with Adam; instead she had pretended that she planned to stay with Jeanette. She would drive to Jeanette's apartment the next morning and have Adam pick her up there. Now she wondered why she hadn't told him to pick her up there this evening, too. It would have saved her a lot of humiliation.

Adam was ten minutes late. It didn't surprise her. He had been closed up in his office with a client when she left work, and Steven Vickers, another lawyer in the firm, had been calling every few minutes to see if he'd finished his appointment yet. Emily wondered whether Adam would be able to get away for dinner at all and dreaded a telephone call telling her that he was still tied up and calling off their date.

When the door bell rang at ten after seven Emily jumped up to answer it, but Rosemary, despite her years, managed to get there before her. Rosemary opened the door, her face as stern as death. Over Rosemary's shoulder Emily saw Adam standing on the front porch. Her aunt glanced pointedly at her watch, and Emily wanted to sink through the floor with embarrassment. She shouldered her way past her aunt and stepped onto the porch.

"Hello, Adam."

His eyes ran rapidly down her and back up to her face. "Emily. You look lovely." A quick smile lightened his face, turning his eyes a vivid blue. "It's a good thing you don't look like that at the office, or I'd never get any work done."

Emily knew it was a flattering lie, but it was sweet to hear it anyway. She'd always wanted to have a man flirt with her, but she didn't know how to respond. She smiled, and her cheeks were tinged a brighter pink with pleasure. Adam had been holding one hand behind his back, and now he brought it out. He held a fresh, spring bouquet of daisies. Emily gasped with pleasure and took the flowers.

"Oh, Adam, they're beautiful!" She gazed at the bouquet, entranced, then looked back up at him, her face glowing. Something tightened in Adam's chest, and he wondered why he'd never noticed how pretty she was before.

Nancy squeezed into the doorway next to her sister. "Well, Emily, why don't you bring the young man in here instead of standing around on the porch?"

"Oh, no, we better leave. I imagine Adam has reservations, and—"

But Adam put his hand at the small of Emily's back and guided her into the house, saying, "We have a few minutes. The reservation's not till seven-thirty. Besides, you need to put those flowers in water."

"Oh. Yes, of course." She couldn't get out of it now. She would be forced to introduce him to her mother and aunt. She led Adam inside and introduced him to the other women, then hurried into the kitchen to find a vase for the flowers.

When she returned moments later, the vase of daisies in hand, she found Adam ensconced on the couch, chatting with Rosemary and Nancy. He flirted with her mother and answered her aunt's stern questions with a smile, until Nancy was practically simpering like a teenager and even Rosemary's face had relaxed into a pleasant expression. When Emily returned Adam glanced at his watch and rose smoothly. "I'm sorry, but I'm afraid we have to run now. It was nice talking to you."

"Oh, yes," Nancy was quick to agree. "Please do come back. Anytime."

"I'm glad to have met you." Rosemary said gravely. "Emily has talked about you often."

Emily quickly crossed to the front door, with Adam following at a more leisurely pace. Rosemary saw them to the door and stood watching as they walked to the car and got in. It wasn't until they backed out of the driveway that Emily saw the front door close. She leaned back in her seat with a sigh. Adam glanced at her, a smile hovering about his lips. "It wasn't that bad, was it?"

Emily turned a startled glance toward him. "Not that bad! It was awful. I'm so embarrassed. I apologize for them"

"Why?"

"The way they acted. My mother flirting with you, and Aunt Rosemary grilling you like you were a criminal."

He chuckled. "Only natural, I imagine. Your mother wants you to have a good time, and your aunt wants to protect you."

Emily shot him an appreciative look. "Thank you. You're very kind."

"You mean you're just now noticing?" he joked.

They fell into silence as Adam drove to the restaurant. Emily could think of nothing to say. She laced her hands together and cleared her throat, then glanced over at Adam.

He seemed entirely untroubled, driving along and humming under his breath. Emily wondered if he had no qualms about going through with this, no uneasiness at being with her. Probably not. Adam was always self-assured. She wished she had even a tenth of his calm confidence. It came, she supposed, from always having known that his place was at the top of any group, intellectually and socially.

Adam turned off Coliseum and into the lot of Ryan's, a wooden building nestled among the trees. He came around the car to politely help her out and escort her into the restaurant, his hand resting lightly behind her waist.

Inside a waiter whisked them up and down various levels to their table, which looked out on the surrounding trees. "It's lovely," Emily commented.

"Haven't you been here before?" Adam asked, surprised, and Emily shook her head. "Then I'm glad I decided on this restaurant."

Emily struggled to think of something to say. She refused to sit there like a mute all evening on her once-in-a-lifetime date with Adam! "Are you still floating on air about the verdict?"

"I've come down a little," Adam admitted. "But it was great. Now if I can only get the Johansens to settle..."

"You think they might?"

"Yeah. They haven't got that strong a case. Unfortunately, neither have we. Johansen's attorney is urging him to settle out of court, and I think he's beginning to see the light."

"Good."

"But Steve Vickers is trying to get me into a doozy now."

"I saw him lurking around your office late this afternoon."

"Yeah. He caught me when Jim left. He has a couple of discontented heirs who want to sue their mother's estate."

"And he wants you to try it?"

"It looks like they're going to need a trial lawyer. Steve's two heirs are fit to be tied because their mother left most of her estate to an evangelistic preacher with a highway church. Nondenominational. The kicker is that our firm wrote the mother's will."

"The one they want to contest?"

"Yeah. Wild, huh?"

"It sounds it."

"It's a good will, naturally; Milton Colby wrote it. But the heirs are claiming undue influence from the preacher. He visited the woman every day, going on and on about saving herself from hell. She was bedridden, and the nurse who looked after her belonged to the guy's congregation. She was the one who suggested that the preacher come visit the old lady. So Mrs. Wheeler got it all the time from one or the other of them. She refused to listen to her son or daughter. She wouldn't get another nurse or see any other minister, including the one from the church they'd attended all their lives. Apparently she seemed to have her wits about her. She wasn't incompetent, just under this guy's spell. Milton didn't like the situation when he wrote up the will. He tried to get her to decrease the donation to the church, or set up a trust for the kids, with the remainder going to the church after their deaths, but Mrs. Wheeler wouldn't have any of it. Milt even delayed writing it for several weeks, but eventually he had to go through with it."

"Could you win the case?"

Adam shrugged. "Who knows? I hate to go up against a charity, especially a religious one. You know, 'money-hungry children and attorneys versus God.' You have a strike or two against you from the very start." He paused, then smiled at her. "What am I doing going on about a case: Let's talk about something more interesting."

"But I think your cases are interesting," Emily protested. Adam's conversation had relaxed her, and she no longer felt so ill at ease.

"I think you really mean that. You like law, don't you?" Emily nodded.

"Why didn't you go to law school? You certainly have the brains for it."

"I don't know. I never considered it, really. Lack of money, for one major thing."

"There are scholarships."

She made a dismissive gesture. "I don't think I have what it takes to get through law school or be a lawyer. I don't have the drive."

"I bet you'd surprise yourself."

Emily was sitting with her hands resting on the table, and Adam reached across and tapped one of her hands with his forefinger. "You put yourself down too much. You have a lot going for you that I don't think you recognize."

She didn't know what to answer. His hand settled on top of hers, and that drove whatever thoughts she might have had straight out of her head. It was difficult to think anything sane when she was sitting across the table from Adam; with him touching her, it was impossible.

He continued to talk, covering her silence, changing the topic to more impersonal, inconsequential things. He told a funny story about one of the lawyers in the firm; he mentioned the upcoming Steeplechase; he inquired after a secretary who had taken maternity leave. Emily recovered her wits enough to answer him, though as long as his hand remained on hers a tingling warmth coursed through her, touching off a submerged excitement.

Their food arrived, and Adam's hand left hers. Emily wished she could call it back; she'd rather not eat. They talked desultorily as they ate, and their silences were companionable, not nerve-racking. Emily was glad Adam had thought of going out tonight as a way to ease into the weekend. The next day would be tense enough without having to go through this period of adjusting to being together socially. At least now she was able to sit with him and feel somewhat relaxed.

After dinner Adam drove to a small nightclub, where they had an after-dinner drink and danced. Emily felt awkward and nervous on the dance floor with him. She rarely danced and had never really learned how, and she didn't have the lack of inhibition necessary to simply move to the music. Still, they managed passably well on the slow dances. It seemed like heaven to be enfolded in Adam's arms, surrounded by his warmth and strength and scent. Their thighs brushed as they moved, and the contact set off sudden sparks of eagerness in Emily's abdomen. She thought about Adam touching her, their naked flesh meeting in a far more intimate way. Suddenly the next day was more real to her than it had been before, more exciting and scary.

Adam pointed out that they would be driving to the mountains early the next morning, so they left the nightclub before too long. When Adam stopped the car on the street in front of her house, Emily was thankful to see that all the lights in the house were out. Rosemary had gone to bed and wasn't waiting up for her, as Emily had half feared she would. Emily turned to Adam and smiled. "Thank you. It was a lovely evening."

"Thank you. I enjoyed it."

"Then I'll see you tomorrow morning? And remember to pick me up at the address I gave you."

"I will." Adam had turned toward her, his arm stretched out along the back seat. He made no move to get out of the car. Instead he reached out and touched her face, a fingertip tracing the line of her cheek and jaw, the swirl of her ear.

Emily's breath caught in her throat. "You look very pretty tonight," Adam said. "Did I tell you that?"

Wordlessly Emily nodded. Her throat muscles were too frozen to speak. His hand slid behind her neck, curving around it; his fingers splayed across her soft flesh, gently pressing. He slid across the seat until he was beside her, his face looming closer. This was it, Emily thought. He was going to kiss her. She closed her eyes. Her heart hammered against her ribs. She realized that she wasn't at all prepared for this. She wanted him too much, loved him too much. She was too inexperienced. She was too—then his lips were on hers, light and warm and soft, and all her thoughts went flying.

## Chapter 5

Adam kissed her without demand, touching her nowhere except where his hand cradled her neck and his mouth caressed her lips. He kissed first her bottom lip, then the upper one, his tongue stealing out to trace the sensitive cupid's bow. The kiss deepened, his tongue teasing her lips open, and hesitantly Emily's mouth began to respond to his. His hand tightened slightly against her neck; his other hand came up to rest on her waist. Unconsciously Emily leaned closer to him, and his lips smiled against hers. His arms went around her then, pulling her into him, and he sank his lips into hers, his tongue roaming with breathtaking care and slowness.

Emily trembled, her hands stealing up to curl around the lapels of his jacket. There was an open, yearning ache growing between her legs. She wanted to touch Adam, to run her hands over his arms and shoulders and chest, but she was too uncertain and shy. His head lifted, but he only changed the slant of his mouth and returned to kiss her again. His hands began to move over her back, sliding down to her hips and back up, threading through her hair and massaging her scalp with his fingertips. He kissed her on either side of her mouth, sharp, quick kisses; then his lips moved across her cheek, moist and velvety on her skin, until he reached her ear.

Emily couldn't hold back a small sound of pleasure as his lips began to work. He traced the lines of her ear with his tongue and tickled her earlobe, tracing around the tiny ball of her earring. She heard his breath, harsh and rapid against her ear, and the tiny click of his teeth against the earring as he nibbled her earlobe. Desire flooded her at the faint, erotic sounds. She was bombarded by new, thrilling sensations— the sharp nip of his teeth colliding with the soothing warmth of his tongue, the velvet invitation of his lips. Emily trembled, and her hands clenched tightly on his jacket.

She wanted to twist and clutch and wrap herself around him. The delightful feelings he was evoking in her were so sharply pleasurable they were almost scary. It was if something in her wanted to break free, would break free. It was unknown, inviting, frightening.

As if he felt the spark of fear in her, Adam pulled away and his arms relaxed, letting her ease back against the seat. Emily looked at him. His face was a little taut, his eyes dark; he was watching her. Emily closed her eyes, afraid of what he might see on her face. Her lips felt swollen and sensitive, and she ran her tongue over them soothingly. She tasted him on her lips. Another quiver of desire ran through her. Adam spread out his hand on her waist and moved it slowly up her. The touch surprised her. She hoped he couldn't see on her face how much she enjoyed it, how wantonly she wanted to move her body against it in counterpoint. She hated for him to think she was so starved for a man's touch.

Adam's hand moved over her breasts, neither light nor pressing, simply touching and learning her. It caressed her chest and shoulders and curled around her throat. It moved downward slowly, at last coming to rest on the flat plain of her abdomen, hovering enticingly above where she wanted most to feel him.

"Tomorrow," Adam said huskily, "I want to undress you. I want to look at you. Touch you."

Emily's lashes fluttered against her cheeks, the only sign that she had heard him. Adam gazed down at her; she looked utterly vulnerable and open to him. It stirred him. He would have liked to continue to explore her body with his hands, to kiss the tender flesh of her throat, to nuzzle and caress her until she was on fire for him. He considered taking her back to his condominium and making love to her tonight.

But no, he knew better. He must move slowly. That had been the whole purpose of this evening—to let Emily get used to his lovemaking by degrees. He had wanted to make it seem more like a real relationship, with a progression from meeting to dating to bedroom. He had intended only a few preliminary kisses tonight, just to set the stage. Adam smiled to himself. They had been necking in the car like two teenagers. Emily had stirred him more than he had dreamed she would. She looked so pretty tonight, and it had been fun talking to her. It had been so pleasant not to have to worry that she would be bored if he started talking about law or the firm. Then, when he had started kissing her, her hesitant, naive response, which quickly flamed into passion, had sparked an answering passion in himself.

He leaned over and kissed her forehead. "We better stop this and get some sleep." Reluctantly his hand left her stomach, and he slid across the seat and opened his door.

Emily opened her eyes and straightened up, trying to pull herself back into some semblance of mental order. As Adam walked around the car to her door she smoothed down her clothes and opened her door herself. He was there as she stepped out of the car, extending a hand to help her. She took his hand, but couldn't quite bring herself to meet his eyes. He said nothing, merely walked her to her front door. There he took the key from her hand and unlocked the door for her, opened it and stepped back.

"I'll see you tomorrow. Nine o'clock," he told her softly. Emily nodded. Adam bent and planted a swift, firm kiss on her lips. "Good night."

"Good night."

Emily went inside the house, and Adam walked quickly to his car. He swung into the driver's seat and turned on the engine. He pulled away from the curb and glanced back at Emily's dark house. He wondered why she had wanted him to pick her up someplace else tomorrow. Probably didn't want the dragon aunt to know she was leaving with him for the weekend. It was no wonder that Emily hadn't had any sexual experience with Rosemary around to guard her chastity.

Adam smiled to himself. Frankly, at the moment, he was rather glad Emily hadn't had any experience. He was looking forward to educating her.

Emily had trouble going to sleep that night, and awakened early the next morning. She rose and showered, dressed in the pale mauve sweater and slacks, and tried applying a little makeup herself. Though she wasn't as skillful or as daring as Jeanette, she was pleased with the result. She packed her small case and took it downstairs. Rosemary was there, sipping her coffee and reading the newspaper. She gave Emily a surprised look, because Emily rarely got up so early on a Saturday morning. Rosemary stared at her, taking in the makeup, the clothes and Emily's hair hanging loose around her shoulders. Emily knew she must be suspicious, but Rosemary made no comment except to say, "You're up early."

"Yeah. Uh, Jeanette and I wanted to get an early start." Emily had told her aunt that she and Jeanette planned a shopping trip to some of the furniture discount stores near High Point.

"You want eggs and toast?" Rosemary rose to make Emily's usual breakfast.

"No!" The way her stomach was flip-flopping around, Emily couldn't imagine eating anything. "I'm not hungry. I must still be full from dinner last night."

"You gotta eat something. I could make pancakes."

Emily thought of the pancakes lying like lead in her stomach. "No, thanks. Really. How about if I have some toast and coffee?" Rosemary shrugged and started toward the ancient toaster on their cabinet, but Emily stopped her. "I'll get it. Sit down and enjoy your paper. Heavens, you fix my breakfast every morning. The least I can do is make toast on Saturdays."

"I enjoy doing it."

"I know. And I appreciate it." Emily popped two slices of bread into the toaster and poured a cup of coffee while she waited for them to brown. Quickly she buttered the toast, laid it on a small plate and cut it crosswise. She sat down at the table across from Rosemary and began to eat. Rosemary watched her, her arms folded on the table. "How was your date?"

"Fine." Emily gave her a perfunctory smile. She didn't want to start talking about Adam to her aunt.

"What did you do? You couldn't have eaten dinner until eleven o'clock."

"No. We went out dancing afterward. It was fun."

There was a long pause and Emily hoped that the subject was closed. Then her aunt spoke again. "You sure sat out in the car an awful long time with him last night."

Emily swallowed the piece of toast in her mouth; it seemed to turn into a lump of concrete in her throat. She washed it down with a gulp of coffee and countered faintly, "Oh? You were still up? I thought you'd gone to bed."

"I had trouble sleeping with you out." Rosemary waited.

Emily took another sip of coffee. "We, uh, sat out there and talked for a while."

Rosemary said nothing. Emily forced down another half piece of toast, then took her plate and cup to the sink so she could clean them. She dried her hands off on a dish towel and turned back to the table. "I'm going to Jeanette's now. You have any message for her?"

Rosemary frowned. Emily felt sure there were a hundred things Rosemary would like to tell her daughter; she disapproved heartily of almost everything that Jeanette did. But Rosemary shook her head. "No. Just tell her to call me sometime. I won't lecture her."

"Okay. And I'll give her your love."

Rosemary nodded. Emily grabbed her case, picked up her purse and hurried out of the house. She was at her cousin's apartment in minutes. She doubted that Jeanette was up yet; she loved to sleep late on the weekends, so Emily let herself in with the extra key Jeanette had given her. The apartment was dark and hushed. Emily sat down on the couch to wait. It was only eight o'clock.

Her hands were icy, and her stomach quivered. She wondered why she had ever agreed to a scheme like this. Why had she told Adam about her feelings on reaching thirty and still being an inexperienced old maid? She must have been insane.

At fifteen till nine the door bell rang, shrilling through the silence and making Emily jump. She hurried to open the door. Adam stood outside, dressed in jeans and a short-sleeved University of North Carolina sweatshirt. It was Carolina-blue, the color of the sky, and it made his eyes startlingly blue. Emily had never seen him so casually dressed. Even when they had worked on Saturdays at the office, he had worn slacks and a long sleeved shirt or sweater. He had nice arms, firmly muscled, though not bulging, and lightly covered with black hair. The jeans had obviously seen many wearings and washings, and were molded to his legs like a second skin. Emily decided Adam was even more good-looking dressed like this than in his tailored suits.

"Hi."

"Hello." Emily smiled shyly. After the kisses that had passed between them last night, she felt a trifle shy with him.

"You ready to go?"

"Yes." Adam picked up her small bag, and they went down to his car.

The trip to the mountains was quiet. Adam made a few comments at first about the weather or business, but then he fell silent. Emily could think of nothing to say. She was gripped by anxiety, and her brain refused to function. The closer they got to the mountains, the greater her tension grew, until by the time they reached the town of Blowing Rock she was sizzling with nerves. Even the beauty of the blue-tinged mountains couldn't calm her.

They took a small highway out of Blowing Rock and before long reached Fender's Gap, a village straggling single file through a narrow valley, a rushing stream snaking along beside it. Adam turned right and took a small wooden bridge across the stream. The road curved around the base of a mountain and began to climb. Soon the village was out of sight. Adam took a dirt track that disappeared into the trees and ended at a small log cabin. In front of the cabin a meadow dropped away, affording a beautiful view of the valley and the mountains beyond. On the other three sides of the cabin the trees grew close: thick, dark evergreens; slim-trunked trees feathered with pale green buds; mountain laurels dangling heavy clusters of purple blossoms like grapes; fragile, white-flowering dogwoods; and bright, pink-blossomed redbuds. A wisteria vine covered with lavender flowers climbed up one side of the rustic cabin.

"Oh, Adam!" Emily breathed, jolted from her anxiety by such beauty. "It's gorgeous!"

He stopped the car to give Emily a full view of the land and turned to her with a grin. "Yeah, isn't it? When I saw this land I had to have it. There was just this side section of the cabin then. It's the original log cabin built in the 1800s. The other side is another old log cabin I had moved in and joined to it."

He started the car forward again and pulled up behind the house. Emily slipped out of the car and walked around to the front porch, where she turned to admire the view. Adam followed, carrying their suitcases. He unlocked the front door and held it open for her to pass through. Emily stepped inside and fell even more in love with the place.

Adam had added some creature comforts, including a modern kitchen in one corner of the room and large, plate-glass windows in each wall to catch the view from every angle. But the cabin retained its essential rustic quality. The floors were smooth wooden planks; the unadorned walls were logs and mortar. A huge stone fireplace dominated the back wall, a long-handled, metal popcorn popper hanging on the wall beside it. A large, cherry red and white braided rug covered much of the floor, while a conversational grouping of chairs and couch sat in front of the fireplace.

A small dining table and chairs stood near the kitchen area. The furniture was modern, but sturdy and plain, and blended well with the cabin.

A door in the far wall opened onto another room, the added cabin Adam had spoken of. Smaller than the other cabin, it had been turned into a bedroom and bath. Another braided rug decorated the floor. The dresser, wardrobe and high, dark four-poster bed were obviously antique. The bed was covered with a colorful quilt in a star design. Emily's eyes skittered away from the bed, and she quickly opened the far door and peeked into the bathroom.

There was an antique porcelain sink beside the door, matched by an enormous antique bathtub, claw-footed and raised high off the floor. Above and beside the tub was a large, plate-glass window, and sun filtered through the newly leafed trees and into the room, sparkling on the porcelain fixtures and ceramic tile. It looked cool and restful and almost sybaritically luxurious. Emily thought of lying back in that enormous tub, warm water lapping all around her, and lazily watching the changing patterns of leaves and clouds and the never-changing solidity of the mountain. She let out a sigh of contentment at just the thought.

"It feels as wonderful as it looks." Adam agreed, coming up behind her and looking over her shoulder into the room. "Sometimes after a really rough week, when I come up here, I spend half my time in the tub, soaking and looking at the scenery."

The thought of Adam in the bathtub quickly dispelled the sense of peace that had touched Emily. Just the idea of him naked and water-slick was enough to set up a tingle all over her. She gave him a nervous, little half smile and stepped back into the bedroom. She glanced around for something to say that wasn't related to her thoughts, but her gaze fell on the bed, which made her even more nervous. Emily cleared her throat and laced her hands together. "Well, uh...."

Adam came up behind her and grasped her shoulders. "Hey. We've got all weekend. We don't have to jump right into bed. Don't worry about it."

"It's silly to be so nervous. I'm sorry."

"Now you *are* being silly. It's natural. There's no problem." He began to knead the knotted muscles in her shoulders and upper back. "Just relax. You're as tight as a drum."

Her muscles loosened beneath his hard, skillful fingers. She felt as if heat flowed from his hands down through her, liquid, molten. How could it be? How could she feel so anxious and scared, yet still go all hot and weak at his touch? How could she want something so badly and yet be frightened of it?

"That's better." Adam went to work on her neck, and bright shivers radiated out from his hands. Emily went limp, leaning into his massage. She had a wild desire to rub her body against him as a cat does when it's stroked. He ran his hands down her back and around to her front, crossing his arms over her stomach and holding her against him, enfolding her. He leaned his cheek against her hair. "We could take a walk. A brook runs down the mountain not far from here and empties into a small pond. It's a beautiful place. You want to see it?"

Emily nodded. "Yes. Please."

His arms slid away from her, leaving Emily a little cold and lonely. But he took her hand as they walked out of the cabin and into the trees, following a faint trail. His hand was warm and slightly rough and large, almost completely covering hers. She liked the feel of it around hers.

"There's nothing wrong with being nervous," Adam began conversationally as they strolled along. "I am, too."

Emily glanced at him, surprised. "But why would you be nervous? You know what you're doing, and you're—well, any woman would love to go to bed with you."

His eyebrows shot up. "Why, thank you. But that's not the issue. I worry that I won't do it well, that I won't arouse you or give you enough time or pleasure. It scares me a little, thinking that I won't make it good enough. It ought to be very special the first time."

Emily smiled and shot him a teasing glance. "But that's no problem. You see, I won't know the difference."

Adam burst into surprised laughter and looped an arm around her shoulders, pulling her against him and squeezing her briefly. "Ah, Emily, you are one in a million." He dropped a kiss onto the top of her head.

Soon they came across a small brook, gurgling over rocks on its way down the hill. Adam turned, and they followed the water's twisting, meandering course until it splashed over a stair of rocks into a small, mountain pool. Emily leaned over and touched the water with her hand. It was icy. Adam led her around to the side of the pool where a large, flat rock jutted out into the water. He jumped up onto the rock and pulled her up with him.

"Here. Sit down." He directed her to the edge, where it extended over the pool. "You can hang your feet over the side without getting them in the water."

Emily sat down where he directed and let her feet dangle. She gazed out over the pond, drinking in the picture of mountains, trees and flowers framing the placid water. To her surprise Adam sat down behind her, his legs on either side of hers and her back flush against his chest. One arm curled around her from behind, looping over her shoulder and down across her chest, his hand cupping her opposite arm. Emily couldn't help but lean back against his support; it made her feel delightfully warm and cherished.

It wasn't real, her mind told her. Adam was simply acting a part, playing a role whose mechanics he knew because he had loved other women. It had nothing to do with her. Perhaps he was even pretending that she was Cassie. Emily knew he'd never gotten over his ex-wife. She closed her eyes against the slash of pain.

But another, kinder, part of her mind warned her not to think about it. There was no need to interject reality into this scene. This was her weekend, her fairy-tale chance at romance. Like all fairy tales, it didn't matter whether it was realistic. The only important thing was enjoying it. For once she could let down her defenses. She could pretend that everything Adam did and said was true, that he loved her, that he wanted her. This was her story to mold, and for these two brief days she was going to live out her fantasy. And she wouldn't let the nasty face of reality stick itself in anywhere.

Emily let out a small sigh and relaxed even more against Adam. She turned her face up to the warm sun and let it pour through her, melting her bones and muscles. There were faint, hushed noises around them: the crackle of a twig, the scamper of a squirrel, the chatter of a bird. The sun glimmered against her closed eyelids. Adam's heartbeat was a deep, steady rhythm against her back; his body was warm around hers. A faint breeze skimmed her cheek and lifted tendrils of her hair. Emily felt almost as if she were drifting on the surface of the sparkling water itself, relaxed and warm, not far from sleep.

Adam's other hand came up to rest on her waist, then moved in a slow, lazy glide up her torso. His hand was firm and knowledgeable, on no tentative exploration, but stroking her body with loving possession. His other arm slipped back to allow him access to her. His hand moved over her breasts and up to her neck. Instinctively Emily arched her head back against his shoulder to expose her vulnerable throat. His fingertips sought out every sensitive inch of her throat, exploring the contrast of hard bone and tender flesh, riding the pulse of her heating blood.

Her lips parted slightly, and color tinged her cheeks. Looking down on her, Adam saw the face of a woman melting into passion, trusting and intensely vulnerable, yet savoring the sweet surrender. It was as if she offered herself to him without barriers, opening up her soul and heart as well as her body. His own blood leaped in response, and his body grew tight and hard. Suddenly he wanted much more. He wanted to be in her, to feel her take him in and accept his thrusting gift. He ached to see her naked body beneath him, her face dissolving into shattering joy. He thought he couldn't wait, yet the delay and anticipation spurred his desire. He would take his time, as he had planned, and his reward would be the sweet ache, the panting, desperate eagerness that had been lost to him for so long.

Adam left her throat at last, his hand gliding to her shoulder. Then both hands moved with agonizing slowness down her front, touching her hardened nipples and pausing to caress them, rubbing the cloth of her sweater against them and arousing them still further. He slid his hands down her rib cage and over her stomach, converging at the joinder of her legs. Emily tightened, catching her lip between her teeth. Adam smiled with lazy pleasure and pressed his hands against her, then let them drift out along her thighs. With infinite slowness he moved back up the same path he had followed before.

Adam buried his face in Emily's hair, as if to shut out the rest of the world and to enjoy the exquisite pleasure in his hands. He kissed her hair and slid down to nuzzle her neck, nibbling at the delicate cord, causing her to let out an involuntary moan. One hand moved to the V of her legs, pressing her back against his burgeoning desire, and the other one stole beneath her sweater, exploring the soft skin of her stomach and lace-shielded breasts. His teeth seized Emily's earlobe and worried it gently. His tongue delved into the sensitive whorls of her ear.

An ever-rising hunger propelled him. His mouth moved across her cheek to kiss her, his lips greedy and insistent, taking the full sweetness of her mouth. The hand that had pressed her tightly against him came up to hold her head, as if she might escape his hungry mouth before he was through tasting her. Her breast was small in his other hand, completely covered; the pebbly hardness of her nipple pushed against his palm. Inwardly he cursed the reins of responsibility holding him back. *Damn it, he wanted her!*

But the rock was no place to make love. That was precisely why he had chosen it. He'd meant only to arouse her, to let Emily explore her passion in a safer setting than the bedroom. Reluctantly Adam pulled his mouth from hers and rested his forehead against her head. His breath came in ragged gasps. "Damn. I didn't mean to come on so strong." He kissed her ear. "I'm sorry."

"Sorry?" Emily opened her eyes and twisted around to look at him. Her eyes were dazed, the pupils huge, and her lips were soft and faintly bruised. She was such a picture of a woman in the throes of passion that it was all Adam could do not to snatch her back to him and kiss her until they were both senseless with desire.

"Yeah." His voice was husky. Adam couldn't keep from nipping at her ear as he talked. "For rushing you. For pushing. I got carried away."

"I didn't mind," she replied, her voice filled with an innocent disappointment that fired his loins. "I liked it. I—are you going to stop?"

"Oh, sweetheart." He grazed her neck with his lips. "You're going to make me lose what little sense I have left. A rock is a very uncomfortable place to make love."

Emily was limp and liquid with desire. She'd never felt anything like the hunger and excitement and intense pleasure that assailed her as Adam kissed and caressed her. She wished it would never end. "But I don't mind," she told him gravely.

Adam groaned and kissed her deeply, then pulled away from her and stood up. He reached down to take Emily's hands and hauled her to her feet, then wrapped his arms around her. "We have to go back to the house." He punctuated each of his words with a hard kiss, the last one long and grinding.

"What's at the house?"

"The one thing that's on my mind right now." His hands slid down her body and came to rest on her hips, twisting her against him. "A bed."

Emily smiled. Even someone as inexperienced as herself could recognize the hard bulge of desire pressed against her. Earlier she had doubted whether Adam would be able to make love to her because his body would desire her so little. But now she knew that he wanted her. It didn't matter that lots of other women had doubtless caused the same reaction in him. It didn't matter that it might take very little to bring him to that state. All that was important was that he wanted her, that his body was sending the same message as his words.

"That amuses you?" he asked, mock indignantly, and rubbed her body back over his.

"It pleases me," she confessed softly.

He grinned, his fingers pressing into her buttocks. "I can please you a lot more." His voice was rich and dark as honey. "Come back to the cabin with me."

"All right."

Adam moved away from her enough to slip an arm around her shoulders and settle her snugly against his side. They started toward the house. Gradually, as they walked, the fever in Emily's blood cooled. She thought about undressing before Adam, and it scared her. It would be humiliating to reveal her naked body to him; it was so imperfect—too long, too thin, too flat. He was bound to be disappointed. Whatever desire he felt for her would fly away. She would be gawky and awkward. She wouldn't know when to undress, whether to touch him . . . and when . . . and where.

Still, her nerves fizzed with excitement, her skin tingled, and there was a throbbing ache deep within her. The ache didn't diminish; rather, it fed on the warm weight of Adam's arm around her shoulders, the hard length of his side, the friction of his leg against hers as they walked. She was hungry for him. She wanted him in a primitive way that outweighed her fears and insecurities. No matter how nervous she was, she was equally eager to reach the cabin.

As they walked Adam leaned down once or twice to brush his lips against her hair. Deep in the shadowy coolness of the trees he stopped and pulled Emily to him to kiss her, and when they reached the porch of the cabin he wrapped his arms around her and kissed her again, pressing her back against the cabin wall. The rough logs caught at the fabric of her sweater; the wall was hard and cool, unyielding. Emily felt every inch of his body pressing into hers: the solid bone of his chest, the long muscles of his thighs, the sharp points of his pelvic bones. Again he pulled back. Emily knew that this was the last time he would stop. His face was flushed, and his pupils were huge and black, turning his eyes a midnight blue. She could see the pulse throbbing in his throat.

He opened the door. A thrill raced through Emily, part fear, part excitement. Her knees began to wobble. She managed to turn and walk through the door. Adam followed, shutting the door behind them. Emily started toward the bedroom, then hesitated. It seemed too bold for her to march right through to the bedroom. Adam took her hand and led her through the connecting door.

Emily thought of the sex manual she had read in a hidden alcove of the library. Despite pages of detailed descriptions of the act in many different positions and numerous anatomically accurate illustrations, it had not provided her with the really important information she needed now. Such as: Who undressed first? Or did they take their clothes off at the same time? Did one disrobe at once or do it in shifts, a few items at a time? And what did one do about the fact that the hand Adam held in his was suddenly sweaty? Should she talk or keep silent? And if she talked, what could she possibly say?

Adam stopped beside the bed. He felt the tension in Emily's hand, saw how stiff her body had become. She was probably scared to death. He tried to remember how he had felt the first time—how long ago it was! He could recall the nerves that had tightened his stomach and closed his throat, the adrenaline racing through him, the excitement thudding in his chest. But he had been a teenager then, and excited even by fear. How much worse it must be to come to it as an adult, having suffered from doubts and insecurities that much longer, certain that you were alone and laughable in your naiveté.

Adam took Emily's other hand and turned her to face him. He kneaded her hands gently, then began a slow, massaging slide up her arms to her shoulders. "Scared?" Emily nodded, refusing to look at him. "This may not help any, but I want you to know that there's no need to be. I won't rush you past where you want to go. I promise. I'll go very slow. You believe me?''

Again Emily nodded. "It's not that. I trust you. You're always kind, even with idiot temporaries who can hardly type."

A faint smile touched his lips. "Not exactly the same situation, but I'll accept that you trust me to deal gently with you. What's the fear, then? Can you tell me?''

"It's unknown, and that's scary.''

"I know." He nodded, and his hands squeezed her arms reassuringly.

"But it's not just that. It's—oh, Adam, I feel like such an idiot! I don't know what to do!'' She spoke in a rush, her head turned from him, her cheeks flushed. "I went to the library and read a sex manual because I didn't want to look like a fool. I thought if I read up on it, I wouldn't be so incompetent.''

Adam's lips twitched. How like Emily—to study the subject so she'd handle it letter-perfectly. It made him want to chuckle and hug her, but he refrained from doing either, sensing that Emily would not share his affectionate amusement. "And?''

"It didn't help. Well, not much. I mean, it talked about intercourse and gave all these technical names and everything. But I still don't know how to act.''

"What do you mean? You don't have to 'act'. Just be yourself. Do what you want.''

"But I mean—oh, undressing and everything!''

"Undressing?''

Now her face was beet red, and Emily felt even more foolish. "Please, let's drop it. Forget I said anything.''

"No. Don't be silly. If you're thinking about it, it's important. Believe me, nothing about sex is ever too silly. Tell me.''

Emily had never been able to refuse Adam anything, and she couldn't now, either. She swallowed, and in a low voice said, "I feel embarrassed and awkward about undressing in front of you. I don't know when to undress. Or how. I don't know what to say or what I should do."

"Ah, Emily, Emily." Adam curved a hand around the nape of her neck and pulled her close so that her head nestled against his chest. Emily could hear the steady, reassuring thrum of his heart and the low vibration of his voice, and the sounds soothed her. "What am I going to do with you?" He kissed the top of her head. "You always try to do too much. That stuff's my job. Remember? That's why you hired me."

Emily smiled a little. "I didn't exactly 'hire' you. You—" She was about to say that he had offered out of charity, but Adam cut in, forestalling her words.

"I know; I know. I admit it. I pushed my way into the job. Even more reason to leave it to me. I asked for it." His fingers began a slow, delicate massage of her neck. His voice was low and soothing, almost hypnotic. "Let me worry about it. I'll take care of everything. That's my forte, remember? I take care of the details. Isn't that right?"

"Yes. That's right." Her voice was faint and muffled against his chest.

"Good." He kissed the top of her head and rubbed his cheek against it. "You don't need to do a thing. Don't worry about it. Just relax and let me do it." His hands began a slow, rhythmical stroking of her back, wandering ever farther around her sides until his thumbs brushed the edge of her breasts. "I'll undress you; I'll kiss you; I'll touch you. You simply let go and enjoy it. Do what you want, as much or as little. There's no right and no wrong. All that counts right now is what you want."

His lips wandered across her hair and down to her ear. His voice was husky, his breathing irregular. "Maybe later we'll get into what you can do to me to drive me crazy. But right now...right now I'm going to make love to you."

## Chapter 6

Emily had done little for the past two weeks but daydream about making love with Adam, but her imagination hadn't even come close to what he was doing to her now. His hands moved slowly, expertly over her clothed body, caressing her waist and hips and thighs, slipping between their bodies to stroke her stomach and breasts. He was leisurely. Enflaming. Emily felt herself going limp against him, her head growing too heavy for her neck, so that she had to rest it on his chest. The warmth in her stomach was growing, melting and spreading all through her. She sucked in her breath as his hand crept down to the juncture of her legs and settled there, not straying from the spot, yet never still.

He nuzzled her ears and neck. He trailed hot kisses along her jaw and across her cheek. He bathed the hollow of her throat with his tongue. Finally, when she was on fire for him to kiss her mouth and beginning to think he never would, his lips settled on hers, and, with a long sigh of pleasure, he drank the nectar of her mouth. His tongue slid across hers, as his fingers slid between her legs. His lips ground into her, as his palm pressed against the fleshy mound of her femininity. His teeth teased and nipped, as his fingers tantalized her throbbing flesh through the cloth.

· All Emily's fears were fast flying away. Her fevered body twisted beneath Adam's ministrations, aching now to be free of the restrictions of her clothing, yearning to feel his hands upon her bare skin. She moaned softly, her hips arching up into his hand. Adam smiled at her movement, the flame in him flaring higher. He took her hips in his hands, pulling her up and into him, rubbing her lower body suggestively against him, frustrating and enflaming them both with the cloth that lay between them. His fingers dug into the soft flesh of her buttocks, and his mouth was fierce on hers, greedily consuming its sweetness.

They tumbled onto the bed, as though their straining muscles could no longer hold them up. Adam lay half on her, pressing her into the infinite softness of the feather mattress, one leg thrown across her and moving slowly up and down her legs. His tongue teased the soft inner flesh of her cheeks, rasped along her tongue, slid over the edges of her teeth. He explored and enticed and demanded. Emily's tongue moved tentatively into his mouth, and he greeted it with a delicate, sliding dance, coaxing her into more fervent forays.

His breath shuddered out as Emily's kisses grew more passionate, and the muscles in his arms bunched. His hand moved beneath her sweater and grappled with the fastener of her bra, then slid the lacy cloth from her breasts. His fingertips caressed the taut, sensitive nipples and gently rubbed them between forefinger and thumb until they were hot and engorged, aching to be cooled, yearning for his touch. Emily imagined his mouth and tongue upon them, and a liquid heat flooded her at the thought.

His lips left hers to move voraciously down her throat while his fingers continued to tease her breasts. One hand moved downward to the waistband of her slacks. The button came open easily, and he slid down the zipper. His hand slipped inside the opened clothes and drifted downward. Emily made a noise deep in her throat and moved her legs restlessly. His fingers roamed over the slick material of her panties, exploring the lace-trimmed edges and barely grazing the skin below. He delved beneath the fabric, easing it away from her moist flesh. She was embarrassed by the wetness he found there, but he gave her no time to move or think before he continued his slow, almost lazy discovery of her intimate secrets.

Emily trembled at the wild sensations his touch aroused in her, her breath rasping in her throat. His skin was rough against her slickness, heat against her heat. There was a knot coiling in her abdomen, a tightness that grew and grew until she wanted to sob for release. His finger entered her, stroking, and the butt of his palm kept up a rhythmical, circular movement. Emily gasped and dug her heels into the bed, astounded by the intense, unbelievably pleasurable feelings radiating out from the gentle caresses of his hand, astounded by the unmanageable force gathering within her abdomen, hot and pounding and demanding. She felt reason spinning from her, replaced by purely physical sensations. She ached. She wanted. Her breath came in rapid pants.

Then the surging force within her exploded, and she jerked, a groan escaping her clenched teeth. For an instant she felt suspended, without reality, flung into some remote world of pleasure so intense it was almost impossible to grasp. Then waves of pleasure poured out, pulsing through her body and washing her with warmth. Slowly she went limp.

Adam let out a low groan and buried his face against her neck. His skin was like fire. "Oh, baby. I never dreamed you were so responsive."

He raised his head and looked down at her. Her face was flushed, dreamy and slack with satisfaction. He wet his lips, desire surging in him. The look she wore, of a woman well loved, aroused him almost past reason. He wanted to take her, plunge into her and push her past the ecstasy she had already reached. He wanted to take her farther and higher, until she melted into joy.

Adam trembled from the effort it took to hold back. He slipped his hand back from her. Her eyes fluttered open, dazed and wide with wonder. "Adam," she breathed.

He bent and brushed a light kiss across her mouth. "Emily."

"Oh my." A darker flush tinged her cheeks, and he saw embarrassment creep into her eyes. "I don't—I mean—" She halted, nonplussed. That had been an orgasm. It must have been. But never in her wildest dreams had she imagined that it could be anything like that. Certainly not for her, who'd always been so shy, so self-contained. That shy, self-contained person was the only Emily Adam knew; he had no idea of the secret longings and dreams that lay deep within her. He must be shocked at her response. It had happened so quickly, before they even had intercourse—before they even removed their clothes! He would think she was vulgar and common and . . . and . . . well, she didn't know what.

She closed her eyes. "I'm sorry," she whispered.

"Sorry! Oh, Emily, no." He began to rain soft, light kisses over her face. "There's nothing to be sorry for. You were marvelous. You made me feel . . . powerful. Sexy. Like ten times the man I am. It was beautiful. *You* were beautiful." He paused for a moment, looking down at her, and smiled. "And now we can start all over again."

He slid from the bed and stood up, pulling his knit shirt off over his head in one smooth motion. He tossed it on the floor and stepped out of his shoes, unsnapped his jeans and pulled down the zipper, then shucked them off. His brief underwear quickly joined the pile of clothes on the floor. Emily watched him with wide, love-darkened eyes, far past embarrassment now at seeing him unclothed. He was powerful, male and very beautiful. His arms were corded and tight with a waiting strength that rarely showed in the world where Emily knew him. His chest was smoothly padded with muscle and lightly covered with dark, curling hair, tapering down to a V at the deep indentation of his navel. His stomach was flat below the shelf of his rib cage, and his thighs were long, lean and muscled, his hips narrow, with long hollows running beside the pelvic bones. It was obvious that he still wanted her. Suddenly Emily longed to feel the smooth skin overlying his muscles. She wanted to caress his naked flesh, to feel the bunching of muscle, the strength, the hardness.

Adam looked down at her for a long moment, then sat on the bed beside her. He reached out and grasped the hem of her sweater and pulled it up over her head. He removed the scrap of her lacy brassiere, already unfastened, and tossed it away. "Don't wear that. I'd like to watch you move with your breasts free and soft."

He cupped one of her breasts and ran his thumb gently around the aureole of her nipple. The pinkish brown circle darkened beneath his touch, the nipple budding to sharp life. He smiled a little at the response, his eyes darkening with desire, and leaned over to graze her breast with a kiss. Lips sheathing his teeth, Adam worried the dark bud, then laved it with his tongue.

Emily sucked in her breath sharply. Having flowered into passion so recently, she was acutely aware of every sensation. Her skin was wildly alive, her nerve endings tingling. The pleasure of his touch was magnified, and now, as he drew the nipple into his warm mouth and began to suckle, it was all she could do not to cry out with pleasure. His mouth tugged at her, a hot, wet cave of passion, and she felt the sensation viscerally. The hot throbbing in her abdomen, eased only moments before, began to thrum again.

He moved to her other breast, and this time she couldn't stifle the moan of intense joy as he played with it, teasing the nipple with his lips and tongue until it was hard and thrusting. Adam pulled back slightly. He smiled, but his lids were heavy with longing and his arms taut with the effort of holding back. "You distract me," he murmured, and kissed the nipple softly. "I planned to undress you." He kissed the other nipple again. "If I stay here much longer, I'll have to have you. And I want to see those long, long legs first."

He slid down to plant a kiss on her stomach, then hooked his fingers in the sides of her slacks. Slowly he pulled them off her legs and sat for a long moment admiring her long, slender legs. His hand skimmed up one leg, defining the shape of her calf and thigh, and back down the other. "Beautiful."

Adam bent and kissed her thigh, and Emily quivered. He moved her legs a little apart and kissed the inside of her thigh. Emily jerked, and he grinned up at her, then lifted her leg in his hands, bringing it up to his mouth and planting a hot trail of kisses along her thigh to the knee. His mouth moved back up, not stopping until he reached the lace trim of her panties, and again Emily moved involuntarily, this time arching upward. His tongue flickered out and traced the lace rim. Emily gasped.

He looked up, concern creasing his brow. "Too much? You want me to stop?"

Emily shook her head. It was too much, but she definitely didn't want him to stop.

"Good." He pressed his lips against the sheer fabric stretched across her abdomen, then slid his tongue along the edge of the opposite leg. "Though I ought to stop for my own sake. I'm driving myself crazy." He moved upward and ran his tongue beneath the lacy waistband, delving into her navel.

He was pounding with desire, so hot he felt as if he would explode any minute, but the torment was sweet, the anticipation exciting. He wanted her. And he wanted her to peak again. Just the thought of the way her face had looked afterward flooded him with desire. This time he wanted to see her face as she reached the pinnacle, to see her features shine with joy and soften into satisfaction.

Adam rolled her panties down and took them off, then let his eyes explore her. His hands reached out to touch where his eyes wandered, traveling the length of her body, skimming over her breasts and stomach, the shallow hollow of her abdomen and the upthrusting hipbones, the long, well-shaped legs. He enjoyed looking at her; he enjoyed even more touching her. His hands traveled up the insides of her thighs, and her legs fell apart, inviting him. He moved in between them, and his hands moved under her hips, lifting her slightly to receive him. He moved into her, pausing at the threshold of her femininity, then pressing inexorably in. Emily's eyes widened at the sudden stab of pain, and she clamped her teeth down on her lip to keep from crying out. Then the pain was gone, and Adam was inside her, full and hard. He stopped, resting on his elbows above her, and looked down at her. His forehead was damp, his arms almost quivering with the strain of holding himself back.

"Are you all right?" he whispered hoarsely.

Emily nodded. "Yes. Please." Her hands went to his waist, sliding over the smooth skin, touching it as she had wanted to earlier. "I want you to."

But he did not begin to move immediately. Instead he lay still within her and bent his head to feast on her breasts. Emily almost whimpered at the sharp joy as his mouth caressed and pulled at her taut nipples. Then he began to move slowly, carefully, aching to thrust into her wildly, but determined not to do it. It must be gentle for her; he must do nothing to exacerbate the pain he'd already given her.

As he moved Emily reveled in the fullness of him inside her. It seemed everything she could possibly want in the world, Adam deep within her, part of her, taking pleasure from her body. But then another need began to grow in her again, the same knotting, yearning tension, and she wondered if it could happen to her again so soon. Surely not, not this first time. Yet there it was, growing, fueled by Adam's movements, by his harsh, rapid breathing, by the heat of his body against hers and the dampness of his sweat. His desire spurred hers; the exquisite pleasure of his deep strokes sent her soaring higher. And higher. Until she was taut and eager again, reaching...reaching.... Again the explosion rocked her, this time deeper and stronger, shaking Emily to her very core. She cried out, and Adam's arms went around her tightly as he, too, groaned aloud and shuddered violently.

Emily lay quietly, watching the play of light across the ceiling as it shifted with the movement of the tree limbs outside the window. Adam lay beside her, asleep, one arm and leg flung across her. After that cataclysmic burst of pleasure he had collapsed against her, damp with sweat, and in a moment he had rolled his weight from her, but curled his arm and leg around her to hold her close. He had kissed her shoulder languidly and asked if she was all right before he drifted into a shallow sleep. Emily hadn't slept, hadn't wanted to. Though physically she felt utterly relaxed, she was too full of swelling emotions to sleep.

It had been more than she had ever dreamed of. She hadn't imagined that anything could be so blissful, so shattering. Not even with Adam. For a moment she had felt intertwined with him, their souls meeting and converging, much as their bodies had. It had been pleasure, but it had also been more than that, something grander and deeper, something that reached in and touched the very core of her being. It had left her awed and joyful—and very eager.

She couldn't stop grinning; she wanted to laugh out loud. She felt like dancing around the room or running crazily across the meadow in front of the house, but she wasn't about to separate her body from the warm weight of Adam's.

Adam's head turned, and his eyelids opened. He stared at her without expression for a moment, then smiled. "Hi."

"Hi." Emily felt as if she might fly apart from sheer happiness, yet she was also a trifle shy at meeting his gaze.

"I'm sorry. I fell asleep, didn't I?"

She nodded. "That's all right. I didn't mind."

He rose on his elbow and leaned over to kiss her. His other hand came up to touch her face and brush her hair back from it. "Are you okay?"

"Yes. You asked me that before."

"Did I?" He hesitated for a moment, looking at her. "I guess what I'm really saying is: Did you enjoy it? Was it all right for you?"

"Oh, yes!" She had thought he had been inquiring about her physical well-being after losing her virginity. It had never occurred to her that he might be feeling uncertain about whether he had pleased her. "Heavens, yes. It was—marvelous." She cupped his face in both her hands. "Thank you. I can't begin to tell you how much I—thank you."

"There's no need to thank me. It was my pleasure." He grinned a little devilishly. "Believe me."

He slipped his arm around her and rolled over onto his back, pulling her on top of him. Emily propped herself up on her forearms and gazed down into his face. She didn't think she could get enough of looking at him. She was too happy to even worry about how much her face revealed of her true feelings. "You know what?" Adam asked.

"What?"

"I'm as hungry as a bear. What about you?"

She hadn't noticed it, but she nodded her head. "Shall I fix us something to eat?"

"Let's see what we've got." He sat up, and she moved back, shy at the idea of getting out of bed stark naked and dressing in front of him. Adam seemed to have no such compunction. He swung out of bed and strode across the room toward the door.

Emily clutched the bed sheet to her chest. "Uh, if you don't mind, I thought I'd take a quick bath first."

He swung around. "Sure. I'll check out the supplies and make up a list of what we need. Why don't we go down to the Gap to eat lunch? Then we can grab some groceries for the rest of the weekend. There's a nice restaurant there, if you like good old greasy home cooking."

Emily smiled. "Sounds wonderful."

He padded into the kitchen area, and Emily jumped out of bed and swooped up her clothes from the scattered places where they lay, cursing when she had to go halfway across the room to retrieve her brassiere from a drawer pull of the dresser. She slipped into the bathroom and ran water in the huge tub. She studied her face in the mirror as the water ran, wondering if there was a difference. It seemed so to her. Her cheeks appeared rosier, her skin softer, her eyes brighter. She looked happy and . . . pretty.

Surely that couldn't be true. Her looks couldn't have changed so dramatically. Yet she did seem prettier. She felt pretty. Adam had desired her. She had felt his desire, heard it. Surely if a man like Adam, who had known as many sophisticated beauties as he had, whose ex-wife was one of the most glamorous women in the state, surely if he had felt passion for her, there must be something more to her than she had ever realized. Emily smiled gaily at her image. She *was* pretty, at least for this brief moment. She turned away, still smiling, and stepped into the bathtub.

She would have liked to have stayed in the tub and soaked for a long time, gazing out at the scenery. But she knew Adam was waiting for her and hungry, so she quickly soaped her body and rinsed it off. Within minutes she was out of the tub and drying off with one of the large, luxurious bath towels hanging on the old-fashioned bar beside the tub. She pulled her clothes back on but left her brassiere off. Adam had asked her not to wear it. There wasn't much need to, unfortunately, as her breasts were small. And if it pleased Adam to see them unrestrained, why not do it? She looked in the mirror to see if she could see any difference. She brushed her hands down the front of the sweater. The tightening of her nipples was faintly evident. She wondered if that was too brazen. But, no, Adam had asked for it, and she would do it.

Emily went into the bedroom and stuffed her bra into her overnight bag. The room was empty. She crossed into the living room beyond and found Adam waiting for her on the sofa, legs stretched out in front of him. He rose as she entered the room and came toward her. She saw that his eyes flickered down to her breasts, and just the touch of his gaze made her nipples grow tight. A faint smile touched his lips, but he said nothing, merely put his arm around her shoulders and started out the door.

The town of Fender Gap interested Emily far more now than when they had first driven in. Quaint and small, it nestled into the magnificent land around it rather than trying to compete. The buildings were wooden and plain, with an old-fashioned air. There were a few small motels and several places renting cabins. The rest of the buildings were tourist-related businesses—real estate offices, gas stations, souvenir shops, stores featuring the work of local artisans, grocery stores, and two or three unpretentious restaurants.

Adam parked in front of a narrow, weather-beaten storefront that bore a small sign stating simply "Granny's." They went inside, and Emily found to her surprise that she was in a small, old-fashioned grocery store. "I thought we were going to a restaurant before we shopped."

"We are. It's in the back. Very convenient." He steered Emily down the aisle and through a door in the back. They emerged into a small dining room furnished with rustic wooden tables and chairs. The back wall had two large, plate-glass windows looking out onto the creek and the towering mountains beyond.

"Oh!" Emily gasped. "How lovely!"

"I know. It's a marvelous surprise, isn't it?"

"Oh, yes." It was almost the middle of the afternoon, and the dining room was empty, so they were able to sit right by the windows. Emily gazed out at the view for a moment, then looked back at Adam, her eyes bright with happiness.

Adam smiled at her. How pretty she looked this afternoon, her face glowing, her mouth softly curved, her eyes alive with a wondrous joy. Had he put that look in her eyes? It made him feel strong and strangely tender. Their lovemaking earlier had been something special for him, as well. He couldn't remember the last time he had made love with such driving passion or known such an exquisite release. It had been different. Unique. Perhaps it had been Emily's unfeigned pleasure that had made it so.

He never would have imagined that his quiet little Emily could have that much passion inside her. When he had planned this weekend he had assumed that it would take long, concentrated effort on his part to break through her reserve. He had never dreamed that when he brought her to pleasure, it would be such intense and unbridled ecstasy. Yet she had writhed beneath him, hot and hungry, little whimpers of pleasure rising from her throat. She had hurtled into climax under only his touch, and then had scaled the heights again, crying out in her joy. She had tried to conceal some of her response, he knew; probably she had been shy at revealing her passion. But there had been no way she could clamp down on the supremely sensual woman within; she had broken out in radiant ecstasy. He wondered how Emily had managed to keep that woman so well hidden all these years.

Emily opened one of the small menus on the table and perused it. "This must be a dieter's purgatory!"

Adam chuckled. "They go in for heavy home cooking. But it's good. The pan-fried trout's delicious, and so's the fried chicken."

"Mmm. With gravy and biscuits."

"Delicious biscuits. And green beans cooked with bacon drippings."

"You made up my mind. That's what I'll have—with the chicken."

Adam ordered for them, and they settled back with their huge glasses of sweet, golden-brown iced tea, content to look at each other and smile. The table between them was small. Adam reached across it and took Emily's hand. His thumb made slow, lazy circles on her palm. They were alone in the room and close, and it seemed very private and intimate, almost as if they were in their own house.

"I'm glad I came into the office late that day and found you crying," Adam said. "I'm glad you told me what was troubling you, and that it led to this afternoon. Are you?" His gaze was direct and probing.

Emily nodded. "Yes." She suspected she might be sorry for it later, but right now she was brimming with happiness.

"Do you feel better about yourself now?"

"Yes. I feel more . . . normal, I guess. I've been such a freak for years." Emily found she could talk to him freely, without embarrassment. They had been too intimate this afternoon for her to hold back her feelings. "Different from everyone else. Unfulfilled. Too unattractive to be loved or desired."

"I don't understand it. You aren't unattractive. You're very pretty."

She smiled shyly at him. "Thank you. Do you really think so?"

"Of course. I wouldn't say it if I didn't. You have big, pretty eyes, a nice mouth. Your features are even. You're slender; your legs are gorgeous. What is there about you that's not attractive?"

"You're joking!" Emily stared at him. "I'm skinny. I've always been a bean pole. Too tall and too thin."

"I know lots of women who would give anything to have that problem."

"I doubt it. I'm flat."

"Now, Emily . . ."

"It's true. You can't tell me you didn't notice. I've always been so embarrassed about it." A faint flush stained her cheeks, and she looked down at her plate. Perhaps it wasn't true that all embarrassment was gone with Adam.

Still she felt a need to continue, an overwhelming drive to tell him about herself. "When I was a teenager, I used to cry over how small they were. I'd go to sleep at night hoping, praying that the next morning I'd wake up and they'd magically be bigger. It never worked. Once I heard about an old home remedy, that rubbing honey on your breasts would make them grow. Janie Sizemore swore it had worked for her. So I even tried that; I'd rub honey on them every night."

Adam's eyes darkened, and his lids lowered a little to hide the sudden heat that had flooded him at the image she created. "And what happened?"

Emily gave him a wry smile. "I got a lot of nightgowns very sticky. But I never grew one inch."

"Ah, but did you use natural, organic honey?"

Emily made a face at him. "All right. All right."

He gave her hand a squeeze. "Sweetheart, you're fine. You don't have to have gigantic mammary glands to be pleasing to a man. Your body is lovely. Your breasts fit nicely in my hand. They feel beautiful to touch. That's all you need."

She went warm all over. "Thank you."

He raised her hand and kissed it. "You're welcome. Just remember that everything I said is true. I enjoyed making love to you more than I have in a long time. You're a passionate, desirable woman."

So desirable that after this weekend he would never make love to her again, Emily thought sourly, but then dismissed the idea. She wasn't going to let any negative thoughts spoil her time with Adam. This weekend would provide her with the beautiful memories she would hold the rest of her life.

Adam glanced toward the door. "Now I think we better stop this discussion, or we'll give our waitress the shock of her career."

He released her hand, and Emily pulled it back into her lap as their waitress approached, bearing a round tray. She set the tray down and laid out their dinners on the table. Emily's eyes widened at the enormous amount of food piled on her plate, but she dug in gamely and found that she was far hungrier than she had realized. She ate crisp, browned chicken and butter, homemade mashed potatoes, tender green beans, and thick biscuits dripping with golden honey. Honey clung to her fingertips when she finished the biscuit, and she licked it off. She glanced up to find Adam watching her, his eyes dark and hooded. There was something different about his face, something loose and almost hungry. It made her pulse beat faster and her mouth go dry. She thought of making love with him and wondered if he would do it again tonight.

Emily wiped her fingers off with the napkin.

"Ready?" Adam asked, and it was as if the strange look had never been there. Emily nodded. "Then let's make a pass through the grocery store. I have a list here somewhere." He dug through his pockets and brought out a folded piece of notepaper, then fumbled for his glasses so he could read it. "Here we go. I had beer and soft drinks at the cabin. Some canned goods—tuna fish, soup, stuff like that. There's a jar of instant coffee there, too, but it's solidified into rock now. What do you think we need?"

Emily gave him an odd look. "I thought you made a list?"

"I did." He extended it for her to see. "It seemed easier to write down what we had, though; there wasn't much of it."

Emily laughed. "That's a weird way to shop."

"I eat out a lot," he confessed.

"Well, let's see." Emily took the piece of paper from his hands and perused it. "What do you like to eat?"

"The country-cured ham's great around here. Better than Virginia ham—don't tell Larry Sansing I said that."

"You want that?"

"If you do. I didn't know what you liked. That's why it was so hard making a list."

"Well, I like ham, so why don't we start with that? We can have ham sandwiches tonight. And we know we need coffee. I can brew it if you have a pot." He shook his head. "We'll stick to instant, then. Okay, grab a shopping basket and let's go."

They roamed around the store, buying haphazardly, picking up thick slices of ham at the meat counter, packets of cheese, bread, chips, hot dogs, eggs, milk and whatever else caught their fancy, joking and laughing as they went. Everything they said seemed hilarious. There was a bright, mushrooming happiness inside Emily that made her feel as though she would probably float off if she let go of Adam's hand. She hoped they were getting most of what they needed, but she was having too much fun to really care about the practicalities.

They left the store, Adam carrying their brimming sack of groceries. Adam stuck the sack in the trunk of his car and they strolled down the street to look at the shops. The town was a treasure trove of mountain crafts. Lovely old-fashioned quilts hung in the windows, beckoning to Emily. Inside the stores were dolls handcrafted out of wood, corn husks and dried apples. There were carved wooden figures and hand-embroidered tablecloths and blouses. Jars of homemade jellies and jams, corn relish, sweet relish, dill pickles, sweet pickles, pickled onions and okra lined the shelves, all decorated with simple, hand-printed labels.

Emily was fascinated. She roamed through the plank-floored stores, peering at all the items. Adam followed her, amused by her interest and enjoying the eagerness that lit her face. Once he had thought Emily completely reserved—to be honest, he hadn't really thought of her as having emotions. She had been the most efficient employee he had ever seen, always willing to work extra time or do a document over because he had decided to change something, able to lay her hands on whatever he needed to find or to screen his phone calls or to find a case in the library when he didn't have the time. She had been so uncomplaining, businesslike and stable that she been almost a machine. She was so eminently satisfactory and he was so happy to have a rock like her amidst his harried, hurried practice, that he had never really wondered if there was any more to her. He hadn't stopped to ask whether she really was a superwoman or merely hiding her human frailties.

But now he saw her with her frailties, her fears and sorrows. He saw her laughter, her excitement, her interest in things, and he found that he enjoyed her. Adam had always respected Emily and had liked her, but he had never guessed that it would give him pleasure to hear her chuckle or see her eyes light up when she picked up a delicate wood carving, that he would find it a joy to be with her.

He bought the wood carving for her despite her protests that she didn't need it. "That's not the point," he replied firmly. "I want to buy it for you." He did want to; there was more fun in giving Emily the relatively inexpensive carving than he had found in giving Cassie a diamond pendant. Cassie had taken all gifts as her right—and usually less than what she deserved. Her pleasure in jewelry was more in seeing it lying against her creamy skin, enhancing her beauty, than in the present itself or in his giving it to her. When Adam had been disappointed in her reaction, Cassie would accuse him of demanding that she be grateful to him, like a puppy wriggling at his master's feet. He hadn't wanted gratitude; at least, he didn't think so. He couldn't express

# Take 4 Books
# –and a Tote Bag–
# FREE

**And preview exciting new Silhouette Intimate Moments
novels every month—as soon as they're published!**

# Silhouette Intimate Moments®

# Yes...Get 4 Silhouette Intimate Moments novels (a $10.00 value) and a Tote Bag FREE!

**SLIP AWAY FOR AWHILE**...Let Silhouette Intimate Moments novels draw you into a world of love and romance as it is experienced by real men and women. You'll find it's easy to close the door on the cares and concerns of everyday life as you lose yourself in the timeless drama of love, played out in exotic locations the world over.

**EVERY BOOK AN ORIGINAL**...Every Silhouette Intimate Moments novel is a full-length story, never before in print, superbly written to give you more of what you want from romance. Start with 4 new Silhouette Intimate Moments novels—a $10.00 gift from us to you—along with a free Tote Bag, with no obligation to buy another book now or ever.

**YOUR FAVORITE AUTHORS**...Let your favorite authors—such as Elizabeth Lowell, Maura Seger, Heather Graham Pozzessere, Erin St. Clair, Mary Lynn Baxter, and others—take you to a whole other world.

**ROMANCE-FILLED READING**...Each month you'll receive novels created especially for you—a woman who wants a more intense, passionate reading experience. Every book offers you romantic fantasy...dynamic, contemporary characters...involving stories...and stirring passion.

**NO OBLIGATION** ... Each month we'll send you 4 new Silhouette Intimate Moments novels as soon as they are published, without obligation. If not enchanted, simply return them within 15 days and owe nothing. Or keep them, and pay just $9.00 for all four books. And there's never an additional charge for shipping or handling.

**SPECIAL EXTRAS FOR HOME SUBSCRIBERS ONLY** ... When you take advantage of this offer and become a home subscriber, we'll also send you the Silhouette Books Newsletter FREE with each book shipment. Every informative issue features news about upcoming titles, interviews with your favorite authors, even their favorite recipes.

So send in the postage-paid card today, and take your fantasies further than they've ever been. The trip will do you good!

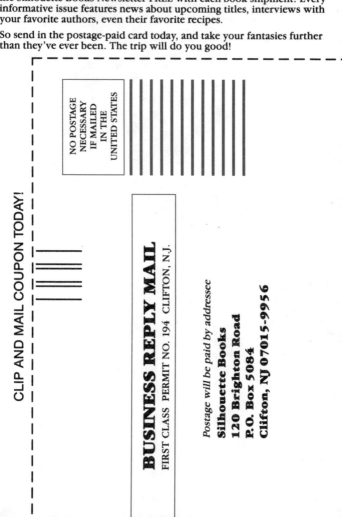

CLIP AND MAIL COUPON TODAY!

NO POSTAGE
NECESSARY
IF MAILED
IN THE
UNITED STATES

**BUSINESS REPLY MAIL**

FIRST CLASS   PERMIT NO. 194   CLIFTON, N.J.

Postage will be paid by addressee

**Silhouette Books**
**120 Brighton Road**
**P.O. Box 5084**
**Clifton, NJ 07015-9956**

# Take your fantasies further than they've ever been. Get 4 Silhouette Intimate Moments novels (a $10.00 value) plus a Tote Bag FREE!

Then preview future novels for 15 days—
FREE and without obligation. Details inside.

## Your happy endings begin right here.

*Silhouette Intimate Moments*®

**Silhouette Books, 120 Brighton Rd., P.O. Box 5084, Clifton, NJ 07015-9956**

☐ Yes, please send me FREE and without obligation, 4 brand new Silhouette Intimate Moments novels along with my Tote Bag. Unless you hear from me after I receive my 4 FREE books, please send me 4 new Silhouette Intimate Moments novels to preview each month as soon as they are published.

I understand that you will bill me a total of just $9.00, with no additional charges of any kind. There is no minimum number of books that I must buy, and I can cancel at any time. The first 4 books and Tote Bag are mine to keep.

NAME _____
(please print)

ADDRESS _____

CITY _____ STATE _____ ZIP _____

Prices and terms subject to change.
Your enrollment is subject to acceptance by Silhouette Books.

SILHOUETTE INTIMATE MOMENTS is a registered trademark.

CTMN65

exactly what it was that he *had* wanted, yet he knew there had been some element missing, some joy or pleasure whose absence had sapped his own pleasure in the gift.

Whatever it was, it wasn't missing in Emily. After her initial heartfelt protest that he didn't need to buy her a present, she had accepted it with pleasure. Her eyes shone as she held it in her palm and ran a finger over its delicate ridges and curves. "It's beautiful," she breathed. "Oh, Adam, thank you. I'll keep it always." She looked up at him, her face glowing, her pale, gray eyes sparkling with unshed tears. Unconsciously she closed her hand around the carving and brought her hand to her chest, to her heart. She went up on tiptoe and brushed her lips against his. "Thank you."

His arm came around her shoulders, holding her there, and he kissed her deeply, his tongue seeking its home in her mouth. When they parted, her eyes were even shinier and her lips were soft and suffused with color. "I think I'm ready to go home," Adam said softly. "How about you?"

Emily nodded, and they left the store and walked to their car. When they reached the car, Adam opened Emily's door for her, then stepped back. "I'm going to run into the store for something. Back in a second."

He closed her door and trotted lightly up the steps to the grocery store. Moments later he returned, carrying a small brown sack in his hand. He slid into the driver's seat and set the bag down on the floor next to the door, then started the engine and backed out into the empty street.

"What'd you buy?" Emily asked casually, wondering which of the no doubt many essentials they had forgotten.

"Nothing much." He glanced at her, and there was a teasing spark in his eyes. "I'll show you later."

Emily's eyebrows went up. "A surprise?"

"Yeah. I guess."

"What?"

He chuckled. "It's not a surprise if I tell you."

"Oh, all right." Emily made a face at him. She supposed he must have bought a dessert for supper, but the sack looked awfully small for anything like that. Certainly not a pie or cake, maybe a small container of ice cream.

When they reached the cabin, he carried in the sack of groceries, the other small bag tucked in on top. He set the large bag down on the kitchen counter, then lifted out the smaller one and took it into the bedroom. Not ice cream, then, Emily thought. She shrugged. Well, she'd find out sometime, she supposed. She began to remove the groceries and put them away. Adam returned and helped her put away the rest of their supplies.

Then he sat down on one of the dining chairs and pulled Emily between his legs. He wrapped his arms around her and leaned against her stomach. Emily laid her hands on his shoulders and began to knead his shoulders. She let her hands slide out to his arms and down his back. Adam made a soft noise and snuggled closer. "Mmm. That feels good. Will you rub my back when I come back in?"

"Come back?" Emily repeated.

"Yeah. It's still chilly in the evenings in the mountains, so I thought we'd have a fire in the fireplace tonight. I need to chop some wood."

"Honestly?" Emily leaned away from him to look at his face. "You can chop wood? Like with an axe?"

He grinned "Yeah. Like with an axe. It's my one and only pioneer skill. Mom and Dad have a house near Asheville, where I used to spend the summer when I was a kid. There was a man down the road who taught me how to use an axe. I like it; it's a great way to take out your frustrations. When Cassie and I were arguing over the divorce settlement, sometimes I'd come up here and cut down a tree and chop enough firewood for here and my condominium in Winston-Salem...and my parent's fireplace...and Tag's. Even wearing gloves, I got blisters all over my hands."

"Did it help?"

"Yeah, it helped." For a moment his face was grim, then it shifted back into a pleasant expression. "At least it kept me from going crazy. And we all had plenty of firewood for the year." Adam rose and kissed her. "But this afternoon all I plan to do is chop enough for this evening. You want to come watch?"

"Sure."

Emily followed him around to the back of the cabin where a small, wooden lean-to stood. Inside Adam kept the few tools that he and the caretaker needed around the place. He removed a pair of heavy work gloves and a long-handled, double-headed axe. Emily grimaced. She had never seen one before except in a movie. "Good grief! That looks lethal."

"It could be," he agreed. "Come on. There's a big dead tree in the woods that I've been taking limbs off of the past few times I've been here. I haven't come up here as often lately, or created so much firewood."

Emily followed him into the woods and watched as he cut off a medium-size limb. Then he dragged it back to the area behind the house, where he chopped it into numerous pieces of approximately equal lengths. Emily watched him, fascinated by his grace and strength as he swung the axe high over his head and brought it down again, biting cleanly into the wood. He soon grew warm from his exertions and removed his shirt. His muscles bunched and relaxed with his movements, rippling beneath his smooth skin, and Emily felt a warmth start in her veins. It was obvious to her now how he had acquired the lean muscles in his arms, so at odds with his desk job.

Adam was soon finished and he carried the pile of wood inside and set it in the wood box beside the fireplace, bringing in smaller branches and wood shavings to get the fire started. Afterward he showered, while Emily sat on the porch and watched the early mountain sunset. Adam was right. As the sun dropped it became distinctly cool, even with a sweater on.

Adam joined her later, and they watched the orange-yellow glow give way to the purplish shadows. They went back inside, and Adam laid the fire in the fireplace and lit it. He opened the chilled bottle of wine they'd bought at the store earlier and they sat on the rug in front of the crackling fire, sipping their drinks and luxuriating in the mellow warmth and mesmerizing sight of the flames. The tangy scent of the pine cones Adam had tossed in on top tinged the air.

Adam leaned back on his elbow, watching her, and Emily was acutely aware of his eyes on her. She glanced over at him, and her breath caught in her throat. His gaze was intense, visible even through the dim light. His eyes traveled over her body, almost tangibly touching her. He wanted her. Every line of his face bespoke desire. Emily felt as if her bones were melting. She eased down on her side, and they gazed at each other, separated by less than a foot. The fire popped and sparked; the heat caressed their feet and legs.

Slowly Adam leaned across the narrow space between them, and his lips moved down to meet hers.

## Chapter 7

Adam's mouth was slow and sweet on hers. Emily's arms curled around his neck. The kiss went on and on, his tongue and lips coaxing her to passion. When at last the kiss ended his mouth trailed across her cheek to her ear and down her throat, nibbling at the sensitive cords of her neck. Emily moved her hands restlessly across his back and shoulders, caressing him through the soft flannel shirt. She loved the feel of his firm muscles beneath her fingers. She wanted to touch his naked flesh, to feel the hot, smooth skin stretched over the muscles.

"You wanted me to massage your back," she reminded him softly. "Would you like me to do it now?"

Adam raised his head. His blue eyes gleamed. "Yes. If you want to."

"I want to."

He sat up and stripped off his shirt. Emily rose up on her knees and positioned herself behind him. She began to knead his shoulders, her thumbs digging into the muscles, taut from his exertion that afternoon. The knots loosened under her probing fingers, and Adam let out a sigh of contentment. His head lolled forward, inviting her hands, and Emily slid up to his neck. Her fingers moved over him, exploring the new textures of flesh and muscle, bone and tendons. It was erotic, and warmth spread through Emily, yet there was a masculine vulnerability to his bowed neck and naked shoulders that inspired a tender ache deep in her chest. Love for him swelled in her. Once she had thought it would be impossible to love Adam any more than she already did, but now she knew that wasn't true. She loved him more with each passing second, each thing she learned about him, each way she expressed her love physically. Love wasn't static, just as desire could never be fully satisfied. It grew and expanded all the time.

She bent down and kissed the arch of his neck, and he let out a low rumble of pleasure. "I like the way you give a massage."

"Really?" She kissed him again, her lips following the hard line of his spinal column. "You mean like this?"

"Yeah. Like that."

She moved over his neck, nuzzling and kissing him, nipping lightly at his skin with her teeth. When she pulled back he said quickly, hoarsely, "Don't stop."

Emily smiled and moved her hands across his shoulders and down his back, then kissed the base of his neck and trailed a line of kisses across his broad shoulders, moving with the same slow sensuality she had used on his neck. He had given her license to explore him, and Emily was eager to do it. She wanted to touch him all over and feel the different textures of his hair and skin. Was the hair on his chest as silky as that on his head? Was the skin of his abdomen as smooth as it looked?

She curved over, her mouth roaming his back, and her hands slid down to his jeans and around to the front. Her fingers traveled up his chest, tangling in the curling hairs, tracing the solid sternum, seeking out the small, pointing buttons of his nipples. She caressed him as he had caressed her, making love to every inch of his skin. Adam's breath scraped in sharply as her fingertips circled his nipples, and he gave a wordless murmur of pleasure. Her hands moved down to the rough denim of his jeans, gliding over the cool, metal snap and lower, and Adam groaned softly.

"Ah, sweetheart, you're a fast learner."

Emily smiled, breathing in the tangy scent of his skin mingled with masculine cologne. Her tongue flickered out to trace a design over his flesh, delighting in the warm, salty taste. She rubbed her cheek against his back, learning yet a new sensation of touch. She felt as if she could lose herself in him, drown in the sight and scent and feel of him.

Adam turned around and clasped her arms, pulling her to him so that their bodies were flattened against each other all the way up and down. They kissed, their mouths clinging and avid, drinking deeply of the sweetness. Finally Adam raised his head. His eyes burned down into her. "Wait here," he ordered huskily. "I've got to get something."

Startled, Emily stared as he rose and crossed the room to the bedroom. Almost immediately he returned, holding the small brown sack he had purchased before they left Fender's Gap. "The surprise?" Emily asked, her eyebrows going up. She tried in vain to recall anything remotely sexual in the little country store.

"The surprise," he confirmed, setting it down on the floor and kneeling beside her again. He reached out and grasped the hem of her sweater and tugged upward. "May I undress you?" Emily nodded wordlessly, raising her arms to aid him. "I've been thinking about seeing you naked all afternoon."

He laid the sweater on the couch and gazed at her. "I saw that you did what I asked." He reached out to touch her breasts, naked and free of restraint. "I probably shouldn't have requested it. It kept me turned on all afternoon. I could see your nipples harden every time I touched you. I wanted desperately to run my hand over them and watch them tighten even more." His voice dropped, becoming lower and hoarser.

Adam unbuttoned her slacks and lowered the zipper, slipping them down. Emily lay back on the braided rug and let him pull the trousers from her legs. He rose and removed his jeans, his eyes steadily on her the whole time, stoking the fire in her loins. When he was naked he knelt beside her and eased the lacy panties off her legs. "When you told me the story about putting honey on your breasts, it was all I could do not to leave the restaurant and bring you straight back to the cabin. I couldn't stop thinking about it. I kept seeing the honey, thick and golden on your breasts, your nipples." His voice was husky, his eyes dark with desire.

He reached into the sack and removed a small jar of dark golden liquid. Emily's eyes flew open wide. "Honey!"

"Yeah." His voice was as rich and thick as the syrup itself. He opened the jar and set it down beside her. He scooped up the viscous liquid with his forefinger and trailed it across her breasts, tracing a line of golden drops around her breast, spiraling inward to the rosy point of her nipple. Then he laced the other breast with the same golden web. Emily watched him silently, the fire in her abdomen flickering outward and consuming her whole body. Just the touch of the thick liquid on her skin, just the dark, hot look in Adam's eyes, aroused Emily almost beyond bearing.

Unconsciously she squeezed her legs together, as if to still the growing ache there. But nothing could ease that ache except Adam's touch. Adam's flesh.

When he finished he licked the honey from his finger and smiled slowly. "I always loved the taste of honey." He stretched out beside her. His mouth hovered over her breast, and then slowly, leisurely, his tongue came out and scooped up the droplets of honey, moving around her breasts, spiraling up until it rimmed her nipple. His tongue skimmed the hard point, then returned, dragging over the golden-coated nipple. Again and again his faintly rough tongue crossed her nipple, bringing Emily to a fever pitch of desire, and then his mouth came down to suckle the sweet tip.

Emily arched, moaning, and Adam widened his mouth, pulling in more of her breast in response. At last he left the nipple, dark and love-swollen, and trailed his tongue across her skin to the other breast. With great care he licked the honey from it, too, but this time, as his mouth drank the sweet syrup from her skin, his hand slid between her legs and lightly stroked the tender folds of flesh there. Emily was flooded with desire, so assaulted by delicious sensations that she writhed and groaned, pressing her lower body up against his hand, mutely begging for the blissful release only he could give her.

She felt mindless, a quivering knot of physical sensations and hunger. She murmured his name over and over, her body moving in the ageless rhythms of passion. But Adam took his time, loving this breast with equal thoroughness, suckling and laving it, until he, too, was quivering under the force of his desire and the effort of delaying what he so desperately wanted to have. At last he moved between her legs and entered her, filling the aching void within her. Emily wrapped her legs around him and moved her hips against him wantonly. His mouth came down to seize hers, harsh with need, his tongue ravaging and wild. He tasted of honey and the faint salt of her skin. He began to stroke within her, building the exquisite friction to an almost unbearable heat. Emily was pressed back into the rug, her back slightly abraded with each hard thrust, but the tiny nip of pain merely emphasized her burgeoning pleasure. Adam's breath was hot against her cheek, coming in quick, harsh gasps; his skin burned. Emily moved with him, circling and matching his strokes. His arms tightened convulsively, and he cried out as his seed poured into her. Emily burst into flames with him, her pleasure released from its bonds and flooding her body. They hung for an instant in eternity together, almost insensate and wrapped in bliss.

Then, slowly, they drifted down from the heights. Adam moved a little, groaning, and sank down upon her. For a long time they lay pressed together, damp and exhausted, still too stunned by their passion to speak or move. Finally Adam kissed her neck softly and started to roll off her. Their skin clung, and Adam chuckled, rolling onto his side and carrying her with him in his arms. "I think we're stuck together."

Emily giggled. They lay for a long while that way, softly murmuring and kissing, until at last even the heat of the fire wasn't quite enough to keep their naked bodies warm. Then they rose, separating reluctantly, and went into the bathroom, where they soaked together in the enormous, old claw-footed tub. They bathed each other, Adam solicitously soaping Emily's breasts until they were free of every last vestige of honey. By the time he finished, they were both so aroused that they made love again, there in the tub, with the warm water lapping around them caressingly.

Afterward they toweled each other dry and snuggled together in their robes before the dying fire, a quilt thrown over their legs. They drank more wine and talked, drifting from their work to their relatives, coming to rest on Adam's brother.

"Tag's not really a rebel," Adam mused, sipping from his glass.

"Really? I would have thought he was. Why not?" Emily asked, encouraging him to expound. She loved to listen to Adam, to learn about the people close to him, the things that he liked.

"He's not interested enough to be a rebel," Adam answered. "Not sincere and dedicated enough."

Emily smiled. "I guess you're right about that."

"James is more of a rebel than Tag when you think about it. James pursues his field of law with such zeal, and I think he enjoys flying in the teeth of family tradition. He's almost a Puritan." He paused and flashed her a grin. "Not, mind you, that he follows Puritan ideals. But in regard to his own ideals, he has that sort of purity of belief, that complete dedication. He's always on some personal crusade. But Taggart—ah, Taggart. I don't think Tag would know a crusade if he met it face-to-face. His philosophy is live-and-let-live. He has a good heart; he's kind. I think people assume from his life-style that he must be a callous, carousing son-of-a-bitch, but he's the one in the family who remembers everyone's birthday or anniversary, who comes by to see you if you're sick or down or hurting."

"You sound as if you have a special soft spot for Tag."

Adam shrugged in a self-deprecating gesture. "He's the youngest of us, the baby. James is a year and a half younger than I am, and he and I were always in competition. I don't mean we don't love each other; we do. But everyone compared us, and we pushed to see which one of us could beat the other. We were friends, but there was always a secret score-keeping going on between us, to see who made the best grades, who dated the prettiest girls. That kind of thing.

But Tag is five years younger than I am, and I didn't feel any competition with him. He seemed like a marvelous, living toy to me. He adored me, like children usually do a much older sibling, and I took care of him. I was his protector, the guy who fixed his toys or, later, covered for him when he got into trouble."

He smiled to himself. "Tag's worth a million other guys. The thing about him is, he just isn't interested in the things the rest of us are interested in. He's different. And I don't think he's ever found what he really wants out of life."

"Somehow I suspect that your father has trouble understanding that," Emily commented wryly.

"Dad?" Adam gave a bark of laughter. "He thinks Tag is a lazy, irresponsible parasite. 'At thirty-two?' he'll say. 'At thirty-two he still doesn't know what he wants to do?'"

Adam's imitation of his father's aristocratic indignation was so accurate that Emily had to laugh. Adam shook his head in amused exasperation. "I love them both, but they can't understand each other. I don't think they'll ever get along."

"I know. It's the same way with my aunt and cousin. They're completely different. I'm more like my aunt than Jeanette is."

"Your aunt? The dragon lady? You're not like her!"

Laughter bubbled up out of Emily. "No, I'm not stern or judgmental like she is. I don't go around trying to catch sinners. What I meant was, I'm more the kind of person Rosemary wanted Jeanette and me to be. Quiet and retiring. Not one to get myself noticed."

"That's putting it mildly."

Emily gave him a small smile. "But Jeanette is outgoing, very personable and attractive. She dresses fashionably; in fact, she's a buyer for a clothing store."

"What about your mother? What's she like?"

Emily stiffened. "Mother? Couldn't you tell?"

"Tell what?"

"Mother was the wild sister of their family. She's always been a partyer. She dresses flashily, wears too much makeup, talks too loud."

"A brazen hussy, in other words."

Emily sighed. "Yeah. I guess so."

"Well, if the rest of your family is like your aunt, she must have had some rough times at home."

"Rosemary's mild compared to my grandfather. I imagine a lot of the way Mother is was simply rebellion against her family's strictness. I'm glad I didn't have to grow up the way she did. But she was pretty unsettling to have as a mother. I remember being embarrassed by her lots of times. Other kids' mothers would come to school for a visit looking like nice, normal housewives. Mother'd show up at school looking like she worked in a bar—which she did part of the time. She was usually gone in the evenings; she either worked or she'd go out. She and Dad fought a lot. Then, after Dad left us, she got worse. That's when she sent me to live with Aunt Rosemary."

Adam's arm was around her shoulders, and he gave her a comforting squeeze. He kissed the top of her head, and she snuggled closer against his chest. "How old were you then?"

"About eight or nine. I don't remember exactly. I lived on and off with Rosemary until after high school. It was nice being with Jeanette; it was like having a sister. And I got along with Aunt Rosemary better than Jeanette did; they were always fighting. Still, I missed Mother; she could be fun, and Aunt Rosemary was never fun. But Mother was unreliable. She'd stay out till all hours of the night. She'd show up one day and whisk me away to live with her for a few months. Then she'd get restless or decide her life-style was bad for me, and back I'd go to Aunt Rosemary. When I was in high school she lived in Florida, and I'd spend most of the summers with her. She's calmed down a lot now. Why, she's lived in that house and held the same job for almost five years."

"Why do you still live with them?"

"I don't know. It's economical. And I've never exactly been a 'swinging single,' so having them around didn't affect my life-style." Emily shrugged. "We're an odd crew. But we manage to struggle along together well enough, except that Rosemary and Mother fight all the time."

"And you try to make peace between them?"

She shook her head. "I've given up on that. Sometimes I think they get a kick out of fighting. It gives Mother a chance to still act wild, and it gives my aunt a chance to condemn someone."

"Do you ever think about moving out?"

"I hadn't, at least not until recently. The past couple of weeks I've felt sort of constrained by living with them. Aunt Rosemary interrogates and lectures me as if I were still a teenager. Mother's not condemnatory, but she's horribly curious. Plus, they use me as an issue to fight over. I suppose I could move. Since Rosemary's living there, Mother doesn't need my financial help."

"If I had to live with my parents, I'd probably die within about three days. When Cassie kicked me out I went back home for a couple of days. I couldn't hack it."

"But I thought you and your father got along well."

"We do—at work. Somehow, at the office, he's able to accept me as an individual and an adult. But there's something about living under the same roof that sets them back into the old relationship of parent and child. Mother worried about my health and reminded me of all the things she'd never liked about Cassie. Dad pontificated on divorce and the structure and psychological makeup of Cassie's family, both past and present, and hounded me about the state of my cases. It was awful. I moved into a hotel until I could find a condominium.''

Emily's spirits slipped a little. She hated any mention of Cassie. Because she loved Adam, she had always envied Cassie for having Adam's love. When Cassie had divorced Adam, she had been amazed that his wife could be that crazy, and furious that she had hurt Adam so deeply. Now she couldn't think of Cassie or hear her name without the bitter twist of knowledge that Adam had loved Cassie so much that he had been decimated by her leaving him. Since then he had dated women like a wild man, but Emily gathered, from office gossip and Adam's own chance remarks, that there wasn't any woman among them who meant anything to him, or with whom he had spent more than one or two nights. That proved to Emily that Adam was still in love with his ex-wife, still enmeshed in her beauty and glittering personality. Emily had seen Cassie Marshall many times; she knew no woman could stand a chance against even her memory—especially no one as ordinary as herself.

"I know it was a bad time for you," Emily said cautiously, not really wanting to hear about his sorrow over Cassie, yet desperately wanting to hear his feelings, to know him better, to be his confidante.

"I was crazy for a while. It's weird, you know. It feels like the world just fell in on you. I walked in one night, late as always, of course. It was about nine o'clock. And there was Cassie, all made up and dressed in a classy slacks suit. She looked as good as I ever remember her. As soon as I saw her, I thought about how infrequently we'd made love recently—we'd both been busy. I'd been gone a lot or worried about a case; she'd been tired. The next thing I thought was that I wanted to make love to her that night; she looked so beautiful. Then she hit me with it. She handed me a Blackjack and water and told me to sit down. She said she wanted a divorce. She wanted me to move out. It was her home, she said, because only she had ever spent any time in it. My only home was Marshall, Pierson, Tidrell, and Sommers, and for all she cared I could sleep there as well as live there." His mouth twisted into a wry smile. "Sometimes I did."

"I know," Emily put in softly, torn with sympathy for his remembered pain.

"Yeah. You found me there once or twice, didn't you?"

"Yes."

"You were good to me then. It was service above and beyond the call of duty for a secretary."

"I didn't do it as your secretary. I did it as your friend."

He pulled her against his chest, wrapping his arms around her. "Thank you. You were the best kind of friend. You didn't snoop; you didn't pry; you didn't push. You just covered for me and helped me silently and let me cry on your shoulder."

Emily understood then why Adam had offered her this weekend. He was returning her acts of friendship. He was doing what he could for her, as she had done what she could for him. He was kind; he was generous. He was grateful.

The idea squeezed her heart, but she stubbornly pushed it away. She would lock it up in some remote corner of her being with any other negative thoughts, and maybe sometime later she would let it out and examine it. Accept it. But not now. At this moment she had Adam, and it didn't matter why he was there. It only mattered that he was.

Adam woke her the next morning by making sweet, slow love to her, pulling her from her sleep into drowsy pleasure, then vibrant passion. He ran his hands over her body, arousing every sensitive spot of her skin, and all the while he watched her, enjoying the play of passion across her face and the responsive moves of her body. One hand went between her legs and sought out the fleshy button of pleasure there, stroking and laving it gently with the moisture of her own desire. With each soft movement he spiraled her passion ever higher, until she quivered from the force of it. Then, at last, she exploded into the world of wild joy she had discovered this weekend, shattering into glittering, shimmering pieces and moaning out her ecstasy.

"I love to watch you," Adam murmured huskily. "I love to see your face when you melt into satisfaction." Then he moved between her legs and entered her, and took them both to another peak of blissful union. Afterward, Emily lay quietly by his side and thought that she would never again feel the kind of joy that she had known this weekend. It was a curiously bittersweet emotion, a mingling of supreme contentment and wistful sorrow.

They walked in the woods again after breakfast, crossing the brook and going farther up the mountain, until they reached a rock ledge that was one of Adam's favorite spots. There they sat and held hands, talking and gazing at the panoramic view before them. They returned almost reluctantly to the cabin, as if doing so signaled an end to the weekend. They made a detour to the pond, and Adam attempted to skim a few stones across it, another skill he had acquired in his boyhood summers near Asheville. He failed miserably each time, the rocks plopping and sinking straight to the bottom. They laughed, and he hugged her.

"It must be the rocks," he said. "You need them flat and smooth to do it successfully." Emily hooted with laughter, and he gave her a rib-cracking squeeze. "All right, all right. Pipe down. I get your point."

They returned to the cabin then, and Emily threw together a small lunch. But she only ate a little of her sandwich, the ache in her chest mushrooming and filling her up inside. They packed their bags quickly, and Adam put them in the car. Still they hesitated. Suddenly Adam swooped her up into his arms. "One last time," he murmured.

He started for the bedroom.

It was several hours later that Adam's BMW rolled down I-40 into Winston-Salem. The town looked strange to Emily. It felt as if she had been away for months, as if everything had changed. Yet it all seemed too familiar; it hadn't changed at all, and it seemed as if it should have.

Adam drove her to Jeanette's apartment. Emily glanced up at Jeanette's door and decided that she would get in her car and go straight home. She didn't think she could face even Jeanette's friendly questions about the weekend and Adam right now. She was too close to tears.

She swallowed and grasped the door handle. "Well. I guess this is it. Thank you. I—anything I can say is terribly inadequate."

"Don't thank me." Adam's voice was quick and sharp and strangely thin. "There's no question of thanks. I—let me get your bag."

He left the car and opened the trunk to take out her small suitcase. He insisted on carrying it to her car and settling it into the seat beside her. Emily dug her keys out of her purse, and they stood for a moment, looking at each other awkwardly. There seemed no appropriate way to end the moment. It seemed bizarre not to touch or kiss after the passion they'd shared this weekend, yet they were back in the real world now. That time was over. Finally Adam moved forward and put his hands on her upper arms, a light, undemanding touch, and bent to kiss her forehead. He stepped back. She backed up, too, and reached to open her door, half turning from him. He turned away and walked a few steps.

Adam turned. Emily was in the car, fitting her key into the ignition, her door still open. There was a strange, heavy lump in the pit of his stomach. He felt—he wasn't sure what. Cheated? Disappointed? She was leaving without a single gesture or even a backward look, as if there had been nothing more between them than a one night stand. But then, he reminded himself, that was really all he was to her, wasn't it? That was all that had happened between them. A few bouts of passion. A favor for a friend. Nothing more. It was part of the agreement.

"See you tomorrow," he called, and walked back to his car.

## Chapter 8

Emily hadn't thought it would hurt so much. Because she had loved Adam for so long and with no hope of ever attaining his love, she had thought she knew the pain involved and her capacity to handle it. She had agreed and accepted that after the weekend their relationship would return to what it had always been. She had expected to lose Adam after those two days, and had believed that knowing it would make the pain less. She found out it didn't.

She drove home from Jeanette's apartment and went straight upstairs to her room, locked her door and burst into tears. She kept remembering how beautiful it had been, recalling every touch, every word, every feeling. She dreaded going to the office the next day and having to face Adam. How could she possibly pretend that nothing had happened between them? She realized now that she had been fooling herself when she had said that they could go back to their former relationship. Or perhaps she'd just been too unknowing to realize how intensely their lovemaking would affect her emotions.

She loved Adam more than ever. She knew him now in a far more intimate way than before. She had learned the taste of his skin, its warm, masculine scent, its smooth feel beneath her fingers. She had seen Adam's face in the throes of passion. She had heard his low moans of pleasure. Emily didn't know how she could face him and discuss business matters without constantly thinking about those things. Moreover, she knew that he knew the same things about her. In the context of this weekend, his knowledge had been exciting. In the context of the office, she was afraid it would be embarrassing.

This weekend she had become used to touching Adam, and she was afraid she might forget herself and reach out to take his hand or lay a hand on his arm. She might stand too close. Worse yet, she had become used to his touching her, and she knew that she would miss it, would wish, even ache, for it. It would be pure torture, she thought, to have him stand beside her, going over something with her, yet without the intimacy or the touching she craved. She didn't know how she would bear it.

Yet she had to. She had managed for ten years, loving him and never showing it. Somehow she must manage not to show her longing now, either.

She went to bed early and slept the night through, as though sleeping would make her problems disappear. That didn't happen, but she did find the next morning that there was another feeling mixed in with her anxiety and pain. She couldn't quite put her finger on it, but there was something almost happy inside her, a small comforting rock of knowledge deep within her. Adam had made love to her; she had been desired. Nothing could change that. Nothing could detract from it. She felt more of a woman, as if now she *knew*. As if now there was something of worth to her. Adam had said she was pretty; Adam had caressed her body and turned hot with passion doing so. There was a confidence inside her, a spark that had never been there before.

Emily thought she could see it when she looked in the mirror. There was more color to her face, a new brightness to her eyes. Even her posture looked better, her figure less skinny. As she tied her hair back with a ribbon, she grimaced at her reflection. Maybe Jeanette was right. Perhaps she should cut her hair and let it fluff out more around her face. It certainly wouldn't do any harm to try; if she didn't like it, she could always let it grow back to its present length.

She went to her closet and sifted through her suits and dresses. All of them seemed incredibly ugly. Her clothes were so dark! It was depressing. She couldn't find anything that pleased her. Then she remembered Jeanette's clothes. Her cousin had lent her an extra outfit, just in case, which she hadn't worn with Adam. The slacks were too casual, really, for the office, but she could wear the attractive pink blouse with one of her suits.

She put on the blouse with her tan suit. It was much prettier than the brown, figured blouse she usually wore with that suit, but it still wasn't anything great. Emily removed the suit jacket. There. That looked better. She added a pair of earrings and an enameled locket Jeanette had given her for Christmas two years ago. She looked down at her brown pumps. They were comfortable, but not very attractive. Maybe she ought to buy some sandals. She had pretty feet, really, and sandals would look sexy on them. She could find sandals that were comfortable, too, and it was getting to be the weather for them. She could go shopping on her lunch hour today.

Emily went downstairs, where her mother and aunt were already seated and eating their breakfast. She was later than usual because she'd put on makeup. Nancy glanced up when Emily came in the kitchen and smiled broadly. "Emily! Sweetheart! How nice you look."

"Thank you." Emily sat down and dipped a spoonful of eggs onto her plate from the bowl in the middle of the table.

Rosemary eyed her, suspicious of any change. "I've never seen that blouse before. Is it new?"

"It's Jeanette's. She lent it to me for a few days."

"It's very pretty. So was that dress you had on the other night when you went out with Adam Marshall." Nancy paused, then asked with studied nonchalance, "How was your weekend?"

Emily glanced at her mother sharply. Did Nancy suspect that she had been with Adam this weekend? Not, of course, that Nancy would disapprove. She'd probably be as happy as a lark that her daughter had spent a couple of days with a man. "Yes, it was very nice," Emily answered carefully.

"We were hoping you'd tell us about it last night, but you never came out of your room," Aunt Rosemary put in.

"I was tired."

"And you didn't eat anything."

"I wasn't hungry."

"Did you make yourself sick this weekend? I know Jeanette would drag you around shopping without any regard to whether or not you were feeling well."

"No, I'm not sick. We had fun, and Jeanette bought some furniture at a good discount."

"I can't imagine what she wants with more furniture in that place of hers."

Emily shrugged. "It wasn't much. A set of end tables and a—chair for her bedroom." Her palms began to sweat. Once you started lying, it seemed to mushroom. Thank heavens Rosemary rarely went over to Jeanette's apartment. She began to fork her eggs down rapidly.

"How was Adam?" Nancy asked.

Emily swallowed a solid lump of eggs. "What?"

"'How was Adam?' I said. You left so early Saturday I didn't get to talk to you about your date Friday night."

"Oh. Yeah. It was fine. We went to Ryan's and then out dancing."

"Terrific! What do you think? Is he interested in you? You never told me he was so gorgeous!"

"No! No. I'm sure he's not interested in me. It was really a business thing."

"Taking you dancing?" Nancy interjected skeptically.

"I mean, we didn't discuss business, but he did it kind of as a 'thank you' for my working late several nights on a case."

"But, sweetheart, he took you out to dinner the night before for that case."

"You know, Emily," Rosemary began in her lecturing voice, "it's really not a good idea to go out with one's boss. It can lead to all kinds of complications. You have no idea how many women have gotten into trouble that way."

"Oh, don't be such a spoilsport!" Nancy complained. "This is the 1980s, not last century."

Rosemary frowned at her sister. "High morals are not outdated. I'm glad to say that Emily has held to that precept, unlike most young women. I'm sure Emily realizes that I have only her best interests at heart. She's no match for a handsome, smooth man like Adam Marshall."

"Aunt Rosemary," Emily declared in exasperation, "Adam does not have 'wicked designs' on my virtue. This whole discussion is pointless—and it's really none of your business, either one of you."

Both women stared, openmouthed, and Emily flushed a little. She jumped up and went to the sink to wash off her plate. She felt a little guilty. She usually wasn't that rude to the two older women—or anyone else, for that matter. But she'd had all she could stand of their poking around in her private life. It was time they understood that she was an adult.

Emily left the house, wondering if she ought to move into her own apartment soon, and drove downtown. She dawdled on the walk to the bank building; she wasn't eager to get to work today and come face-to-face with Adam. When she reached her office she was glad to see that Adam's room was still dark and empty. She went to the lounge and poured herself a cup of coffee, then returned to her office. She went about her daily morning routine of turning on the word processor and retrieving her current work from the file drawer of her desk. Finally she settled down to work, though it was difficult to concentrate when she was listening to everyone who passed down the hall, waiting for Adam's footsteps or the sound of his voice.

When she heard Adam's laugh in the distance everything inside her froze. There was the rumble of his voice, and another man's in answer. The two voices came closer, and Emily strained to hear, all her muscles taut. "...So what was I supposed to do? Hell, you know Ingram."

"Don't I, though! Wish I didn't. So what did you tell him?"

"Well—" The voices were almost upon her now, but then she heard the click of a door closing and sudden silence. They'd gone into Adam's office.

Emily relaxed, releasing her breath. He must have an appointment with someone. She hoped it would take a long time. Her concentration greatly improved, she began her work again.

Adam was irritated when he stepped out of the elevator and found Larry Sansing waiting for him in the lobby. Larry was on the in-house counsel staff of Contelco, one of the firm's major corporate clients, and Adam had worked with him several times in the past. He was bright, pleasant and easy to work with, but this morning Adam wasn't interested in getting tied up with him before he even got to his office. He had intended to stop by Emily's office and drink a cup of coffee while he went over his week's schedule with her.

He should have been glad, of course, to delay the moment of meeting Emily. He had been feeling a little nervous and awkward about how he should act. But mixed with the nervousness had been a certain amount of eagerness. He was the kind who liked to face things and get them over with. Besides, he'd been bored and restless the whole evening after he said good-bye to Emily. He had missed her intelligent conversation and genuine interest in his work, and he'd been looking forward to talking to her again this morning.

But Larry had his briefcase and a look on his face that told Adam he'd be here most of the morning. His instincts were right: Larry stayed until noon, then suggested they go out to lunch on top of the office building, where Contelco was housed.

"Sure," Adam agreed, wishing Larry hadn't asked. He would have preferred a corned beef sandwich in his office and a chance to catch up on some of his work. The unexpected, morning-long appointment with Larry had thrown him even further behind. And he still hadn't had a chance to talk to Emily. She was here; it was obvious from the silence of his phone that she'd been holding all his calls. "Let me grab my messages and tell Emily where I'm going."

He went down the hall to Emily's office, Larry trailing along behind him. Emily was typing in front of her large word processor, and when she heard him, she looked up and smiled. It was like a beam of sunlight spreading across her face. Adam grinned back, and a prickle of warmth touched his abdomen. He remembered her after their lovemaking, smiling up at him like that, as though she'd been touched with joy. He forgot what he was going to say.

"Hello, Adam. Mr. Sansing." Emily spoke to Larry, who had come up beside Adam in the doorway.

Adam glanced at Sansing and saw the other man's eyes widen. Larry straightened, his hands coming out of his pockets. "Emily." It came out more as a question than a greeting.

Larry was amazed at the way Emily looked, Adam knew. He had to admit that she was much prettier than she used to be, though he'd grown rather used to it this weekend at the cabin. What had made the change in her? Surely it wasn't simply leaving off her glasses. There was a glow in her face that had never been there before. He wondered if it was a result of their lovemaking and again felt the little tongue of warmth inside.

"I'm going for lunch with Larry. I'll be back soon. Any messages?"

Emily indicated the message spike, decorated with a sheaf of message slips. "Nothing that won't wait."

"Okay. Good. Well, see you." He backed out of the office. It was decidedly unsatisfactory talking to her with Larry Sansing around. Still, at least they had gotten through the awkward moment. They had met and exchanged the kind of words they had always exchanged. Now they could return to normal.

As they walked down the hall Larry murmured, "Is that the same Emily who's always worked for you? What happened to her?"

"Of course it's the same woman," Adam retorted, a little irritated. You'd think Emily had been ugly before, the way Larry acted. "Nothing happened to her." Except a weekend in bed with him.

"You're joking. Something must have. I can't remember exactly what she looked like . . . but she wasn't pretty. That girl is pretty."

"It's the same woman, Larry. She got contacts, that's all. By the way, how is Catherine? You still dating her?"

They rounded the corner, talking. Emily watched them until they were out of sight, then leaned back in her chair with a sigh. She had made an idiot of herself, grinning like that when Adam appeared in her doorway. But she'd been concentrating on her work and hadn't heard him open his office door, so he had caught her by surprise. Her immediate, natural reaction on looking up and seeing him there had been a joyous smile. She wondered what he'd thought when she greeted him with too intimate and happy a face. It certainly wasn't a typical secretary-to-boss smile. If she weren't careful he might become afraid that she would try to pursue their brief intimacy. She would have to watch herself next time.

Emily decided to break for lunch. Her nerves had been unsettled by seeing Adam, and her concentration was shot. She'd do better after lunch. Besides, she was eager to go shopping.

Emily took the whole lunch hour, and a little bit more. She found sandals quickly, then spent the rest of the time trying on dress after dress. Practically every one seemed a vast improvement over her present wardrobe, and it was a real struggle to limit her choices. But at last she settled on just three: a sundress of shiny pastel stripes, with a cropped, short-sleeved jacket that matched one of the stripes; a crisp, white jacket and skirt with a bold turquoise underblouse;

and a narrow-lined black dress with puffed, white-and-black, patterned sleeves and a kicky, short, pleated underskirt. They would knock a hole in her savings, of course, but she'd saved a great deal of money on her clothes over the years, so it seemed only fair that clothes should take something out of her savings for once.

When she returned to the office she phoned her cousin. Jeanette's voice when she came on the line was bright and full of curiosity. "Emily! Why didn't you come inside yesterday? I was dying to hear what happened."

Emily smiled. "You won't ever hear that."

Jeanette chuckled. "That good? Congratulations."

"Yeah. It was that good. The only bad part is the fact that it's over."

"Don't give up hope."

"I told you. We agreed. Nothing's going to come of it. But I called you about something else."

"What?"

"You remember what you were saying about my hair?"

"Of course I do. You mean you're going to take my advice?"

"I'm not completely sure about streaking it, but I think I'll get a cut and permanent. I wanted to know where you'd recommend."

"Emily, you have made my day! I'll do better than recommend. I'll make you an appointment myself at my hairdresser's, and I'll tell him that he's got to do an extra special good job for you. This is so exciting! When do you want it?"

"Whenever he can do it, I guess. Sometime after work or on Saturday. Does he work on Saturday?"

"Yeah. But I'll push for an evening this week. I want to get you in there before you get cold feet."

"I won't get cold feet." She paused. "I went shopping today and bought three new outfits."

Emily had to hold the phone away from her ear, the shriek on the other end of the line was so loud. "You're joking! This man must really have had a powerful effect on you."

Emily smiled. "Yeah. I guess he did. I don't know. I looked at my clothes this morning and they were so drab. Your clothes had looked so good on me. All of a sudden I couldn't stand to wear mine anymore."

"You've made me an extremely happy woman. I feel like a mother whose daughter just got engaged to a doctor. Listen, you come over to my apartment tonight and we'll go through my clothes. I've got a bunch of things I don't wear that you can have. They'll look super on you."

"Oh, yeah? If they're so super, why don't you wear them?"

"You know me. I love to buy clothes. I wear them a few times and then I get bored with them. Honestly, I bet I have five or six dresses you can have. Then I'm going to take you shopping. We'll use my employee discount, and you'll save a ton of money."

"I don't know..." Emily demurred. She'd already spent more money on clothes today than she normally did in a whole season. But she thought of the joy of trying on the clothes at lunch and seeing herself in the mirror; she thought of wearing them at the office, where Adam could see her. "All right. But if I use up my life's savings, it'll be your fault."

"Are you sure you haven't developed a split personality? Is this my cousin I'm talking to?"

Emily laughed. "Jeanette..."

"Okay, okay. No more teasing. I'm going to hang up and call Randall right now. I'll let you know when I set up an appointment for your hair. And remember—you're coming over tonight to go through my wardrobe. Right?"

"Right."

"Great. See you. Bye."

"Bye." Emily hung up the receiver and sat for a moment, staring off into space. It was hard for her, too, to believe what she'd done today. She hardly recognized herself—but she thought she liked this stranger better.

Adam arrived a few minutes later to retrieve his messages. Emily heard him coming and was able to greet him with a circumspect smile and cool professionalism. "Hello, Adam. How was your lunch?"

He shrugged. "As usual." Adam slipped the stack of messages off the metal spindle and leafed through them. He knew he was buying time; he wanted to remain here a bit longer, but he didn't know what to say. The rather cool tone with which Emily had greeted him had set him back. Now she had turned her attention to her word processor and was reading through the text for errors. "Would you call Carey Browder for me, please? I've got a securities problem I need to talk over with him. Tell him any time this afternoon would be fine. My schedule's clear, isn't it?"

Emily looked at her daily calendar. "Yeah. No appointments till four."

"Four? Who am I seeing then?"

"Amanda Ritter."

"Who? Oh, yeah, I remember. That's in connection with that contested will. Okay. Tell Carey before four, then. Whet his curiosity—let him know it's something big."

Emily's eyes widened with interest, and Adam knew she wanted him to tell her. He barely stopped himself from leaning over and kissing her—the habits of even a weekend were hard to break. "Uh..." He cleared his throat.

"Top secret, huh? Is that what Larry Sansing was talking to you about so long this morning?"

"Yeah. It's going to be quite a surprise to this town."

"Now don't tease my curiosity like that." Emily pulled a stern face, and Adam grinned.

He flopped down on the straight chair beside her desk. He wanted to talk to her about the case. God knows, Emily could be relied upon to keep her mouth shut. Working for him, she was privy to almost every piece of confidential information he received. He reached back with his hand and closed her door. Emily leaned forward, crossing her arms on her desk and giving him her undivided attention. "This must be something."

"It is. It should be all over the newspapers tomorrow. The feds are arresting him this afternoon."

"Who?"

"Jack Larson."

Emily's eyes grew round. "Jack Larson! At Contelco?"

Adam nodded. "That's right. One of the three senior VPs."

"You're joking! Arresting him for what?" Then she recalled that he had asked to see the firm's securities laws expert. "A securities violation?"

"Yeah. He's been selling insider information. Contelco's going to buy out a firm in Virginia that's been a little shaky the past couple of years. Their stock's gone way down. Jack sold the information to a stockbroker, who then bought stock in the Virginia company for several of his clients. Of course, when news of the sale broke, the value of that stock would have zoomed right up. It was a flagrant violation."

"Wow." Emily sat back in her chair, absorbing the news. "I can hardly believe it. Jack Larson!"

"I know. Civic leader, responsible church member, family man. He's on the board of two banks—fortunately not Allied's, or my uncle would have a coronary. His wife's big in cultural charities. She's from a tobacco family in the eastern part of the state."

"But why?"

Adam shrugged. "Who knows? It's hard to figure. Maybe they had financial problems, though with her family and his salary, I wouldn't have figured money to be a problem."

"What will happen to him?"

"He and the stockbroker are both in hot water. The broker's a cousin of the president of Western Hills Savings and Loan. The country club will be buzzing tomorrow. The SEC's bringing charges against them; they'll be tried on securities violations. They could be sentenced to time in prison if they're found guilty."

"But, wait. How are you involved? This all sounds like a criminal case."

"It is. But Contelco plans to bring a civil suit against Larson. Their deal, you see, has gone down the tubes because of this. So they have a good case for loss of corporate opportunity. There might even be an unfair trade practice case here, which is treble damages. I'll have to check into it. That's why I need to talk to Browder. Sansing's also scared that stockholders might bring a suit against Contelco because of what their employee did to the detriment of the company. Darryl Simpson, the president of Contelco, is really steamed about the whole thing. You see, he was the one who hired Jack; Jack was Darryl's fair-haired boy."

"I see. So you're going to represent Contelco in a civil suit against Jack Larson."

"Right. After the criminal case."

Emily shook her head in disbelief. "This is too wild. I can hardly believe it."

"You won't be the only one. I bet even James'll be shocked, and he's usually unshockable. It should be quite a trial."

"Think of that man's poor family."

"Yeah. They're ruined. Socially. Financially."

"Emotionally," Emily added.

"You're right." He reached over and patted her hand. "Don't look so sad. You're too tender-hearted to work for a law firm."

The touch of his hand was hot and electric on Emily's skin. For one sizzling moment the passion of the past two days sprang up in her, and she thought of the heated slide of his skin over hers as they made love, the fierce blue of his eyes, darkened by desire.

Emily snatched her hand away. She mustn't think that way. It was over. Over. If she couldn't maintain a professional relationship with Adam, she would lose what little she had of him. She crossed her arms and moved her chair a fraction away; it was enough for the emotional distance she needed.

Adam recognized the barrier she put up between them, and the excitement and energy he had felt while talking about the case with her suddenly faded. He looked at the sheaf of pink slips in his hand, as if wondering how they had gotten there. "Well. I better get to these." He rose and opened her door, then hesitated. "You'll call Carey?"

"Yes. Right now." She pulled out the writing board over the first drawer of her desk, where she had taped a list of all the firm's extension numbers, and ran her finger down it, searching for the other attorney's number.

"Good. Well. Good bye, then."

"Bye." Emily raised her hand in a farewell gesture as she picked up the phone and punched out the number of Carey Browder's office.

She didn't see Adam again that day. He spent the afternoon closed up in his office, first talking with Carey Browder, then trying to plow through the stack of work on his desk before his late afternoon appointment arrived. He was still in his office with the last appointment when Emily left for the day. She wished rather wistfully that she had at least seen him again before she left, then reminded herself sternly to stop such nonsense. She had to reaccustom herself to their office lives.

She drove straight to Jeanette's apartment, where she and her cousin shared a salad and sandwich for supper before digging out the clothes Jeanette no longer wanted. By the time they finished Jeanette had convinced Emily to accept seven new dresses and suits for the office, as well as several pairs of slacks and tops, and a strapless, pink satin evening gown.

"But, Jeanette, I'll never wear it!" Emily protested as her cousin added it to the stack of clothes on the bed.

"Never mind. You're taking it anyway. You never know when something might come up. Be prepared, that's my motto."

"I thought that was the Boy Scout's."

"Honorary member." Jeanette surveyed the array of clothes on the bed with satisfaction. "Do you know how long I've been trying to get you to do this?"

"All my life, it seems," Emily responded with a smile.

Jeanette grinned and leaned over to hug Emily. "Oh! Before I forget. Your appointment for your hair is Wednesday at six. Here's Randall's card. And get there on time, no dawdling at the office. He hates latecomers, especially in the evening."

"Okay." Emily pocketed the business card. She grinned up at Jeanette. "I feel like a kid at Christmas. And I love it."

"After thirty years you ought to." Jeanette sat down beside her on the bed.

"You know, it's strange. I miss Adam, and I feel sad and lonely. In fact, in some ways, I'm downright miserable. But at the same time I feel better and more alive than I ever have. Isn't that odd?"

Jeanette turned to her and took both her hands. "Oh, sweetheart, you've finally come alive! You're releasing the restraints you've kept on yourself for so long. Of course it feels great—getting to stretch and move after all that time! I can't tell you how grateful I am to Adam Marshall for springing you from that prison."

Emily chuckled. "I hadn't thought of what he did exactly like that."

"Probably he hasn't, either. No doubt he just regards it as a pleasurable experience. But I'd lay odds he's thinking about it."

Emily shook her head with a wistful smile. "No. I don't think so. I doubt he gives me a thought."

In that Emily was wrong. Adam Marshall did think about her. In fact, he found himself thinking about her far more than was comfortable. He remembered their time together in detail until his blood grew too hot and his brain too fuzzy to think much at all. He imagined lovemaking that hadn't occurred between them. He daydreamed about talking to Emily, seeing the animation on her face and hearing her laugh. He daydreamed about taking her to the family beach house at Hilton Head and strolling with her through the sand, splashing in the cool waves. Adam thought about her in the evening at home and in his bed at night; he thought about her in his office during the day. He went to the office each day with a new eagerness and dreamed up reasons to visit Emily's little office across the hall.

It was crazy. It was absurd. But Emily Townsend was filling his thoughts more and more. He wanted her. He had started missing her as soon as they returned from the mountains. He had thought about her when he went to his solitary bed that night, and, to his amazement, despite the passion he'd expended that weekend, Adam had felt hunger for her rise in him. Seeing her back in their normal surroundings the next day hadn't lessened the desire, as he had hoped. It kept pricking at him, disturbing his work, interrupting his thoughts. The more time that passed, the worse it grew.

Emily seemed to grow prettier daily. He'd never noticed her clothes before, but now she seemed always to be dressed in soft, feminine suits of turquoise or powder-blue or sea-green. One day she came to work in a straight, black dress that outlined her slender figure to perfection. Around the hem of the short skirt was a pleated underskirt that swirled around her legs as she walked, showing flashes of her shapely knees, with an effect that was much more devastating to Adam's senses than if her knees had been bare. That day he had walked to her office every time he wanted to tell her something instead of calling her on the phone as he usually did. Once he had spent ten minutes trying to think up an excuse to get to her office.

Then, on Thursday, she sauntered into work with a new hairdo and floored him. She'd cut off her hair to the shoulders, and it fell around her face in soft, fluffy waves. It seemed brighter somehow, and incredibly feminine, and she looked beautiful. When Adam saw her walk past his office that morning he froze, the pages of the *Southeast 2d Reporter* which he had been reading drifting shut in front of him. He wanted to jump up and follow her to her office and lock the door behind them. He wanted to sink his hands in her hair and kiss her, pulling her hair up to his face and glorying in the scent and silken texture.

Of course, he didn't. After all, he had agreed that the weekend they spent together would be all there was between them. They had pledged to resume their old, perfectly agreeable relationship. Emily was sticking to the agreement. She seemed to have no trouble. She acted cool and at ease with him, friendly, but without a hint of intimacy. She was, as she had always been, the perfect secretary, without a hint of emotional or physical need. Without a hint of interest in him.

Adam found her attitude thoroughly irritating. How did she manage to remain so aloof? How had she gone from the shattering heights of their lovemaking to the placid role of secretary with such ease? To look at her, you'd never suspect that she had writhed and panted beneath him in the grip of passion; you'd never think she had moaned his name, or run her hands over his body. How could she talk to him as if he meant no more to her than any other attorney along the hall?

The answer, unfortunately, was obvious. He *didn't* mean any more to her. She had wanted to rid herself of her awkward virginity. She had told him outright that she had considered picking up someone in a bar or asking Jimmy Swale. She had wanted a man, and it hadn't mattered who that man was. Emily hadn't wanted Adam; she had wanted sex. Once that goal had been accomplished, she had had no problem separating herself from Adam. They'd had a business deal, really. A contract. Emily had lived up to her side of the bargain. He was the one having a problem.

The solution was to bring himself back in line. Emily was acting as she should, as they'd agreed. It was the only reasonable thing to do. An ongoing physical relationship between them would result in a mess. Office romance always did. It had happened before in the firm and had ended in disaster each time.

If he pursued her, Emily might feel pressured to sleep with him because he was her boss. If she made love with him, he would wonder whether she had agreed because she wanted to, or because she had felt that imaginary pressure. Even if they got together willingly, without pressure, without doubts, it would disrupt the easy employer/employee relationship that had existed between them for so long. They would no longer be boss and secretary, but lovers. If he corrected her typing, he'd be afraid he might hurt her feelings; if he asked her to work late, he'd worry about tiring her. She might agree to do more or work harder than she wanted to because she wanted to please him. Or she might think she could slack off because he was too fond of her to correct her.

Worst of all would be ending the relationship. When passion cooled it was hard to avoid hurt feelings. It seemed that one person always wanted to stop before the other one wanted to. There was usually anger, sorrow, bitterness. There were arguments or persistent, pleading phone calls. Most of the time one person wound up hoping they'd never see the other one again. That sort of rift would make a working situation impossible. When it was over Emily would have to quit or transfer to another attorney in the firm. Adam didn't want that. She had been too good a secretary, too kind a friend, to have a messy, unpleasant situation develop.

He could find sex elsewhere, anytime. He'd found that out since his divorce. But the relationship he had with Emily was far more special, and he wanted to keep it. The obvious solution, Adam realized, was to follow Emily's lead and keep their relationship businesslike and platonic. He would cool his passion with another woman and suppress the sparks of desire that shot through him when he was around Emily nowadays. He would make himself act toward her as he had in the past. He would keep his mind off their bodies and on their work.

If only it weren't so damned difficult!

## Chapter 9

Emily had never dreamed that she would suddenly become so popular in the office after she changed her hair. She had visited Jeanette's hairdresser, who gaped at her in horror, then determinedly went to battle with scissors, perm and color. When Emily saw the finished product, streaked with light, buoyant and flirty, she had been stunned by how pretty she looked, but she lacked the confidence to be sure that others would think the same thing when they saw her. What if they stared? What if they talked about her? What if—the absolute worst—they laughed? So the next day, when she went to work, she slipped off the elevator and sneaked around the back way to her office.

Along the way one attorney stopped dead in his tracks and turned around to look at her retreating figure, and another did a quick double take. Neither looked at her with horror or condemnation, but with an amazed admiration. Before she had been in her office ten minutes half the secretaries on the floor had come by to see her new hairdo, and the con-

sensus had been overwhelmingly favorable. Stranger than
that, over the course of the day several attorneys in the firm
dropped by her office to ask if Adam was in or to leave a
message for him, some even coming from the far end of the
office. Two of them—one a thrice-divorced, well-known
ladies' man, and the other a young bachelor—had sat down
and chatted with her for a few minutes. An accountant on
the floor below, with whom she had exchanged casual
greetings a few times on the way to or from work, stopped
by her table in the coffee shop at lunch and talked for almost fifteen minutes. The following Monday morning, as
she came to work, she met him standing in the lobby by the
newspaper machines, perusing the newspaper he'd just
bought. He smiled a greeting and rode up in the elevator
with her. Two days later he asked her out for a date.

It was rather amazing, and flattering. But most of all it
was frustrating, because the one man whose attention she
would have done almost anything for remained oblivious to
her changed looks. When she'd walked past Adam's office
with her new hairdo he hadn't moved a muscle, nor had he
said anything about it later, when he brought in some work
for her to do. She wore her prettiest, most flattering new
clothes, her sexiest new sandals—despite the fact that her
feet were aching by the end of the day—even a deliciously
sultry perfume. None of it brought about any change in
Adam's attitude.

He remained polite, friendly and utterly removed. He
didn't touch her, even accidentally. He didn't wink at her—
which she had seen him do with other secretaries! He didn't
pay her a compliment on her changed looks. Emily decided
that he hadn't even noticed; to Adam she was still only his
secretary and he was about as interested in her as in any
other piece of office furniture.

Adam's passion for her had been real during those two days at his cabin; surely she wasn't mistaken about that. Yet he seemed able to turn his desire on and off at will. Or maybe it was that he lost interest in a woman very quickly. Emily was certain that he still loved Cassie, so his interest in her or any other woman was purely physical and no doubt fleeting. For a short while she had aroused him, but that was over.

There was no reason to think that she could continue to interest him. He was often around women far lovelier than she was, even with her new clothes and hairdo. Besides, an office romance could be messy, and Emily knew she didn't have enough appeal to make him risk such complications. They had made an agreement not to continue their relationship past that weekend; no doubt that was one of the major reasons Adam had been willing to do such a thing. Adam would always stick by his agreement. He wouldn't display any interest in her. He wouldn't even think of continuing the relationship. He would return to viewing her only as his secretary.

Emily knew that she ought to do the same thing. She had agreed to the rules, and she had to live up to her part of the bargain, no matter how painful it was. She had to stop thinking about catching Adam's interest. She must put their weekend in the past and get on with her new life. A life that didn't involve Adam. The next time the accountant asked her out for a date, she accepted him.

His name was Gene Evers, and he was nice looking in a quiet, studious sort of way. He was trim, slightly taller than she was, and had even features, serious brown eyes and short brown hair. There was nothing wrong with him, but there was nothing exciting about him, either. However, Emily was resolved to give him a chance. She couldn't keep comparing all men to Adam, or they would always come up short.

Gene arrived at her house for their date a few minutes early. Emily was sitting in the living room, waiting for him, this time free of nerves. Her aunt and mother had kept out of sight most of the time since dinner, but when Gene's car stopped in front of the house they appeared in the living room as if by magic. Nancy peeked out past the corner of the curtain. "There he is." Her mouth turned down. "He's not nearly as handsome as Adam." She shot her daughter a disappointed look.

Rosemary joined her sister at the window. "He looks much more sober and industrious, though."

"Listen." Emily rose to her feet and faced the two older women sternly. "I refuse to let you do this again. Adam could handle an inquisition, but I'm not so sure about Gene."

"An inquisition! Don't be silly."

"We'd never..."

"Oh, yes, you would. I am thirty years old, and I don't need my aunt and mother in the living room with me when my date comes to pick me up."

"We're just interested, dear," Nancy explained.

"Mother..." The door bell rang, and Emily gave the two women a firm stare.

"Oh, all right." Nancy shrugged and retreated to the den. She paused at the doorway. "Rosemary?"

Rosemary hesitated for another instant, then sighed and followed her sister. Emily blew out her breath in relief and went to answer the door. "Hello, Gene. Would you like to come in for a moment?"

He glanced at his watch. "Yes, I suppose we have enough time before our dinner reservation."

Emily led him inside, and they sat down on the couch. There was no bouquet of flowers in his hand, no light and charming conversation. Emily might not be nervous with Gene, but neither could she think of anything to say, and Gene wasn't much help. The silence from the room beyond the living room was almost tangible. Emily wondered if her aunt and mother would resort to putting a glass against the wall to hear. If so, they would be very disappointed.

She offered Gene a small smile and said the only thing she could think of. "How is your work going?"

"Much better now that tax season is over. Of course, we still have the ones we had to file extensions for, but the heavy load is over. At least I get home before nine o'clock at night now."

Emily smiled again to acknowledge the bit of humor. She kept on smiling because she was stuck for any more conversation. The muscles around her mouth began to hurt. What else could she say? She didn't know the man at all. She supposed she could ask him questions about himself—but when you got right down to it, she wasn't too interested in the answers.

She reminded herself that she was supposed to make an effort. "What sort of work do you do? I mean, mostly corporate or individual?"

"A little of both, actually. With a lot of small businesses they're one and the same."

"Yes. I see."

"But we do more what you'd call corporate work. Besides tax returns, we keep books for several smaller corporations. You know, where they need something more than a secretary who doubles as a bookkeeper, but aren't large enough for an accounting department. We keep everything on computers, of course."

"Of course." Emily tried smiling some more. Even her awkwardness and nerves had been exciting with Adam. This was just awkward and dull. "Well!" She turned to look at the clock. "We better go, don't you think?"

The evening continued in the same vein. By the time Gene brought her home, Emily's entire lower face ached from forcing a smile. He had been nice; the dinner had been good; they had gone to a fairly entertaining movie afterward. But Emily had been bored to tears. The things Gene talked about didn't interest her, and no matter how many times she reminded herself that he was perfectly nice looking, he didn't incite even a spark of desire within her. The kiss he gave her at the front door left her cold. She hoped that he had been just as bored and wouldn't ask her out again.

Emily trailed upstairs to her bedroom and sat down in the easy chair beside the window. She stared out at the night. The moon was full and yellow and huge, hanging low in the sky, casting its bright light over the deserted streets and the tangle of tree branches. It was a beautiful, romantic night. She wished she was sharing it with Adam. How wonderful it would be to sit in the front porch swing with Adam, his arm around her shoulders, and gaze up at the moon, becoming hypnotized by its glow. She could imagine the warmth of his body against her side, the pressure of his fingers on her arm, the musky, mesmerizing scent of his cologne. His hand would slide up and down her arm, making her flesh tingle. He would kiss the top of her head and lean down to murmur against her ear, the breathy rumble sending shivers through her.

Tears sprang into Emily's eyes, and she jumped up from the chair and began to pace the room. Was she condemned to never love anyone but Adam? Would she spend the rest of her life pining after him? That was one part of her "thirties blues" that the weekend with Adam hadn't helped at all.

If anything, it was worse. She loved Adam more than ever, yet she also knew more fully what she was missing. Now she longed for the joy, the laughter, the closeness, that she could have with a man she loved. She wanted to share her life with a man, to feel the consuming fires of love and passion, and the little pleasures of daily life. Her single life seemed ten times lonelier.

That was why she had gone out with Gene Evers. Since Adam was out of the question, in order to have that joy, that sharing, she had decided that she would have to find another man whom she could love. She had to rid herself of her infatuation with Adam, or she would be lonely the rest of her life. Yet when she went out with someone else, she didn't enjoy the evening or the man. She thought only of Adam, missing him, comparing him to Gene, wishing he was the one sitting across the dinner table from her, or beside her in the theater.

Had Adam spoiled her for all men? Or had she tried the wrong man? She wondered if most women's social lives were like this—dating man after man they didn't like in order to find the one man who could light up their world. It seemed a long, hard, unhappy process. Emily sighed. She could hardly say that she had given other men a fair chance after going out with only one. On the other hand, she dreaded going through that again with someone else. She wanted Adam!

Almost angrily Emily undressed and got ready for bed. She would have Adam, all right, tomorrow and every day at the office for years to come. He would be always there, filling her thoughts, her eyes, her life—yet she would never know his love. Damn it! When would she grow up? When would she get over her desperate love for him and make a life for herself?

She had to try dating again; she simply had to. And this time she would find someone better, a man more like Adam, a man who could attract her. Who would help her to forget Adam. If the next one didn't work, either, she would just keep on until she found someone who could make her forget. She wouldn't spend the rest of her life crying for the moon.

"Emily?" Adam stuck his head inside her office door, and Emily looked up, sternly trying to quiet the tumult in her chest that started whenever she saw him. "Grab a notepad and pen and come with me. I'm going to interview Mrs. Van der Bibb, and I want you to take notes. She's scared of using a tape recorder."

"Okay." Emily swept up two pens from their holder, grabbed a small steno pad and her purse, and followed Adam out of her office. "Who's Mrs. Van der Bibb?"

"The sister of Mrs. Eleanor Wheeler."

"Oh. The probate case."

"Yeah." Adam glanced at Emily. She wore a soft, gray-blue suit. Its jacket buttoned at the waist and most of the front was scooped out to reveal a thin blouse of a paler shade of gray-blue that was gathered into a delicate, feminine ruffle around the neck. She looked beautiful, he thought, and he was looking forward to spending the afternoon with her. He had been elated when Mrs. Van der Bibb told him that she'd prefer that he not use a tape recorder during their conversation.

He pushed the button for the elevator, and they rode down to the cool, underground garage where his car was parked. Their steps rang as they walked across the concrete floor of the deserted garage. Adam liked the silence; he liked being alone with Emily. For the past couple of weeks he'd resented the noise and bustle around them, the constant flow and interruption of people. He hadn't been able to have a single decent conversation with her without someone popping in on them.

"How's your mom?" he asked, wanting to start her talking.

"Okay. I think I persuaded her and Aunt Rosemary to stop their interrogation routine."

That meant she had been out with someone else since they'd returned. He almost had to bite his tongue to keep from asking her whom she had gone out with. What had they done? Where had they gone? He wondered how often they'd dated. He wondered if she had slept with him. Surely not. It had been too soon since she'd been in his bed. She couldn't have gone that easily into another man's arms. Could she?

All the way to Mrs. Van der Bibb's house, Adam kept picturing Emily lying naked with another man, her mouth on his, arms and legs entangled. By the time they reached the two-story town house on the golf course at Tanglewood, he was in a thoroughly bad humor. He glared at Emily as they got out of the car, then marched her up to the front door, his hand tight around her arm, his jaw set.

Emily glanced at him in puzzlement. Adam had seemed friendly as they went down to his car, but he'd grown more and more silent on the drive out here, and now he was frowning like a thundercloud. She guessed he must be thinking about his work, but she couldn't imagine what would make him so furious about this contested will.

A plump, white-haired woman opened the door of the exclusive town house and smiled at them. Her hair was short and curled fluffily around her head; her skin was fair, and her eyes were a faded blue, but very alert. She was dressed in a lightweight pants suit, with socks on her feet, but no shoes. A pair of golf shoes and a golf bag stood next to the side door leading into the garage.

"Mrs. Van der Bibb?" Adam forcibly smoothed the frown from his forehead. "I'm Adam Marshall, of Marshall, Pierson, Tidrell, and Sommers. I spoke to you on the phone earlier today."

"I remember," the old woman replied testily. "I'm not senile yet. It was just an hour ago."

"Yes, ma'am." Adam smiled, and Emily could see Mrs. Van der Bibb soften. He was having his usual effect on women. "This is my secretary, Emily Townsend. I'd like her to take notes on what we say, if you don't mind. I'm afraid my memory isn't the greatest."

"Sure." Mrs. Van der Bibb led them through the hallway into the high-ceilinged living room. A bank of large, plate-glass windows looked onto the sculptured landscape of the golf course. "And, please, call me Sissy. Everybody does. Van der Bibb's such a mouthful. I told Len I almost didn't marry him because of his last name."

Adam smiled at her witticism. "All right, Sissy. Thank you."

Sissy plopped down onto a white couch with soft pillows and Adam and Emily arranged themselves in the chairs on either end of it. "Okay. If you want to know about my sister, you better start asking, 'cause it could take hours to tell you how crazy she was, and I don't want to be late for my golf game."

Adam's eyebrows rose, and Emily's pen started scribbling across the empty notepad. "She was crazy?" Adam asked conversationally.

"Only on one subject—that hellfire-and-brimstone preacher of hers. Lucy was scared of dying, and once she found out she had cancer, she sat around and brooded about it. She took to reading the Bible all the time and talking to her minister a lot. That was okay; I figured anybody'd do that when facing death. But then her day nurse introduced her to Bob Cecil, and he made her crazy.''

''Made her crazy? What do you mean? Did he make her angry? Upset her?''

''He scared her to death, first of all. After she'd seen him a couple of times, she was terrified that she was going to hell. Then he convinced her that only by leaving all her wealth to his church could she be saved from it. I tried to talk her out of seeing him. So did her kids. I'm convinced Cecil made her sicker.''

''Intentionally?''

''No, I don't mean he poisoned her or anything. Anybody could see it was a matter of months before she died. Not that I wouldn't have put it past him. That man's no more a man of God than I am. But what I meant was, he worried her to death. He'd tell her stuff to worry and scare her. It made her too nervous to eat or sleep; she'd call me, all het up and jabbering a mile a minute about what wonderful things Cecil was going to do with her money.'' Sissy gave an inelegant snort. ''I imagine the 'wonderful things' all turned out to benefit Bob Cecil and nobody else.''

''Did Mr. Cecil visit your sister frequently?''

''All the time. He didn't give her any peace. He was out there every day, reading the Bible with her and lecturing her, and when he left, that nurse would start in on her. It was pitiful. Lucy's kids tried to talk to her about it, but she wouldn't listen, and they hated haranguing her about it because she was so sick. I did, too. She looked so wasted. Anyway, I never dreamed she'd do what she did. Except for the religion thing, she seemed perfectly sane and sound. Then, after she died, we found out what he'd gotten her to do. It was awful, a man using religion like that to line his pockets and make a woman turn against her own children."

"Sissy, can you remember any of the things Mr. Cecil said to your sister?"

"Sure. She used to repeat them to me all the time."

"But did you ever hear Mr. Cecil himself use them?"

"Yeah. I came in on them once or twice while they were talking, but he'd usually shut up pretty quick and leave when I came in. But once, when they didn't know I was there, I stood outside the door for a bit and listened."

"Can you remember what you heard?"

"Not word for word, but I got the gist of it." She leaned forward and began to reel off the things Bob Cecil had told her sister, anger making her voice fast, and Emily's fingers flew to keep up with her words.

They stayed for almost two hours, Adam skillfully probing, and Sissy Van der Bibb eager to oblige him with descriptions of the ways in which Bob Cecil had exerted influence over her dying, frightened sister. At last they left and walked to their car. Behind them Mrs. Van der Bibb chugged out of her garage in her pink-and-white golf cart and drove around the side of the town house onto the course.

"I bet she really whacks a few golf balls today," Emily commented.

Adam smiled. "I imagine you're right. She was steamed up about the whole thing. She'd make a good witness. Clear and decided and loaded with common sense. Of course, family members are inclined to band together to attack an intruder, and sometimes their very anger can work against them. They can come across as vindictive and unreasonable. But the nice thing about Sissy is that she didn't lose anything by her sister's writing the new will. In the former will, Lucy left her some jewelry and a piece of Tiffany glass, but no money, and in the new will she left that disposition exactly the same. So that makes Van der Bibb a much more unbiased witness than Lucy's children.''

Adam started the car and turned it around, heading back through Tanglewood to I-40. He turned on the air conditioning and loosened his tie. Casually he asked, ''Who did Aunt Rosemary try to grill this time?''

''What? Oh.'' Emily chuckled. ''Gene Evers. He's a C.P.A. who works on the floor below us.''

''Oh. At Fairman and Jones?''

''Yeah.

Adam wrinkled his brow in concentration. ''I don't think I've met him.''

''Probably not. I've just ridden up in the elevator with him a few times.''

''A likely story,'' he teased, and Emily smiled. Adam paused, struggling not to ask the next question, but he couldn't resist. ''You like him?''

''He's a nice guy, but...'' Her voice trailed off, and she shrugged.

Adam pressed his lips together to keep from smiling. He felt inordinately pleased.

Tag Marshall was waiting for Adam when they returned to the office, lounging in the hallway beside Adam's door and talking to one of the paralegals. The girl hastily ended the conversation when she saw Adam approaching and scurried off, and Tag turned toward his brother with a grin. ''Hey, Adam. I was just—'' He broke off and stared at Emily. ''My, my, my. Emily, you look gorgeous.'' His bright blue eyes raked down her appreciatively, and Emily had to smile at his look, which was somehow both sexy and comical.

Adam scowled. ''You were just what?''

"Oh. I had to go to the bank to see my trust officer, so I thought I'd drop by and visit you before I left."

Adam went into his office and held the door open for his brother to follow. Tag remained outside for a moment, watching Emily's backside as she went past them to her room. "Tag..."

"Yeah. I'm coming, I'm coming." Tag grinned and entered his brother's office, and Adam closed the door. "Say, what happened to your secretary? I thought she had potential, but nothing like this!"

Adam's lips thinned. "Do you never think of anything except sex?"

"Oh, every once in a while I consider something else. What's the matter, Adam? Is our Miss Townsend getting you stirred up?"

"Don't be ridiculous."

"*I'm* not being ridiculous," Tag returned pointedly, and sauntered over to a chair. "Come on, big brother." He lounged back in the chair and propped up his feet on top of Adam's desk. "What's going on here? A little extracurricular activity with your secretary?"

"Tag, I'm warning you..."

Tag laughed. "You must have it bad."

"I don't *have* anything!"

"Ahah." Tag nodded his head knowledgeably. "Then that's the problem. I think I understand."

"I doubt it," Adam grated out.

"You want to talk about it?"

Adam sighed and sank into his chair. "I don't think so. It's too silly."

"Silly?"

Adam started to speak, then shook his head. "No. I can't talk about it. It would be betraying a confidence. But, yes, I think I'm attracted to 'our Miss Townsend.' Unfortunately, I know the horrors of letting your social life and your business life get tangled up. Remember Fred Morris?''

''Sure.''

''That's why he left the firm. He started fooling around with Lipscomb's secretary, and the whole thing turned into a horrible mess. Fred left his wife and everything.''

''You don't have a wife,'' his brother pointed out.

''There are lots of other pitfalls. Fred couldn't handle it; his work suffered. The secretaries ostracized the girl, and Fred complained to Dad, of all people. Anyway, he wound up leaving the firm.''

''And you think Dad'll kick you out if you sleep with Emily?''

''No, of course not. But... well, it's a problem. It's always bad enough when you break up with someone, but when she works for you, it's an impossible situation.''

''Why are you talking about breaking up? You haven't even gotten together.''

''It's bound to happen.''

''Why? Emily looks like she might be able to hold your interest.''

''Taggart... Okay, she's attractive, I'll grant you that.''

''You're so generous.''

''I like her. But it's highly unlikely that I'll marry the woman, and any other ending is bound to create unhappiness.''

''Why is it so unlikely?''

Adam stared at his brother blankly. ''Why?'' He repeated. ''Come on. You know how I've been since Cassie and I split up. Face it. I'm dead wood emotionally. I'll admit that I haven't sat around aching for Cassie in a long time; I don't miss her anymore, or even think about her, really. But it killed something inside me.''

"No. I think it just wounded it severely. But now you're coming back. I haven't seen you this upset about anything to do with a woman since Cassie left you. Here you are, ready to take off my head because I teased you about Emily. That's a good sign. A very good sign."

Adam shook his head in exasperation but he had to smile. "You are something else. Have I ever won an argument with you?"

"No." Taggart grinned. "You're too logical."

Adam raised an eyebrow. "Do you think we could drop the subject?"

Tag shrugged. "Whatever you want. But you aren't going to get rid of the problem that easily."

"I'll handle it." Adam sighed unconsciously. "I'll handle it."

Adam spent most of the next morning in the firm library researching a case. He was sitting at one of the two long work tables in the room, a pile of *Reporters* on the table before him, trying to keep his mind on the case, when Emily walked through the door. She smiled at him and passed through the library into the small inner room, which contained the two office copy machines. Adam returned to his book, but he could hear her moving around in the copy room, changing the paper in the machine and setting dials. The machine began clicking and whooshing out copies. They were soft noises, and usually they didn't bother him, but today his concentration was poor. He wondered why they had connected the copy room to the library; it seemed a bad choice.

The noises stopped and Emily emerged from the room carrying a large pile of papers consisting of many smaller stacks, crisscrossed. She set down the pile on the other long table and picked up one of the numerous smaller sections.

She walked around the table, setting out single sheets until the section was laid out all over the table. She took up a second stack and started over the same trail, laying these papers down on top of the others.

Adam groaned mentally. She was going to work here! It wasn't unusual. The secretaries often used the large library tables for work that had to be spread out. Adam had sat in here lots of times with a couple of secretaries working away at the other table, and it hadn't bothered him. This time it bothered him.

He watched Emily move around the table, her pencil-slim skirt emphasizing her silhouette. If it hadn't been for the short slit up the back, the skirt was so narrow it would have hobbled her walk. Adam liked the slit. It exposed little, going up barely past her knees, but the way it opened and closed as Emily walked was enticing. He kept catching glances of her long, slender legs. Her hose gleamed against her skin. Sharp little needles of longing darted through him.

Emily glanced up, feeling his gaze on her, and smiled apologetically. "Sorry. The collator's broken, and I have to do it by hand. I hope I'm not disturbing you."

"No," he lied. "Go right ahead. What are you putting together?"

"The documents you're going to use as exhibits in the Purvey Machine case."

"Oh. Good." He pretended to return to reading the book. His eyes moved, but he didn't register a word. From the corner of his eye he could see Emily as she worked. She was wearing a light, short-sleeved, pink sweater above the narrow skirt. It was soft, and clung to her small, rounded breasts. A pearl drop on a chain nestled in the hollow of her throat. He remembered kissing that hollow. He wanted to move the pearl out of the way with his tongue and run it across the indentation. He wanted to kiss her throat all the

way up to her chin. He wanted to cup her breasts through
the soft material. He wondered if she still went braless beneath her sweater, as he had asked her to. His fingers itched
to find out.

Adam swallowed hard. His eyes had gradually wandered
from the book until he was openly staring at her again. He
forced them back to the printed page.

A faint whiff of her perfume drifted to him. It was elu-
sive, sexy, barely there. She'd started wearing it recently, and
Adam had found that it played havoc with his senses. He
wished she would stop wearing it. He wished she'd come
closer so that he could smell it better.

He thought about the first day at the cabin, when they
had sat on the rock overlooking the pond, and his hands had
roamed about the treasures of her body. She had been so
soft and pliant beneath him. He had wanted to take her right
then and there, but the anticipation had been sweet.

Adam wondered what Emily would do if he came up behind her now and put his arms around her. He imagined
sliding his body up and down against hers. He imagined her
turning in surprise and delight, her arms going up to encir-
cle his neck. He would kiss her as he'd wanted to for days,
hard and deep, drinking in all her sweetness, and his hands
would go to her hips. He saw her lying back on the long table, the skinny skirt riding up her thighs, her legs opening
to him.

"Hey, Adam."

Adam jumped. Thomas Benton, one of the older lawyers in the firm, walked in the door, speaking to Adam and
giving Emily a nod. He never remembered any of the secretaries' names except that of his own. Adam gave him a
sickly smile. "Tom. How's it going?"

"Okay." Benton strode to the far wall and searched
through the CCHs, finally found the one he wanted and

brought it back to the table. Adam scooted his chair farther under the table to hide his lap. The older man sat down and flipped through the large book. Adam adjusted his glasses on his nose and began to read.

Emily leaned across the table to place the next set of sheets on the piles in the farthest corner, lifting one leg slightly in her stretch. Her skirt pulled tightly against her derriere, outlining its smooth curve. The slit in the back fell away from her leg, exposing the long line of calf and the vulnerable flesh at the back of her knee. Her skin there was like silk, Adam remembered.

She began to straighten each stack and staple them. The sheaves of paper were thick, and she had to jam her palm down hard on the top of the stapler. Her breasts jiggled a little under her sweater with the exertion. Adam felt the heat spreading through his abdomen and up his chest to his head. He wondered if his face was flushed. He curled his hand tightly around his pen, watching her. The plastic pen snapped, and ink dribbled across his palm.

"Damn!" Adam whipped out his handkerchief and wiped away most of the blue mess on his palm. Thomas Benton glanced at him curiously, then went back to his book.

Emily stacked the papers together and lifted them in her arms. Adam wanted to offer to carry them down the hall for her; they looked heavy. But he didn't dare stand up right now. He watched her walk out of the room. Slowly his muscles relaxed. He leaned his forehead against his clasped hands, feeling drained and weak all over. He was beginning to wonder if he could handle this.

## *Chapter 10*

Emily walked back to her office, her spirits drooping. It hadn't been absolutely necessary to put those exhibits together this morning. The collator would be fixed by tomorrow morning, and Adam didn't need the documents for a couple of days yet. But she had known Adam was in the library and she hadn't been able to resist making the copies and putting them together on the library table so she could be close to him for a while. She was never around him enough to satisfy her. The afternoon they'd spent together interviewing Mrs. Van der Bibb had merely whetted her appetite. She had purposely gone to the library, wanting the opportunity to look at Adam surreptitiously and hoping that he might be bored and strike up a conversation with her. But he had only stared at her for a moment and gone back to his reading.

In fact, he'd been distinctly unfriendly. He'd hardly said a word, and he'd kept fidgeting in his chair and glancing at her, as if irritated at her for disturbing his peace and quiet.

She understood it, of course. He had no need to be around her as she did to be around him. He'd been hard at work and had resented the break in his concentration. But that didn't make her feel any happier about his attitude.

She slipped the documents into several brown expandable folders and marked them, then slipped them into the empty top drawer of one of the file cabinets. Listlessly she pulled out another drawer of the file cabinet, where old cases were stored, and flipped through it looking for a file. Adam had asked her to locate the name and address of an orthopedic expert who had testified for him at a trial two years ago.

Emily found the file, actually four bulky, expandable folders, and set it on her desk so she could sift through it better. She finally found a letter from the doctor, and she copied down the name, address and telephone number. She dialed long distance information in Los Angeles to ascertain if the number was still correct, and the operator confirmed that it was. She set the slip of paper aside for Adam.

She glanced at her watch. It was time for her lunch break, and today she needed to get away from the office. She was reaching for her purse when Larry Sansing appeared at the door. Swallowing her irritation, she smiled at him. "Hi. I think Adam's in the library. Do you want me to buzz him?"

"No need." Larry moved into the office and sat down beside her desk. "I dropped off something on his desk. I'm sure he'll find it. If he has a question, tell him to call me."

"Okay." Emily didn't know what else to say. This was the second time that Larry had stopped by her office to chat in the past couple of weeks. The other time he'd been waiting for Adam to finish with a client, but now, as far as Emily could see, there wasn't any reason for him to linger. Yet he seemed firmly ensconced in that chair.

"Could I get you a cup of coffee?" she asked, to be polite.

"Sounds great. I'd love it."

"Cream? Sugar?"

"A little of both."

She nodded and smiled and went to the coffee room, returning with a Styrofoam cup of coffee and packets of sugar and cream substitute. Larry poured in the packets and stirred the mixture with a small plastic straw, while Emily watched him and wondered what he was doing here.

"Almost time for the Steeplechase," Larry remarked conversationally.

"What? Oh. Yes, I suppose it is."

"Have you ever been to it?"

Emily shook her head. "No. I'm afraid I know almost nothing about it, either. I'm not very knowledgeable about horses and racing."

"Neither am I. But I always go." He gave her a wink. "Probably for the tailgate parties." He paused and sipped the coffee. "Were you born and raised here?"

"Yes. You're from Virginia, aren't you?"

"How'd you guess? It couldn't be the accent, could it?"

Emily chuckled. Larry had the distinctive vowel sounds that belonged exclusively to Tidewater Virginia. "Accent?" she teased. "What accent?"

"You probably didn't notice. You only hear it when I speak."

Emily smiled. If she had to sit around being nice to one of Adam's business associates, Larry was as good as she could find. He had an easygoing manner and a nice sense of humor, and he was good-looking in a boyish way. Emily suspected that he was the sort of man whom women wanted to mother. She also suspected that he was happy to oblige them.

Larry started a story about the country in Virginia where he had grown up, which he claimed contained more snobs per acre than anywhere else in the country—"Including Charleston, South Carolina"—and soon had Emily giggling. The time passed pleasantly and quickly, though Emily remained puzzled as to why he was in her office. Finally, when the conversation lagged, he glanced at his watch and asked, "When's your lunch hour?"

"Anytime I want, really."

"You mean that tyrant gives you so much freedom? I thought Adam kept you chained to your desk."

"No. My work does that."

"I was about to go to lunch. Would you like to join me?"

Emily stared at him blankly. It took a moment for his words to register. He was asking her out on something resembling a date. Was he interested in her? He and Adam were friends, so it was unlikely that he'd be trying to pump her about Adam or one of his cases. If he was interested in her—well, why not? She had decided she was going to build a new life instead of dreaming about Adam, hadn't she? Larry Sansing was much more the kind of man who could make her get over Adam than Gene Evers was. "Why, yes," she agreed, smiling. "I'd love to. Thank you."

"Great. Then let's hit it. Shall we?" He stood.

"Of course." Emily got her purse and stood up. Larry ushered her out of her office and down the hall to the elevators, his hand resting at the small of her back.

They met Adam striding down the hall from the library toward his office. He glanced at them oddly. "Hello, Larry. Emily. Did you need to see me?"

"No. Emily and I were going out to lunch." Emily noticed that Larry didn't invite Adam to join them. "I left an envelope on your desk. I think it's self-explanatory, but call me if you have any questions."

"Sure." Adam appeared a little stunned. "Have a nice lunch."

"We will," Larry replied cheerfully, then steered Emily toward the elevators.

Adam stared after them for a moment, then turned and slowly walked to his office. He crossed to the plate-glass window on the far wall and stared down somberly at the street below. Larry Sansing! That sneaky—that was why he'd been around the office so much the past couple of weeks. He was interested in Emily! Adam remembered opening his door to usher out a client the other day and finding Larry seated in Emily's office, laughing and talking. At least then he'd been waiting for Adam. But today he hadn't made the token gesture of coming by on business. He hadn't even asked him out to eat with them!

Adam scowled. Gene Evers hadn't been anything to worry about. After Emily told him she had been out with Gene, Adam had made a point of going down to see one of the accountants at Fairman and Jones and looking up Gene Evers while he was there. The man had impressed Adam as being basically dull. But Larry Sansing was something else again. He was bright and nice looking, and he had a thick Tidewater accent that some women practically swooned over. Women liked him; he never lacked for a date. He was the kind of man Emily might fall for.

Adam straightened and peered out the window. Larry and Emily had just crossed the street below and were waiting for the light. Adam jerked off his glasses and tossed them on the desk so he could see better at a distance. They walked across the side street and continued up the block. In the middle of the block they turned into the Hanson Building, a rather smallish office building built years ago by Hanson Textiles. It still housed their offices and boasted a small, expensive and rather quiet restaurant on the ground floor. He worried his lower lip with his teeth, slowly turning away from the window. Suddenly, decisively, he left his office and hurried down the hall. He punched the button for the elevator and glanced at his image in the mirror beside the elevator as he waited, combing his hair with his fingers. When the elevator arrived he pushed his way into it even though it was already full, and rode down to the lobby.

Larry took Emily across the street and down a block to the elegant Salem Room in the Hanson Building. The hostess seated them at a table meant for four toward the front of the small restaurant. Emily settled back in the comfortable, high-backed wing chair and studied the menu. She finally decided on the shrimp salad, and had just given her order to the hovering waiter when Larry glanced toward the door and stopped in mid-sentence, his eyebrows rising in surprise.

"There's Adam!"

Emily peered around the high back of her seat. There, indeed, was Adam Marshall, strolling along toward them behind the hostess. Adam saw them and smiled broadly, veering toward their table. The hostess stopped and waited patiently for him.

"Well, hey!" Adam greeted them jovially. "Fancy meeting you here."

"Yeah."

"Hello, Adam."

He remained standing beside their table, and after a long pause, Larry asked, "You meeting someone here?"

"No. Just ran over for lunch."

The hostess moved closer. "Sir? Shall I show you to a table or . . ." She looked at Larry and Emily.

Emily glanced at Larry, expecting him to invite Adam to join them. He kept his lips firmly shut. Adam turned to the hostess. "I think I'll sit with my friends here." He swiveled back to Emily and Larry, his eyes innocent. "That is, if you don't mind?"

"No. Please, sit down," Larry said grudgingly.

Adam smiled and plopped down across from Larry beside Emily. The hostess handed him a menu, and he snapped it open. "Well! What are you all having? The luncheon special looks good."

"Virginia ham's always good," Larry agreed loyally.

Adam grinned and glanced at Emily. She remembered the ham they'd eaten at his cabin and the warning he'd given her not to tell Larry Sansing that it surpassed Virginia ham. She smiled a little, her face softening with the memory. Larry frowned and looked from her to Adam and back again.

"Is there a joke here that I'm missing?" he asked carefully.

"Not exactly. Emily and I found a ham in Fender's Gap that'd beat Virginia hams all solid, but I told her those would be fighting words to you."

"Fender's Gap?" Larry repeated, even more puzzled.

"Yeah. That's where my cabin is. I've told you about it, haven't I?"

Larry glanced quickly at Emily. She could feel color rising in her cheeks. Adam might as well have told Larry outright that she'd slept with him; it must be obvious to him that they had been to the cabin together. She felt ready to sink through the floor with embarrassment. Adam seemed utterly oblivious to what he'd just revealed, picking through the basket of rolls for the kind he wanted.

"There." He grabbed a sesame bun and looked back up at Larry. "So, how are things in Contelco?"

Adam dominated the conversation throughout lunch, skillfully directing business-related questions at either Emily or Larry, so that the meal turned into little more than a business meeting—and a thoroughly dull one at that. It wasn't until after lunch was over that Emily realized that because of Adam's questions she and Larry had talked primarily to him and had exchanged hardly ten words with each other. Larry had kept casting speculative glances her way throughout the meal, and Emily had grown more embarrassed by the second. She knew he must have wondered whether she had slept with her boss. How could he think anything but that, after what Adam had let slip? Knowing the way lawyers gossiped, the news would be all over Contelco's legal department—not to mention Marshall, Pierson—before the week was out. If it got back to Leith Marshall, he'd probably fire her for corrupting his son.

When they had finished Adam insisted on paying the bill, pointing out that it had to be his business expense since it was his secretary with them. They walked out single file, necessary in the small restaurant, and Adam maneuvered himself in behind Emily and before Larry. When they reached the sidewalk he remained between them. They strolled across the intersection to the Allied Central Building in a rather silent group. Adam stopped when they reached the front of the bank building and reached out to shake Larry's hand.

"Enjoyed it," he told the other attorney jovially. "I'll call you tomorrow on that Larson thing."

"Okay. Thanks for lunch." There was little Larry could do except part from them there.

"Don't mention it. Anytime. I was glad I ran into you."

Amusement suddenly sparkled in Larry's eyes. "I just bet you were." He turned and nodded to Emily. "Emily."

"Good bye, Larry."

He started off briskly down the street, and Adam turned to open the door for Emily. Emily walked past him, frowning. It was crazy. She couldn't understand why Adam would do it. But it seemed that he had arranged what happened at lunch, orchestrating it so that she and Larry were kept apart. Why would he go to that trouble? Why would he even want to? Yet, from Larry's remark before he left them, he apparently suspected that Adam had even arranged to eat at the same restaurant. She didn't know how he could have known where they were going, since Larry hadn't mentioned the Salem Room until they were walking down the street toward it.

Suddenly understanding flashed in her eyes as she pictured the view from Adam's office. The Hanson Building lay on the same street as Adam's office. If he had been looking out his window when they went into the restaurant, he could have seen them. Even from that distance her bright pink sweater would have been clearly visible. He could have gone to the Salem Room specifically to spoil their lunch. And if he had done that, there couldn't have been anything accidental about his hint that he and Emily had spent the night together at his cabin. He had clearly done his best to warn Larry away from her.

She couldn't imagine why. Was he angry with her for dating a man who was, in a sense, a client? It seemed pretty flimsy. Did he know something about Larry that made him unsuitable? Was Larry married, and she didn't know it? Or was it that he thought she was unsuitable for Larry? After all, Larry was a fellow attorney and a friend of Adam's, a member of the same social class. All of which she was not. She was the outsider here, she reminded herself; it was more likely that Adam was trying to protect his friend, not her. He must think that now that he had slept with her, she was trying to encroach where she didn't belong.

The more Emily thought about it, the more hurt and humiliated she became. Even the anger that flashed through her at Adam's jumping in and arranging her life like that quickly turned to hurt. Adam must dislike her. Archaic as it sounded, he must think less of her because she had slept with him. He didn't care for her in any way.

Tears began to batter at the back of her eyelids, and when the elevator opened on their floor Emily rushed through the door and down the hall to her office, leaving Adam without a word. "Emily?" She heard his puzzled voice behind her, but she didn't stop or turn. She didn't dare.

Adam started down the hall after her. Suddenly the sense of elation he'd felt at outmaneuvering Larry Sansing was gone. Was Emily mad at him? "Emily!" Even his raised voice didn't stop her, though one of the other attorneys stuck his head out of his office to see what was going on. Adam increased his pace and rounded the corner just as Emily reached her office door.

"Emily!" It came out in the stentorian tones he used in the courtroom, sudden fear in the pit of his stomach giving his voice impetus.

Emily jumped and whirled to face him. Her eyes glittered. "What!" she snapped back.

Several more people peered from doors on both sides of the hall. Adam jerked his head toward his door. "Come into my office, please." The harsh, stilted tone robbed the words of all politeness. "I want to talk to you."

She couldn't face him right now. She couldn't! She'd burst into tears and probably tell him all sorts of things she'd regret later. Emily took a deep breath. "No." She stepped into her own office.

Adam's eyebrows shot up, and for an instant he was too stunned to move. Then anger flooded him, and he charged down the hall after her. "What the hell do you mean, 'no'?"

His harsh voice sliced through Emily. Tears welled in her eyes and plopped onto her cheeks. She was furious that he had forced the issue, making her humiliate herself further. Emily shot him a glare and stalked past him out the door and down the hall. She entered his office and stood waiting for him, her arms crossed, gazing straight in front of her. Adam followed more slowly and closed the door. He had seen the tears in her eyes, and now he felt like a heel. Never in his life had he experienced so many roiling, conflicting emotions. He'd been an emotional yo-yo for two weeks now. "I'm sorry," he said softly, then had to clear his throat. "I hurt you, didn't I?"

Emily whirled, tears pouring from her eyes. "Hurt me! Yes, you hurt me! What do you think?"

"I'm sorry I yelled. I didn't mean to. I was trying to get you to stop and talk to me, and it came out louder than I meant."

"I'm not talking about yelling at me!" Emily snapped back, her cheeks high with color. "I'm talking about what you did in the restaurant!"

"Oh."

"Yes. Oh. Why did you do it? Why did you say that about Fender Gap? You as good as told him we'd spent the night together."

"You're damn right I did!" he flared back. "It's the truth, isn't it? Are you ashamed of it? Are you afraid Larry might not want you if he knew I'd had you first? Well, you're better off without him."

Emily stared. "He's a friend of yours."

"Friendship has nothing to do with this. I don't want you sleeping with him!"

"I was just having lunch...."

"Lunch! You think I don't know what he wanted? Larry Sansing doesn't take my secretary out for lunch without an ulterior motive. Believe me, baby, he wants you in his bed. He was practically drooling over you the other day."

"Adam..." Emily wiped the wetness from her cheeks. Her tears had dried up. She was too astonished to cry. "What is the matter with you?"

"What's the matter with me!" he repeated explosively, his voice low but no less violent in its intensity. "Good God, Emily, what do you think? That I'm made of steel? That I'm not a man? You think I can watch you day in and day out, see you flirting with other men all the time, and not care?"

Emily's jaw dropped.

"Damn it, I can't handle our agreement! It's too much. It's unfair. You can't expect a man to make love to you one weekend, then never think about you again, never want you. How am I supposed to shut it off? It's inhuman. It's impossible. You can't ask that of me!"

Emily struggled to say something, but her voice was gone. Now she knew how people felt when they stepped into "The Twilight Zone." The whole world was suddenly as distorted as a funhouse mirror.

Adam turned away and began to stride back and forth across the room in his anger, the pent-up feelings of the past two weeks flooding out. "I want you constantly. I see you in the office, looking gorgeous, flirting with Tag or Larry or those hundred other guys who hang around your office, and it nearly kills me. I keep thinking about the cabin and the things we did, the way you looked. I want to take you to bed. I can hardly work anymore, because I can't stop thinking about you. You're driving me crazy. This agreement is driving me crazy! I nearly came unglued this morning in the library, watching you work. I wanted to make love to you so badly I could hardly think or breathe. I wanted to shove those stupid papers onto the floor and lay you back on the table and—" He broke off and slammed his clenched fist down on the credenza. The files and books stacked there jumped, and several papers slid to the floor.

A giggle shot up out of Emily's throat, surprising her. Adam whirled, scowling. "What the hell is so funny?"

"Oh, Adam! Adam! This is insane. I don't care about the agreement; I thought you were the one who wanted it. I don't want Larry or anybody else. I just want you."

Now he was the one who stared. "What did you say?"

"I said, 'I just want—'" But he was across the room before she could finish, pulling her into his arms, his mouth coming down fiercely on hers.

Emily let out a tiny sigh of contentment and melted against him. His mouth was avid, lips grinding into hers as his tongue swept her mouth, velvety and insistent. His hands roamed over her body, pushing up under the soft, pink sweater to glide over the cool satin of her slip. Her breasts were free of a bra beneath the slip, and he cupped them, making a soft noise of pleasure as his thumbs circled the hardening nipples. "Sweet, sweet," he murmured, breaking their kiss to seek the tender flesh of her earlobes and neck.

His mouth moved over her like a starving man, tasting every inch of her skin, and Emily trembled under the caress of his lips and hands. For over two weeks she had missed his lovemaking and thought about it constantly, so her body was primed for his touch and she responded instantly. Her skin flamed like wildfire all over her body. She moved her hands restlessly over him, sliding them beneath his suit jacket and around to his back, seeking the warm delight of his skin. His clothes blocked her, and she tugged at the buttons of his vest and shirt in frustration.

Her movements excited Adam further, and he ground his body against hers, imprinting her with the brand of his desire. Impatiently they ripped at their clothes, too eager and hungry for each other to wait, jerking at buttons and yanking at zippers. They pulled away to undress, yet were unable to stay apart long enough to finish the job, and they moved back together again and again, clothes open or half off. It was enough to be able to reach each other's skin and caress it with hands and mouth; neatness and aesthetics had no place in their fevered rush. They sank to the floor, hot and tangled, and Adam positioned himself between her legs. Emily moved to accept him, her hips arching up and her legs twining around him. He groaned softly as he shoved into her welcoming, moist warmth and muffled the noise against her mouth. Emily moved eagerly against him, matching his wild rhythm, desire knotting ever more tightly within her, until at last it exploded, shooting them both into a mindless realm of ecstasy.

Adam collapsed against her, burying his face in her shoulder, and she hugged him to her tightly. After a long moment he rolled from her and lay on his back, eyes closed, his breath rasping in and out of his chest unevenly. At last, softly, he said, "I think I just died and went to heaven." One heavily lashed eye opened to look at her, and he grinned. "Lawyers' heaven—making love among the files."

Slowly Adam sat up. His gaze went to the door, and he reached over hastily and turned the lock. "Good Lord, I didn't even lock the door." He turned back to Emily and smiled as his eyes ran down her. "What have you done to me?" He reached out and cupped her cheek, his thumb softly caressing the soft flesh. "I wanted you so much I couldn't think of anything else. When you said you wanted me—" He shook his head in bemusement at his own actions. "I didn't hurt you, did I?"

Emily smiled and shook her head as she sat up. She glanced around them. They had indeed been rather hasty. Shoes, underwear and other various bits of their clothing lay all over the room—on the floor, on chairs, on Adam's desk. Her slip had been pushed down from the top, and both it and her skirt were bunched up around her waist. Adam's shirt had been unbuttoned and pushed off one arm, but remained on the other arm and shoulder. And his tie was rather askew but still firmly knotted around his neck.

Emily stifled a giggle. They glanced at each other, and more giggles bubbled up from their throats, until finally they burst into laughter. They laughed so hard they had to hold their sides, and it was several minutes before they subsided into weak, sporadic chuckles. Adam pulled Emily into his arms and sat with his back against the wall, holding her. He kissed her hair and face. "Do you suppose the rest of the firm is standing out there wondering what's going on?"

Emily nodded. "Probably."

"You want to know something? I don't care." He rubbed his cheek against her hair. "After the past two weeks, this feels too good for me to care about anything else."

Emily snuggled into his chest. She agreed wholeheartedly. At the moment she didn't care if Leith Marshall himself was outside.

"Why didn't you tell me?" Adam asked. "I thought you didn't want to have anything to do with me after we got back. You were so cool and businesslike."

Emily looked at him in exasperation. "How could I tell you? We'd agreed that it would be that weekend and nothing else. I figured you were the one who wanted it that way. I thought you didn't want to do me a favor and then have me chasing you around the office."

Adam grinned. "I think I would love to have you chase me around the office. Shall we try it tomorrow?"

Emily shot him a quelling glance and nestled back into his arms. Adam sighed. "It's probably very foolish to get involved. I think that's why we came up with that damned agreement to begin with. But, frankly, right now I'd rather be foolish." He paused. "In fact, I think I'd like to be irresponsible and undutiful, as well. Get dressed. You and I are going to take the afternoon off and spend the rest of the day in my bed."

"All right."

They gathered up their clothes and dressed, glancing at each other with quick, secret smiles, and stopping now and then for a kiss that simply couldn't wait. When they were dressed, straightened and presentable, Adam opened the office door and looked out. The hall was empty. He motioned to Emily and started down the hall. Emily grabbed her purse, which had still been in her hand when she stormed into his office after lunch, and followed him, striving to maintain the same straight, businesslike demeanor that Adam displayed. She wondered if it was obvious to everyone what they had been doing. Though she had straightened her clothes and combed her hair, there had been nothing she could do about the glow on her face or the redness of her much-kissed mouth.

They waited for the elevator, looking everywhere but at each other for fear they would either burst into giggles again or betray their passion in the way they looked at each other. When the elevator arrived they joined the other people already in it and rode very primly to the underground garage. It wasn't until they were ensconced in the partial privacy of Adam's parked car that he pulled her into his arms, as he'd been longing to since they left his office, and kissed her thoroughly.

"You've corrupted me," he told her, smiling. "All the way down I was trying to figure out a way we could make love in the elevator."

Emily laughed, and the sparkling sound touched a chord deep within Adam. He cupped her face and gazed down into her wide, gray eyes. "Ah, Emily. Why did it take me so long to discover you?"

## Chapter 11

Adam and Emily were with each other constantly over the course of the spring and into the summer. They worked together, slept together and played together. Emily quickly realized that she would have to remove herself from her aunt's and mother's watchful eyes, so she moved into her own apartment. However, she spent little time there. Almost every night found her at Adam's luxurious condominium on the old Graylin estate.

Emily was ecstatically happy. If her looks had blossomed after their weekend in the mountain, now she burst into full bloom. Though she changed nothing further in her hairstyle, clothes, or face, no one failed to notice that she had suddenly become beautiful. She knew the change was simply her happiness in the knowledge that Adam desired her. He seemed to want her with him always, and while it amazed her, she was certainly willing to comply.

Their physical relationship outside the office did not harm the comfortable working arrangement they'd had for years.

Though they might smile secretly at one another as Emily jotted down Adam's instructions or handed him a typed letter, or even snatch a kiss behind a closed door, they were still able to work together efficiently. In fact, contented as they were now, they were far more competent in their work than they had been during the weeks following their weekend at the cabin. Somehow the work seemed easier and less tiring, just knowing that they were sharing it, even during the long evening hours at the office during Adam's next trial. Emily cheerfully stayed late to catch Adam up on the things that had happened during the day and to take down his instructions. She listened to his strategy for the next day or complaints about the present one and did all she could to help him with his preparation. When at last he was finished, they would go to his home and Emily would rub the knots of tension from his shoulders, and Adam would forget his responsibilities and worries in her arms.

One night, as they lay quietly holding each other after making love, Adam said, "I like your interest in my work."

Emily smiled. "It's not hard. It's interesting work."

"Not everyone would think so," he commented dryly. "Cassie certainly didn't."

The name pierced Emily's contented mood. Cassie again. Adam couldn't forget her. She was the woman to whom he would compare all other women. But Emily forced the thought out of her mind. At least this time Adam was comparing her favorably to Cassie.

"Cassie hated the time I spent at the office. She told me it was why she found a lover, because I was never there." He sighed. "She was right. I wasn't home enough. But I couldn't give up litigation; it fascinated me. Still does. And you know how time-consuming litigation is if you're going to do it well. I don't know; maybe if we'd had children I would have felt differently. Maybe I could have arranged my schedule differently, not taken on so many cases. Cassie always told me I could have made more time for her, but I was too selfish."

"I don't think it's wrong to want to do the work you enjoy, the work you're so well suited for," Emily defended him to himself. "If you had given up litigation or spent less time on it, it wouldn't have been a loss just to you, but to all your clients, as well."

"Thank you." Adam squeezed her, and she could see the flash of his smile in the darkness. "You always back me. Why is that?"

*Because I love you.* The words were on the tip of her tongue, but Emily managed not to say them. Adam might enjoy her company and desire her in bed, but no man would want the pressure of a declaration of love when he didn't reciprocate the feeling. Adam had never indicated that he had any love for her, and given the way he felt about his ex-wife, Emily doubted there would ever come a time when he did love her. That was too much to ask of fate, which had already been so generous. So she held back her feelings and said simply. "Usually I think you're in the right. You're a good, strong man, and I can't think of a better person to back."

Adam leaned over and gave her a brief, hard kiss, then settled back against his pillow. "Anyway, Cassie hated the law firm. Marshall, Pierson, Tidrell, and Sommers was her deadly enemy. She wouldn't listen to anything about the office or my work. She said the time I spent with her was short enough as it was, and she wouldn't have it spoiled by something as boring as law."

"Boring!" Emily exclaimed. "But it's not boring. I mean, what I do isn't very much, but I think even that much is interesting. And what you do—planning the strategy, doing the research, extracting information from people, then going to court and presenting your case in the best possible way—it's so complex! So difficult." Emily's long-held admiration for him rang out clearly in her voice. "You do something very few people could. You have a rare combination of intelligence, power and skill. It fascinates me to see you lay out your plan of action, to hear you analyze the case. The cases themselves are interesting. Every one is unique. Even when they're the same type of action, the people are different, the injury's different. There's a whole new set of circumstances."

"That's the way it seems to me," Adam replied, his voice rising a little in the excitement of meeting a like mind. "That's why it's so nice to talk to you. You want to know what went on in court, what I plan to do with a case, or how I'll handle a certain witness. It's such a pleasure to know that you understand what I'm saying, that you can discuss it reasonably with me, that you're interested in hearing about it. It makes it so nice to talk to you. It's almost as nice as making love to you." Again his grin cut through the night. "Almost."

He rolled over on his elbow and kissed her, and again Emily opened up her heart and her body to his lovemaking.

Later, after the trial was over, they began to go out sometimes in the evenings, seeing a movie or a play or one of the summer concerts on the Graylin estate. But most of the time they spent at Adam's home, wanting nothing more than to be with each other and make love. The attraction didn't wear thin, as Adam had feared; he didn't feel himself slipping into boredom with Emily. Instead their lovemaking seemed to grow more beautiful each time, and Adam found that he wanted her more than before. They made love at home in his wide bed. They stole away to his mountain retreat and made love there. They spent one weekend at the Marshall family's beach house on Hilton Head Island and made love on the floor before the wide windows looking out onto the rolling, phosphorescent surf. Sometimes their lovemaking was quick and furious, as it had been that day in the office, and they joined together in eager heat. At other times they made love slowly, languidly, savoring each delicious sensation and prolonging the glorious release until they trembled and ached from the force of their desire. Now and then they teased and laughed and tumbled about, playing at their lovemaking. And everything they tried was delicious, ending as it always did in a sweet cataclysm of love.

Adam educated Emily in the ways of love, but he found that their lovemaking led him, too, to heights that he had never known before—or had forgotten long ago. Sometimes he wondered if it had ever been this good with Cassie, but his memory of her was foggy, and he had difficulty envisioning her, let alone recalling how he had felt when they made love. He didn't try very hard to remember; the time with Emily was too sweet and happy to waste it thinking about his ex-wife.

So they floated into summer, wrapped up in one another. It seemed as if the rest of the world hardly existed. Emily noticed that they never went out with anyone else, either Adam's friends or family, and the idea brought a little shaft of pain to her. She wasn't important enough to Adam, she thought, for him to introduce her to his family and friends. He knew she wasn't a woman who he might marry or even date for long. She didn't belong in his world of wealthy, sophisticated people, and it would be pointless to introduce her to people she would never see again once their affair was over.

Emily preferred to be alone with Adam; she had no desire to meet any of those people. She knew she would feel clumsy and inadequate around them, and she didn't want to embarrass Adam with her lack of beauty and polish. Still, she felt a twinge of hurt that Adam didn't think she was worth introducing to the people close to him.

So she felt surprised, elated and scared to death when Adam came into her office one day in July, perched on her desk and said, "Mother's throwing a family thing this Saturday. Can you come?"

Emily's jaw dropped. "Me?"

Adam made a production of glancing around the room as if searching for someone. "Of course, you."

"But, Adam, you don't want to take me! You couldn't."

He gave her an odd look. "Why couldn't I? Who else would I take?"

A flame of jealousy leaped up in her at the idea of his taking anyone else to anything. But the sudden, heart-pounding terror she felt at facing Adam's aristocratic mother was far greater than any amount of jealousy. "Anyone!" she blurted. "Oh, Adam, I couldn't go to a family party."

He frowned. "Why not? I don't understand. Do you have something else to do? Do you not want to go? It'll be pretty dull, I'll admit, but I—"

"Oh, no, no," Emily reassured him hastily. "It's not that I don't *want* to go. Or, at least, well, it's not that I'm afraid I'd be bored."

"Then what is it?"

"I—I'm scared."

"Scared?" His eyebrows shot up. "Of what? It's no big deal, just the family."

"'Just the family,'" Emily repeated in a tone of horror. "Adam . . . it's your family I'm scared of."

"But why? You already know a lot of them. You know Mother and Dad. Tag. James. Have you met James?"

Emily nodded. "Yes, I saw him a couple of times when he came to the firm's Christmas party."

"Well, then. You know my immediate family. The rest are just cousins, aunts and uncles. Grandparents. They're okay people. You'll like them."

"Adam, you don't understand. Meeting your mother once a year at the Christmas party and seeing her in the hall when she comes up to see your father is not the same as 'knowing' her. She always looks like she just stepped out of a fashion magazine. She's on all those charity committees and civic groups. And she's a Taggart!"

"Emily, for Pete's sake…what does that have to do with anything? I'm one of the Taggarts, too, if you want to look at it that way." He grinned devilishly. "And that certainly hasn't kept you from 'knowing' me."

"That's different."

"How? Look, you like Tag, don't you?"

"Yes."

"And you like me?"

"Of course I do."

"So what makes you think the rest of our family is any different? We're fairly likable people. And Mother always throws a nice July party. She has party lights in the trees in the backyard and dancing on the patio and a good buffet."

"I don't doubt the quality of Mrs. Marshall's party—"

"Her name's Joyce."

"And I'm sure your family is very nice," Emily plowed ahead determinedly. "But I don't fit with them!"

"Don't fit? Don't be silly. Of course you fit. You fit with me."

"Do I really? You haven't exactly shown me off to family and friends before this. Because you know as well as I do that I don't belong with the Taggarts and the Marshalls and the Leiths of this world."

Adam stared, then leaned closer, his eyes narrowing to bright slits of blue. "Are you telling me you think I've kept you hidden because I'm ashamed of you? Because I think you aren't good enough for my family and friends?"

Emily swallowed. She wished she'd never let that last remark slip. She managed a small nod.

"I'll be damned." Adam sat back, shaking his head "You come up with the weirdest ideas." He stood up and closed the door into the hall, then turned back to her, putting his hands on his hips, his suit coat shoved back behind his hands. Emily gazed at him, wondering how anyone could be good enough for Adam Marshall. His stance delineated the streamlined perfection of his figure, the silk vest and trousers tailored to his broad chest, narrow waist and long, slender legs. His thick, black hair framed his face; his blue eyes were bright with intelligence. He was the epitome of wealth, breeding and good looks. How could he be anything but too spectacular for her?

"Let me set the record straight. I have not taken you to parties or introduced you to my friends because: A, I've been busy; B, I'm not very fond of social functions; and C most imortant of all, I haven't wanted to share you with anybody else. I enjoyed having you to myself. I wanted to spend my time just with you, do things just with you. didn't have any desire to see anyone else. Because of my work I have precious little time to spend with you as it is and I sure as hell didn't want anyone else horning in on it. thought you felt the same way. I didn't realize you wanted to go out with friends or talk to my family, or I would have arranged it."

A huge lump formed in Emily's throat, and her eye shone. "Oh, Adam," she breathed, "do you honestly fee that way?"

"Of course I do. But I'm confused. What is it you feel? What is it you want?"

Emily reached out and took one of his hands and drew it to her face. Softly she kissed his large palm and held it against her cheek. Her eyes glittered with unshed tears. "I want to be with you. I have no desire to be with anyone else, anytime, anywhere. You're all I want, all I think about. I want to keep you to myself, too. I just never dreamed you felt the same way; I assumed you must not think I was worth introducing to your friends."

"Oh, Emily!" Adam pulled her up and into his arms. "When will you realize that no one would be ashamed to be seen with you? You're gorgeous." He kissed her lips. "Sweet. Bright. Fun." He punctuated each word with a kiss, the kisses growing longer and deeper with every repetition. "A marvelous companion. A marvelous bed partner." He raised his head from their last kiss and drew in a shaky breath, resting his cheek against her shining hair. "And if I don't stop, we're going to have another office seduction."

"I wouldn't mind."

He chuckled. "How do I get any work done with you around?" He kissed her again, then firmly set her aside. "Now, are you going to stop all this nonsense and agree to come to the party Saturday?"

"Yes."

"Good." He turned to leave.

"But, Adam..."

"What?" He turned back, his face so wary that Emily almost laughed.

"Are you sure your mother would really want me there? I mean, if it's for your family..."

"We're entitled to bring dates and spouses. Though not at the same time, of course." That did bring a chuckle from her, and Adam smiled. "Besides, you goose, Mother has specifically requested your presence. She called me three times to ask if I was bringing you.''

''Me!'' Emily repeated, shocked. ''What does she know about me?''

''Only that Dad's told her the office gossip about us, and Tag's given glowing reports of your beauty and charm.'' If possible, Emily's eyes widened even further. ''Only that it's common knowledge that I haven't gone anywhere without you for the past month, except to court, and that I haven't been with a woman for this long since my divorce. And she's dying of curiosity.''

''Oh, my heavens.'' Emily felt another spear of self-doubt—how could she possibly live up to such advance notice? But the insecurity had little chance against the overwhelming tide of warmth and happiness sweeping through her. She was special to Adam. Nothing could have said it more clearly. No other woman had held him this long since Cassie. He wanted to be with her all the time. And alone—he didn't want to share her. Joy swelled within her, threatening to float her away. She wanted suddenly, desperately, to tell him that she loved him. It was all she could do to keep from blurting out the words.

As the days passed and the time for the party grew closer, Emily's joy rapidly diminished, replaced by a burgeoning fear. No matter what Adam said—and no matter how much she loved his saying it—Emily knew she didn't belong with people like his family. She was also certain that his mother and father would be dreadfully disappointed when they met her outside the office, and the idea of having to deal with them on a social level terrified her. She didn't think she had ever spoken more than a few words to either one of them. Joyce Marshall was tall, elegant and poised, the perfect society wife. Her cool smiles and polite chit chat were mea ured out carefully at the Christmas party, the gracefully assumed burden of her husband's business. Emily had never felt that she really saw any of the firm's employees, including some of the associates, as people. As for Leith Marshall—well, Emily had never done more than nod to him in the hall and scurry on past, head down. She knew he had an icy, crackling wit and an equally icy anger, and Emily had always been careful that there was never an occasion for him to turn either on her. He was as incisive and brilliant as his son, but had little of Adam's warmth or kindness.

Emily was sure that the party would be an awful, prolonged test of her social skills and endurance. She was also miserably certain that she would fail in everyone's eyes, including Adam's.

She spent three hours Saturday afternoon getting ready, changing her clothes five times before she finally settled on a crisp, white sundress with a modest, lacy jacket. She had to redo her eye makeup twice because her fingers were trembling so much she couldn't put it on straight, and she popped a run in a brand new pair of hose just pulling them on. By the time she was dressed and ready, Emily was trembling and ice cold all over. Then she had to wait another thirty minutes for Adam to arrive, since her fear had driven her to dress far too early. As she waited the knot in her stomach and the ice in her veins thickened. She had reached the point of calling Adam and telling him that she was too sick to go when he arrived on her doorstep.

Adam smiled at her, and she returned a sickly grin. He ran his eyes down her and leaned forward to kiss her. "You look gorgeous. I'll be the envy of every man there."

Emily wanted to tell him that she couldn't possibly go, that she was on the edge of throwing up just thinking about it, but she found she couldn't back out. Adam expected her to do it, and Emily knew she could never let him down if there were any way she could keep from it.

"I guess I'm ready," she told him, snatching up her purse and turning to march out the door.

Adam glanced at her grim face and smiled. "You aren't going to the guillotine. I promise."

Emily managed another weak smile and forced her legs to move forward, carrying her out the door and on to her fate.

The Marshalls' house was a huge, white mansion on Stratford Road, near Buena Vista, in the heart of the wealthiest section of Winston-Salem. A long driveway led up to the house, which was set well back from the road, and circled in front of it, with another section sprouting off to the massive garage and adjacent porte-cochere. It was a fortunate thing the paved area was wide, for it was jammed with cars. Emily noted that most were Mercedes, BMWs, or Porsches, with a sprinkling of Cadillacs and Lincolns. There was even one elegant, old Rolls Royce in a gleaming, tobacco brown. Emily wet her lips and prayed she wouldn't make a total fool of herself.

Adam stopped in front of the steps, and a valet in a short red jacket hurried forward to take Adam's keys and park the car. Adam put his hand under Emily's elbow and escorted her up the steps to the dark, glass-inset front door. As they approached the door was opened by a tall, regal gentleman who was the personification of everyone's idea of a butler.

"So happy to see you, sir," he said gravely, stepping aside to let them pass. "Shall I announce you to Mr. and Mrs. Marshall?"

"No, that's all right. We'll find them." Adam guided Emily down the hall toward the entertainment area at the back, already alive with noise and laughter.

"A butler?" Emily whispered in amazement. "I'm surprised he didn't call you 'Master Adam.'"

Adam chuckled. "He's supplied by the caterer, too." He grinned down at her. "Mother's housekeeper usually answers the door—and she calls me 'Dadum.'"

"Dadum!"

"It's what James called me when he was little; he had trouble saying Adam. It stuck throughout most of my childhood. Fortunately it was only in the immediate family, or I'd never have gotten rid of it."

They stepped into a large carpeted room filled with furniture and people. There was a long table at one end of the room, laid with a crisp white tablecloth and covered with dishes of hors d'oeuvres. At the opposite end of the room was a bar, behind which stood another red-jacketed attendant. Waiters passed silently through the room with large trays, picking up glasses and taking orders for drinks. A bank of long windows and matching French doors across the far wall looked out onto a flagstone patio, a serene, blue pool and a beautifully landscaped backyard, just slipping into dusk and beginning to glow with a multitude of soft party lanterns. There was a small platform to one side of the patio where three musicians were setting up their instruments. A scattering of people stood on the patio and sat in chairs around the pool. It wasn't Emily's idea of a family party.

Emily surveyed the area and gave Adam a skeptical look. "All those people are your family?"

He grinned. "Family includes every Taggart, Leith and Osgood, as well as Marshall, within driving distance. Mother holds this twice a year, now and before Christmas. Come on, I'll introduce you around; then we can get some food and go out by the pool and enjoy ourselves."

Adam led her around the room, introducing her to a dizzying number of aunts, uncles, cousins and in-laws. "I'll never keep them all straight," Emily whispered to him.

Adam shrugged. "Don't worry. Most of the people in this room don't know all the others. There's a guy over there who I'm sure is an Osgood, but I can't place him for the life of me. Ah, there's Mother. Here's our second most important duty call. Then we'll visit Gran Marshall, and we'll be home free."

Emily had relaxed slightly during the whirlwind of introductions, but now her stomach iced up anew. Joyce Marshall turned and smiled at them, a picture of elegance in a mint green summer dress, and Emily wished she had never come. Adam's grip was impossible to break away from, however, and he led her inexorably to his poised, calm-as-glass mother.

"Hello, Mother." He placed a brief kiss on Joyce's cheek, and Joyce responded by reaching up to pat his face.

"Hello, dear. I'm so glad you could come. This must be Emily." She extended both her hands, enfolding Emily's hand in hers and giving it an extra pat. "How nice to finally meet you."

"Thank you. I—I'm pleased to meet you."

"I'm pleased Adam brought you." Emily could feel Mrs Marshall's pale blue eyes assessing her quickly, without any change in her polite expression. She wondered what the other woman was thinking. Had she passed the test, or had she failed utterly? "I told Adam he'd been very selfish, never bringing you over to meet any of us."

Emily smiled vaguely, hoping that would suffice as a response. She had no idea what to say.

But Joyce Marshall was fully in control of the situation. She took Emily's arm and gently guided her toward an adjacent, much quieter room, saying to her son as she passed him, "Why don't you fetch Emily a drink, dear, while she and I get to know each other?"

"Of course." Adam winked at Emily. "Just don't eat her." Then Adam left her.

Emily followed the other woman up the two steps into a smaller room, where a few people sat conversing in elegant, uncomfortable chairs. They took the most uncomfortable of the lot, a low Empire love seat against the far wall. It was quiet and private, sheltered from the rest of the room by a long, marble-topped coffee table and a spreading schefflera plant.

"I really am happy you could come," Joyce Marshall reiterated as they settled into the low, stiff seats. Emily felt as if her long legs were jackknifed up to her chin. Obviously the women of the Napoleonic era had not been five-foot eight.

"Thank you. It was my pleasure."

"Leith tells me you've worked for Adam for some time."

"Yes, ma'am," Emily replied, feeling a little like a schoolgirl "visiting" with the principal. "Ten years this summer."

"My goodness. That is quite a while. Why, that's since he graduated from law school."

"Yes. He hired me when he joined the firm."

"How nice." A heavy silence settled on them; then Joyce started up again gamely. "Are you from this area?"

"Yes. I was born in Winston-Salem and lived here all my life." Now here would come the questions, Emily thought miserably: Who are your parents and where did you go to school and are those the medical Townsends?

But instead Mrs. Marshall said only, "So was Adam. For that matter, so was I. It's such a lovely town. I don't think I'd ever want to live anyplace else."

Joyce went on to talk about the Little Theater, the summer concerts and her various other charitable activities. Emily did her best to keep up, answering as knowledgeably as she could and smiling when she didn't have any idea what the woman was talking about. Eventually Adam showed up with two drinks in his hand and rescued her.

"All right, Mother. You've had Emily long enough. Gran's wanting to meet her."

"Well, I suppose I shall have to give her up, then." Joyce smiled politely and patted Emily's hand. "I hope we'll have a chance to talk again soon. Make Adam bring you by the house one evening." She rose and walked away.

Adam handed Emily her drink, and she took a large gulp. Adam smiled. "It wasn't that bad, was it?"

"Easier than I expected," Emily admitted, standing up. Adam curled an arm around her shoulders and gave her an encouraging squeeze.

"Another hurdle taken. Now, on to Gran. She's the dragon of the family. Dad's mother. She and Mother have had a quiet, refined feud going on for years—well, ever since Mother dared to take Gran's oldest and dearest son from her thirty-eight years ago."

"You're joking."

He smiled and shook his head. "They unite periodically over some scandal or important family issue, but they never really stop sniping at each other. You'll like Mama Min better. She's Mother's mom, and a real character."

Emily met each of the grandmothers in turn. Mrs. Marshall was a small, slim woman who sat ramrod-straight in her chair and turned a well preserved, cool face upon her grandson and the woman he brought with him. She spoke softly, but in clear, precise tones, and there was an undeniable element of iron in her voice. Emily suspected that the old woman's sons had rarely disobeyed her. Mrs. Taggart, on the other hand, was a plump, soft woman who appeared slightly uncomfortable in her sheer, fluttery summer dress and confessed that she was more at home in her work clothes out digging in her garden. She was a vivacious, talkative woman with whom Emily was quite comfortable, never having to add more to the conversation than an occasional nod or verbal agreement. Oddly enough, Joyce Marshall seemed more similar to her husband's mother than to her own.

Later they met Adam's brother, James, who was accompanied by a small, fragile woman with a cloud of dark hair and a die-away voice. James resembled his older brother, though he was slightly shorter and broader through the shoulders. His hair wasn't as black as Adam's, more a deep brown shot through with red highlights, but his eyes were the same piercing blue. There was a certain similarity in their facial structure, too, though there was a harder, more set quality to James's expression. Adam had charisma, and Tag had charm, but James exuded power. Everything about him bespoke a man who charged at life and bent it to his will. Emily was sure that as a public official he was utterly incorruptible, and that his strict sense of honor, so like Adam's, wasn't tempered with Adam's kindness. It was difficult not to be drawn to him; all the Marshall men were undeniably appealing. But Emily was glad she would never have to face him from the defendant's table.

Adam introduced them, and James reached out to shake her hand. His grip was firm, neither friendly nor remote, and his eyes whisked down her in a brief, masculine assessment. He smiled a fraction, and his intense blue gaze flashed to his brother's face in a quick, meaningful look, then returned to her.

"It's nice to meet you," he said conventionally. "I must congratulate Adam. His taste is improving."

"Thank you." Emily smiled a little shyly. James was unsettling in a way that neither Tag nor Adam was.

"I'm surprised to find you here," Adam told his brother. "You stayed away last Christmas."

"Oh. Yeah, I had a case. Didn't have the time to waste."

"Somehow I thought that altercation with Dad in September might have kept you away."

James grinned. "Nah. If I stayed away every time I locked horns with Dad, you'd never see me. I'm only one notch higher than Tag in his estimation. No, the really serious wrong I committed was being so ungentlemanly as to exchange harsh words with Dad in Gran's presence. She hardly spoke to me today."

"I suspect you'll survive," Adam commented dryly.

"Hopefully."

The four of them visited the long table set up inside the house, which now held the supper buffet, and returned with their full plates to one of the poolside tables. Before long they were joined by Tag and a stunningly attractive woman with thick, rich brown hair and pale, golden eyes. The brothers greeted each other cheerfully, though Emily noted that there was some reserve between Tag and James. However, there was no reserve in either Adam's or James's greeting to the woman. Both stood up, hugged her and gave her a hearty kiss. Emily felt a distinct quiver of jealousy.

"Sammie! Gee, it's good to see you."

"How was Europe?"

The woman smiled with enjoyment and affection. "It was terrific, except that two weeks wasn't long enough. I'm going to have to convince the bank we need longer vacations. How are you guys doing? Making money and locking people up, right?"

"That's one way of putting it." Adam put an arm around the woman's shoulders and turned her toward Emily. "I want you to meet someone." Sammie turned bright, interested eyes on Emily. "Sammie, this is Emily Townsend. Emily, this is my cousin, Sammie Jo Taggart."

Sammie gave him a sharp dig in the ribs with her elbow. "Just Sammie—or Samantha. 'Sammy Jo' lives only in these guys' warped minds." She reached across the table to shake Emily's hand.

Emily beamed back at her, flooded with relief that this gorgeous female was related to Adam. "It's nice to meet you, Sammie."

Tag returned to the house to fetch drinks and dinner for him and his cousin, and Adam went with him. Sammie plopped down in Adam's vacant chair next to Emily. "I'm dying to hear all about you," she said with a vivid smile that softened her bluntness.

"I'm afraid there's not much to tell."

"There must be. You've captured Adam's interest, and that makes you a hot item in this family."

Emily stared. She would have figured that nobody in Adam's family would have cared if she lived or died. Sammie chuckled at her expression. "It's true. We worry about Adam; he took it so hard when Cassie dumped him. I don't think he's gone out with any one woman more than two or three times since then, so everybody was thrilled when they found out he'd been dating somebody hot and heavy. Of course we're dying of curiosity. You're one of the major attractions today."

"I hope I don't disappoint you all."

"Don't worry. You won't. The word's already out that you've gotten the stamp of approval."

"Approval?"

"Yeah. Adam's grandmother admitted that you were 'quite proper.' Mama Min said you were 'a sweet girl' and just what Adam needs.' And Aunt Joyce is very happy."

"Adam's mother?" Emily's voice rose in disbelief. "Adam's mother is happy with me?"

"Sure. Don't let that reserve of hers fool you. She despises Adam's ex-wife. I don't think she ever liked Cassie, but since the divorce—whew!" She raised her eyebrows exaggeratedly. "I mean, we were all angry about the way Cassie treated Adam, even the people who liked her. But Aunt Joyce was livid. Anyway, she likes you, and she's pleased to death that Adam found you, especially now."

"Why especially now?" Emily asked, unable to take it all in.

"Because of the rumors about Cassie. People say she's having trouble with her second husband—the guy she left Adam for. I heard yesterday that she's leaving him. Aunt Joyce is afraid Cassie might try to come back into Adam's life now that it's gone kaput with this other guy. That's why she's so happy that Adam's all wrapped up in you."

"I see," Emily managed to say through colorless lips. Cassie was free and on the prowl? Her stomach felt as if it had just dropped to the floor. Joyce might be able to convince herself that Emily could hold Adam's affection even with Cassie around, but Emily wasn't that foolish. If Cassie wanted him back, Adam was as good as lost to her.

Adam returned to find Emily and Sammie engrossed in conversation, so he set down the drinks he had carried out from the house and wandered off to circulate. There were several people whom he ought to talk to out of politeness, and with Sammie keeping Emily entertained, this was a good opportunity to do so. He went into the house and chatted with a pair of widowed great-aunts, one of whom couldn't see well and the other of whom was almost deaf. It took him nearly five minutes to establish who he was, yet he knew that if he hadn't, one of them would have said later

"Now where was Leith's boy, you know, the oldest one? He never came by and said hello."

After a few minutes he moved on, drifting in and out of several conversations until he decided he had satisfied most of his family responsibilities and could return to Emily. He stepped out the back door onto the patio and looked toward the table near the pool where he had left Emily. James and his date were still there, but there was no sign of Emily, Tag or Sammie. Adam glanced around the porch and pool area, searching for her. He hoped she didn't feel lost and alone, as if he'd deserted her among the wolves.

"Lost her?" A smooth, masculine voice came out of the shadows to his right, and Adam started. He turned and looked at his father.

Leith Marshall wasn't as tall as his sons; their height came from the Taggart side of the family. But the handsome regularity of his features, the vivid blue eyes and the thick dark hair were all assets he had passed on to his heirs, though in his case the hair was now almost half silver. He was a good-looking man, tough as nails, but that was well hidden under a coolly elegant exterior.

"Hello, Dad. Yeah, it looks like Tag and Sammie spirited her away."

Leith casually scanned the party. "Somehow our family seems to multiply every year."

"You just forget how bad it is in between times," Adam joked, and Leith smiled faintly. Adam had an easier time than his brothers in dealing with their father. He wasn't sure if it was that their personalities were more attuned, or simply that his needs and wishes had rarely crossed Leith's.

Leith removed a slender cigar from an inner pocket and began the lengthy ritual of lighting it. "She's changed a lot," he commented, still surveying the party.

"Who? Emily?"

"Yes. She isn't the brown mouse I remember."

Adam frowned. "I don't think Emily was ever unattractive."

His father smiled to himself, rolling the cigar between his fingers. "Not unattractive, no, but I couldn't have told you exactly what she looked like."

It occurred to Adam to point out that that was his father's problem, not Emily's, but he refrained.

"I trust you've thought over what you're doing rather carefully," Leith went on after a moment.

"What I'm doing? What do you mean?"

Leith studied the end of his cigar. "This little office romance. They usually turn out badly."

"I thought about that. But it doesn't have to."

"It's difficult when it ends."

"Who said it's got to end?"

Leith raised an eyebrow at his son. "You planning on marrying the girl?"

"Marry?" Adam shrugged. "I hadn't thought about it one way or the other."

"Relationships don't stay static. You know that. Eventually you'll have to make a decision: either to marry her or let it die."

"Well, it hasn't gone that far. We've only been together a couple of months."

"Sure have been living in each other's pockets, though. It's caused talk at the firm."

"The people in that firm talk about something all the time. It doesn't make much difference what."

"It makes a difference when it's a Marshall they're talking about."

Adam turned to face his father. "Exactly what are you trying to say?"

"You aren't in the same position as every other attorney in that firm. You have to plan ahead. You have to think for the firm instead of just for yourself. And that means thinking with your head, not your glands."

"The firm doesn't run my life," Adam pointed out quietly.

"I'm not telling you to drop the girl," Leith responded mildly. "Just asking you to consider what you're doing."

"I know what I'm doing," Adam surveyed the yard, his mouth tightening.

"Emily's not used to the kind of world you've grown up in."

"I know."

"Think she'll be able to handle your social obligations?"

"In case you haven't noticed, I'm not heavily into 'social obligations.'"

"No. But at least you aren't as bullheaded as your brother James. You attend a few parties; you drop in every once in a while at the club."

"Yes."

Leith drew on his cigar, and the tip glowed red in the dark. Silence spread around them. Then Leith said quietly, "Now that was something Cassie was really good at, keeping up the social end of your life."

"Yeah, and we all know what a wonderful wife Cassie was," Adam retorted sarcastically.

"She was a beautiful woman."

"As far as I know she still is."

"Yeah. Joyce tells me she's leaving her husband."

Adam glanced at him, amazed. "Already?"

"So Joyce says. I figure she probably regrets what happened between you."

"Maybe," Adam replied without much interest, his eye
roaming over the distant yard. Suddenly he straightened
"There she is!"

"Who?"

"Emily. Between Tag and Sammie back by the pine
Sorry, Dad. I've gotta run." He started off across the pa
tio. "Nice talking to you."

Leith watched Adam cross the patio and skirt the poo
heading unswervingly toward a pool of shadow far back i
the yard. Leith blew out a wisp of smoke, watching it cu
upward, and a small smile curved his lips.

## Chapter 12

Emily hardly heard a word that was said the rest of the evening. All she could think of were Sammie's words. Cassie was leaving her husband. She would be free again, and she would want Adam back. How could she not? She'd been crazy to give him up in the first place, and the rapidity with which her second marriage had failed must indicate that she had realized the mistake she'd made. Cassie would come back to Adam, and he would gladly take her in. Emily's brief moment of paradise would be over.

Even after Adam rejoined them, Emily was taut and distracted. It was a relief when he suggested that they return home. However, her mood was no better once she was alone with Adam, and when he took her into his arms that night she was stiff and awkward. She didn't belong there. He would soon leave her. Her thoughts wound her as tight as a spring, and it took a long time and many slow, seductive kisses before her natural desire for Adam welled up and took

over. Then she writhed and twisted in his arms, starved fo
his lovemaking, greedy to taste the delights that she knew
would soon be taken from her.

Her nails left long, red scratches on his back, which sh
was horrified to see the next morning, but Adam merel
grinned and shook his head. "Who'd have guessed you wer
such a wildcat?" he murmured, kissing her.

Emily wanted to cry with love and grief.

She continued to be quiet and moody all week. Adam
seemed preoccupied as well. Emily wondered if he had heard
the news about Cassie. Did he long to go to her? Did he
wonder if she would want him back now? Was he trying to
think of a nice way to let Emily down? Such speculation
increased Emily's gloom, and she almost wished that he
would go ahead and tell her good-bye and get it over with
At least it would be a quick death instead of this slow tor
ture. On the other hand, she thought she'd rather endure
anything, even her miserable uncertainty, than lose him.

In fact, Adam had hardly given a moment's thought to his
father's gossip about Cassie. He was taken up with what
Leith had said about Emily. And marriage. Adam hadn'
thought of marriage in connection with Emily before. Fo
the past two years he had presumed that he wouldn't marry
again. His life-style wasn't suited to having a wife. He wa
out of town frequently, and he worked long, late hours. He
loved his job, and there were times when he was almos
consumed by it. It wasn't a situation where a marriage and
children could thrive. He'd found that out with Cassie. Be
sides, after Cassie, he'd known he wouldn't fall in love
again.

But then, he'd thought he wouldn't ever desire a woman
again as much as he had desired Cassie. Yet for the past few
months he'd been at a fever pitch of passion, making love

to Emily over and over, satisfying his momentary desire without ever eliminating it. He couldn't remember if he'd ever wanted Cassie that much, even in the first spring hunger of their love. If he'd been wrong about his ability to desire a woman, it was just as likely that he'd been wrong about his ability to love. And wrong about marriage.

Did he love Emily? Did he want to marry her? It seemed a bizarre way to think about Emily, but then, in the past couple of months everything he'd thought about her had been turned upside down. He considered what it would be like to share his life with her and realized that that was exactly what he was doing right now. They were together almost constantly, at the office and at home. There was a space in his closet now that was tacitly hers. Her cosmetics lay on the counter of his bathroom. Her favorite coffee was in his kitchen cupboard. In the evening they stretched out in the living room and automatically divvied up the newspaper. And later they made love, which left him with a peace he hadn't known in years. If ever.

Was that love? It was too comfortable, surely, too even and natural. On the other hand, it was too physical, too intensely exciting; that kind of feeling couldn't last. It was too perfect; it wasn't real. How could they be in love if they didn't fight? How could such sweet peace and hot desire continue unabated? Yet how could he survive if they didn't?

The more he thought about marriage and Emily, the more it nagged at him, until sometimes it seemed as if that was all he could think of. He wished he could talk about it with someone, but he couldn't imagine discussing it with Tag or any of his friends. In fact, the only person with whom he felt really able to share his thoughts and feelings was Emily. And she was the one person to whom he couldn't talk about it.

So he kept his confusion locked up inside and hoped that it would somehow untangle itself.

Mindful of Emily's assumption that he had kept her to himself because he was ashamed of her, Adam took her to a summer dance at the country club the next week. The Forsyth Country Club was the oldest and most prestigious club in Winston-Salem, the innermost sanctum of the elite. The Marshalls and Leiths had belonged to it from its inception. It was an imposing building, set back from the street and surrounded by beautifully landscaped grounds, like a green island in the middle of the city. Looking at it as they approached along the long, tree-lined driveway, Emily felt slightly sick to her stomach. There was no way that she fit in here.

An attendant parked their car, and they walked inside, Emily holding up the skirt of her formal dress so that it wouldn't touch the sidewalk and steps. It was the gorgeous, pink, strapless concoction that Jeanette had given her. A simple chain with a pearl drop encircled her throat.

They strolled through the hall to the doorway of the elegant ballroom and paused. Emily surveyed the crowd of expensively dressed, coiffed and jeweled people within the large room. She felt rather like Cinderella at the ball, wearing someone else's dress and hoping that everyone would be kind enough not to point out that she didn't belong. She glanced at Adam beside her and wondered how much longer her Prince Charming would be hers.

He looked down at her and smiled. "Well? Are you game?"

"I guess."

They strolled around the edge of the room. Adam nodded and spoke to people as they passed. "You know everybody," Emily commented.

"Not quite. But I grew up here. Mother and Dad are still pillars of the place, even if we kids don't frequent it much."

"Why not?"

He shrugged. "Oh, Tag comes some, but he's out of town a lot—at the beach or on his boat. Besides, he usually goes in for more, uh, flamboyant activities. James hates it, wouldn't set foot inside the place. He's very much against elitism and most social functions; he has high ideals. And I—oh, I used to come when Cassie and I were married. She liked this kind of thing. I enjoy more solitary evenings, really. Besides, my work doesn't allow much time for it."

Adam introduced her to so many people that the names were soon spinning in her head; she was sure she'd never remember half of them. They danced and had some refreshments, and Emily's nerves unlocked a little. Then Sammie Taggart came by, with her escort in tow, and chatted for a while. Later Tag spotted them and asked Emily to dance. Adam danced with her again, and she realized that she was floating in his arms and having a marvelous time. She smiled up at him brilliantly, and Adam's heart turned over.

She enjoyed the rest of the evening, chatting with Adam's friends, none of whom looked at her oddly or asked her embarrassing questions, and dancing. It was far less frightening than she had expected, and at the same time far more ordinary. She decided she preferred to spend her evenings alone with Adam. Still, it was nice to know that she could attend a function like this without falling apart, that she could hold her own even among the upper crust of Winston-Salem society.

The pleasant glow lasted until shortly before they left. Adam whispered a decidedly lewd proposition in her ear, and she giggled and nodded, and they started making their way around the dance floor to the exit. It was then that she glanced across the room and saw Cassie. Emily turned to ice.

Cassie was beautiful, as always. Her cinnamon-brown hair was cut short in a vibrant, windblown style that gave her a touch of wildness. Her large, melting, brown eyes and the exquisite bone structure of her face were as beautiful as ever, and her makeup emphasized them to advantage. Her small, perfectly proportioned body was encased in a coppery, satin dress with wide ruffles drawing attention to the bottom of the narrow skirt and to the neckline, scooped out to reveal the smooth skin of her shoulders and the creamy tops of her breasts. Her skin was golden and glowing, with a tinge of apricot in her cheeks. She looked utterly devastating, and Emily was sure there wasn't a man in the room who hadn't noticed her.

Emily glanced up at Adam. He, too, was looking at Cassie. Emily couldn't read his expression. Cassie turned just then and saw Adam, and she smiled, her mouth warm and beckoning. Adam nodded to her, and put his arm around Emily's waist, but Emily suspected there was more defiance than affection in the gesture. They continued out of the room. Emily felt like running. Cinderella's clock had just struck midnight.

Late the following Monday afternoon Emily sat in her office, typing up the first draft of a settlement agreement. Adam had spent the last week hammering out an out-of-court settlement with the opposing counsel in the Wheeler will case. Bob Cecil, the minister involved, had tentatively agreed to sign the settlement, as had the children of Mrs. Wheeler. As soon as Emily had typed it, Adam would present it to Cecil's attorney, and they would iron out whatever details remained. With luck, in a couple of weeks, they'd get both parties to sign.

Emily sighed and rolled her shoulders. She felt tired and blue, although the week had only begun. She knew she felt this way because she had spent the weekend under such tension, watching Adam for signs that he wished she were gone, or that he still loved Cassie, unable even to enjoy their lovemaking. Adam had seemed lost in thought, and once they had gotten into a brief, unresolved spat when he had asked what was wrong with her and Emily had refused to admit that anything was the matter.

Emily rubbed the base of her skull, where a headache was beginning to form, and thought about leaving work early. Maybe if she went home and had a nice, long soak in the tub she would relax a little. At the rate she was going her silences and bad temper would drive Adam away even if his love for Cassie didn't. She glanced up casually at the sound of footsteps in the hall, then froze as she saw who it was. Cassie Marshall Hyde was walking down the hall to Adam's office. She was as lovely close up as she had been the other night across the width of the ballroom.

She glanced into Emily's office and smiled carefully. She paused. "Is Adam in his office?"

For a second Emily didn't think she could force any air up her throat to speak, but to her surprise the words tumbled out. "As far as I know. Would you like me to tell him you're here?"

Cassie gave a languid wave of the hand. "Don't bother." She winked. "I know my way."

She disappeared, and Emily fought the urge to run to her door and watch Cassie enter Adam's office. She heard Adam's startled exclamation as Cassie stepped into his office, then the sharp click of his door as she closed it behind her. Emily set the papers down on her desk with shaking hands. It was over now. Over. Cassie had come for Adam. Emily began to tremble. She grabbed her purse and left her office, hurrying down the hall to the women's rest room.

Adam sat at his desk frowning, a file laid out before him. Someone stopped outside his open door, and he looked up. Cassie stood in the doorway, her delicately rounded figure outlined in a pale yellow dress, her face and hair artfully arranged. "Cassie!" He stared at her.

She took his exclamation as an invitation and entered the room, closing the solid door behind her. "Hello, Adam. Surprised to see me?"

"You could say that." Belatedly Adam remembered his manners and stood up. What was she doing here? It had been over two years since she'd set foot inside his office. Even during their divorce negotiations she had refused to meet at Adam's firm. "Please, sit down." He indicated a chair on the other side of his desk.

She was still beautiful. There was no denying that. He'd known it when he saw her the other night at the dance, and this afternoon only confirmed it close up. There were few women who could compete with Cassie on the basis of face and form. And, of course, she was impeccably dressed. He couldn't remember her ever being anything less than neat. Even in the midst of lovemaking she'd never had a hair out of place. He thought of Emily lying beneath him, her face sweetly contorted in passion, her hair wild and tumbled on the pillow, the sheen of love-sweat on her brow, dampening her hair. He smiled to himself.

Firmly Adam forced his attention back to his ex-wife. "Well. What brings you here today?"

"No wasting time on social amenities with you, right?" Cassie responded.

Adam shrugged. "Since you haven't graced this room for two years, I assumed you didn't come here for a chat."

"Are you still bitter?"

Adam frowned. "I don't know what you mean."

"About my leaving."

"I don't think so. It was a long time ago. Wounds heal, Cassie."

"I hope so." Cassie paused and gazed at her hands, which she had laced together in her lap. "I need your help." She looked up, tears sparkling in her eyes, turning them luminous and huge. "Your professional help, I guess. I left Daniel. I want to file for a divorce."

Adam sighed. "Oh, Cassie. I'd heard you left him, but I had hoped it was just gossip."

Cassie seemed surprised. "You'd hoped? And here I thought you would be glad I'd gotten it all back in my face."

Adam smiled sadly. "Once I probably would have been. But not now. I wish you were happy, too."

Her eyebrows rose, but she said nothing and quickly returned her gaze to her lap.

"I don't do divorces. You know that. But I can recommend a good attorney. Frank Jarma does what divorces we handle in the firm. Ed Shields, with the Levinson firm, is good. Frankly, the guy you had last time is one of the best. Why not stick with him?"

Cassie looked up. Her face was pale, and she appeared rattled. "I—I suppose I will. I was—I don't know. I guess I was hoping more for emotional support."

"From me?" It was Adam's turn to look surprised. "Why?"

Cassie wet her lips nervously, and her fingernails dug into her stylish, lemon-yellow handbag. "This isn't going at all as I'd imagined."

"Why not? What did you want to happen?"

"I was thinking you might hold me, comfort me—that we might—oh, hell! I might as well be honest. I came here to ask you to take me back."

"What!"

"Adam, please, listen to me." Cassie rose, the handbag sliding unnoticed to the floor, and took a step toward him, her hands clutched earnestly in front of her. "I was so angry with you when we split up. I was hurt because I thought you didn't love me, didn't pay enough attention to me. Your secretary saw more of you than I did." She paused and added cattily, "Now I can understand that a little better."

Adam shot to his feet. "If you're implying that I had an affair with Emily while we were married—"

"No, no." She made a dismissive gesture with her hand. "I'm sure you didn't. You were far too perfect to do something like that."

"Cassie, why are you bringing this up again? There's no reason to rehash it."

"I didn't mean to start an argument. I was trying to explain how I felt, how angry and hurt I was with you at that time. So angry and hurt that I had an affair. I guess because of who I am and how I was raised, the only way I could justify going to bed with Daniel was to believe that I loved him. Somehow, probably through sheer stubbornness, I managed to keep up the pretense the whole year it took for our divorce to become final. And I married him. But the past few months, I started coming to my senses. I guess the craziness of the divorce is finally out of my system. Anyway, I began to see things more clearly. I saw what an idiot I'd been."

Adam watched her, saying nothing. He didn't know how to respond.

Cassie gazed straight at him with her liquid, brown eyes. "I wanted to tell you that I was wrong. I realize that now. So much of what went wrong between us was my fault. But I didn't want to see that; I preferred to cast you as the villain. I didn't take any interest in your work; I didn't think about what was important to you, what I could do to help you. All I thought about was myself. Now I can see how stupid I was. I don't love Daniel; I never did. The only person I've ever loved was you." Her eyes sparkled with unshed tears. "I still love you."

Adam stared at her, dumbfounded. He had never expected to hear those words from Cassie. Once he would have done anything to get her to say them. He would have shouted for joy once she did. He would have swung her up into his arms and kissed her breathless. Now he simply stared and wondered what he ought to say to end the scene gracefully.

He cleared his throat. "Uh, Cassie, I . . . I'm at a loss for words."

Cassie emitted a small, nervous laugh. "That must be a first." Tears spilled out of her eyes and down her cheeks. "Oh, Adam. It's too late, isn't it? I was a fool too long. You don't want me anymore."

"No," he admitted softly. "I don't." How strange. It was true. He didn't want her, not even to salve the pride she had hurt by cheating on him and leaving him for another man. He had dreamed of Cassie returning to him, begging him to take her back. But now that she had done it, he felt only a faint pity. There was no longer any room in his heart for her.

Because his heart was completely filled with Emily.

He loved Emily. Adam felt like laughing out loud, and it was all he could do to refrain from breaking into a grin that would be inappropriate to their conversation. He loved Emily. Why had it taken him so long to realize it? He couldn't believe he'd spent the past week analyzing his feelings, trying to figure out if he loved her, when it was so blindingly obvious that he did.

For some reason it had taken Cassie's asking him to take her back to make him realize it. It was only when he had the chance to get what he had thought he wanted so badly, Cassie's love, that he knew he didn't want it at all. His love and life were already given to Emily.

It had snuck up on him over the past few months, growing slowly and steadily from a desire to help her to a physical desire for her to a strong, sure love. Or perhaps it had been coming on even longer than that. Perhaps the roots of his feelings for Emily had been there for years, growing in the sun of their friendship and their easy working relationship. Could it be that Cassie had been on the right track when she'd hinted that Emily had kept him at the office? He knew he hadn't stayed at the office nearly as much the past few weeks as he had when he was married to Cassie. Was it because now he could take Emily home with him?

Well, it didn't matter now. For once he wasn't going to waste time trying to analyze, categorize or understand. It was enough simply to feel. He loved Emily. He wanted to marry her. That conclusion flowed readily now from the other one. He wanted to spend his life with her. And he wanted to rush to her and tell her.

Which brought him back to Cassie. He glanced at her uncertainly. She had turned and picked up her purse, and was now rummaging through it for a tissue. "I'm sorry." She wiped away her tears. "I've made an idiot of myself."

"Don't say that."

"No. It's the truth. I should have known." Cassie offered him a brittle smile. "It's too late for us. You can't go back and mend things once you've torn them up. It's crazy to even try. They're never the same." She tucked her purse under her arm. "I guess I'll get the same attorney." She paused. "I'm sorry for the pain I caused you."

He shook his head, struggling to hold in his glee until after she had gone. "It's long over, Cass. Don't worry about it."

She smiled again, a tremulous smile that once would have torn him in two. Now he simply smiled perfunctorily, waiting for her to leave. She was turning away when suddenly the door opened, cracking loudly in the silence, and they both jumped and whirled to face it.

Emily had managed to reach the bathroom and lock herself in one of the stalls before the tears came. She had leaned against the cool, metal wall and cried for her shattered dreams. She had known. She had known that it couldn't last, that Adam still loved his ex-wife. Why in the world had she allowed herself to hope?

Finally, when her sobs quieted, Emily had dug several tissues out of her purse and wiped away the tears, then blown her nose. Thank heavens no one had come into the rest room while she was crying. The humiliation on top of all the rest would have been too much. She left the stall and went to the mirror above the sink to inspect the damage. She looked a mess, just as she'd expected. Her eyes were red and puffy from crying, her face blotched.

Emily sighed, wet a paper towel, and wiped her face with it, then blotted her face dry. She stared at herself in the mirror as if her image would somehow give her the answers. What should she do?

Well, she certainly couldn't stay in there hiding the rest of her life. She had to face Adam sometime. It would be easier to get it over with now. No doubt he would be embarrassed about facing her, looking for a way to break it to her gently that he and Cassie were back together. There was no point in making it any harder for him than it already was.

She should gather her courage and go back to her office. When Adam came in she would tell him that she understood. She would say that he didn't need to explain. She had seen Cassie going into his office, and she had known immediately that he and Cassie would get back together. She pictured herself shrugging and smiling gamely, pretending that she had never considered their affair to be anything more than a temporary diversion. She had known all along that Adam still loved Cassie. Naturally, if Cassie was free again....

Tears sprang into her eyes, and Emily moaned softly. She put her palms down on the counter and leaned forward. Her head touched the mirror, and she knocked it against the glass again, harder. How could she possibly say that? How could she smile and let Adam go gracefully, when all she wanted to do was cry? Yet she knew that she had to let him go; there was no way she could hold him. If she didn't struggle, there would be less pain. Maybe she could retain some small relationship with him.

But, no, that was impossible. She wouldn't be able to work for him any longer. She couldn't stand to go to the office day after day and be in close contact with him, to hear him and see him and not be able to touch him, to feel the

ove pouring through her and not be able to express it. It
vould be too awful to bear. She couldn't. The only thing to
lo was to quit her job and never see Adam. She'd tell him
hat, too. She would hand in her resignation this afternoon
ind stay only long enough to train another secretary.

She closed her eyes, but the searing tears leaked through
ind streamed down her cheeks. Oh, Adam! How could she
tand it? It wasn't just that her heart was breaking. Her
vhole world was crumbling.

Why hadn't she left well enough alone? Why had she ever
igreed to Adam's crazy scheme in the first place? Why had
he let herself get so involved with him? If only things had
emained as they were she wouldn't be experiencing such
iurt now. She had known she wasn't woman enough to keep
\dam. Why hadn't she simply stayed the way she was? Why
iad she fixed her hair and bought new clothes and tried to
urn herself into something she was not? Why had she de-
:ided to change?

Because Adam had made love to her. He had been with
ier and enjoyed her company. He had wanted her. And that
iad changed her. Emily looked up and met her reflection in
he mirror. Wide, gray eyes gazed back at her gravely.

Once she had been a mouse, creeping through life—
Ireaming, but never hoping; wanting, but never trying;
vishing, but never believing. Then Adam had taken her in
iis arms and made love to her and showed her a whole new
elf. Bathed in the warmth of his affection and passion, she
iad uncurled from her cocoon and stretched her damp, bent
vings. She had tried at last, and she had obtained some-
hing because of it, more than she had ever dreamed she
vould have. She had discovered that there was beauty in her,
ind she had released it. She had released her passion. Her
ove. Her soul.

Emily stared at herself in the mirror. She wasn't the sam
She could no longer believe that she wasn't pretty. She ha
seen the proof of it in men's eyes. She had seen the truth
the mirror. She wasn't unattractive. She wasn't benea
Adam's touch. His family hadn't scorned her, had they? H
friends hadn't laughed her out of the club, had they? SI
wasn't the same person. She couldn't fool herself ai
longer.

And she couldn't go back to being the little mouse sI
once had been.

Emily set down her purse on the counter. She took ai
other tissue from it and blew her nose again. She looke
down at her purse for a moment, then opened it and wit
shaking fingers pulled out the small, floral-patterned co
metics bag inside. It scared her to death. She could hard
bear to think about it. There was no way she could be
Cassie in battle over Adam. Yet she knew that she could r
longer simply stand back and not even try.

She repaired her makeup as quickly and neatly as he
trembling fingers allowed, often having to stop and redo
spot. But soon she had wiped away the smudged masca
and highlighted her eyes once more, had hidden the blotch
with foundation, and had turned her colorless lips pin
again. Then she took out her brush and ran it through he
hair, fluffing it out around her face, soft and sunny.

She repacked her purse and studied her reflection. SI
looked a great deal better, but it wasn't enough. This bus
ness suit, while attractive, wasn't alluring. A wicked smi
curved her lips, and Emily slipped off the suit jacket.

Beneath the jacket she wore a soft, sheer blouse of pale
lavender. It went beautifully with the suit, and that was wl
she had bought it. But it was very sheer, so she always ke
her jacket on over it, buttoned, so that only the high, fra

le, fluted collar and a V of material were visible within the neckline of the jacket. Without the jacket it would make quite an impact on the male senses.

She could see the outline of her slip beneath the blouse. Emily frowned. That wasn't the effect she wanted. She went into a stall, stripped off the blouse and slip, and replaced the blouse. She returned to the mirror and smiled. That was more like it. The soft lavender material fell over her breasts, light as a spiderweb, its touch making her nipples tighten. It veiled her breasts, not quite concealing, yet not brazenly revealing, either. One could see the darker shadow of her nipples just enough to entice a man and make him long to see more.

Satisfied, Emily slipped her jacket back on and stuffed her slip into her purse. She left the bathroom and walked down the long hall, then turned the corner. The door to Adam's office was still closed. She stepped into her own office and set down her purse, then removed the concealing jacket and tossed it across the chair. Taking a deep breath, she walked across the hall and opened the door to Adam's office.

Cassie was standing on this side of Adam's desk, facing him, her purse tucked under her arm. Adam stood on the other side of the desk, his face filled with emotion. They both swung toward the door, startled, as Emily came in. Emily's heart sank at the sight of Adam's glowing face, but she refused to cave in now. She pasted a bright smile on her face. "Why, hello, Cassie. I didn't realize you were still here."

Cassie stared at her blankly. Emily sauntered across the room to stand beside Adam. Adam watched her approach, his eyes dropping to the front of her blouse. He wet his lips.

Neither he nor Cassie spoke. Emily didn't stop until she wa standing so close to Adam that they were almost touching "Hello, sweetheart," she greeted him, gazing up with wid flirtatious eyes. She laid a proprietary hand on his chest an went up on tiptoe to kiss him.

For a moment Adam didn't respond, but Emily presse her mouth firmly against his, sliding the tip of her tongu between his lips, and then suddenly, fervently, he was kis ing her back. One of his hands came up to cup Emily's nec and the other went to her back, pulling her closer. His r sponse startled Emily so much that she almost drew bacl but his hands tightened and wouldn't let her go until he ha kissed her thoroughly. Only then did his fingers relax, an Emily slid back down, her feet once again flat on the floo She stared at him, bemused and aroused, her cheeks flushe with heat. She glanced around the room and saw that it wa empty. Cassie had left sometime during their kiss, closin the door behind her.

Emily looked back at Adam. She didn't know what to say What in the world was going on?

Adam grinned down at her. He knew he looked perfectl sappy, but he didn't care. He felt perfectly sappy. "Wha was that for?"

"What?"

He chuckled. "Did it blow a fuse? The kiss, silly. An that less-than-subtle bursting-in on Cassie and me. Th stroll across the room." He ran a hand slowly down fror her shoulder to her waist, sliding it amorously over he breast, and his eyes darkened. "That come-hither blouse. got the feeling you were establishing your territory. Am right?"

Emily tilted her chin. "Maybe. What was Cassie her for?"

"Jealous?" he asked, a faint smile clinging to his lips. His and stole back up, seemingly fascinated by the dark circle f her nipple. His thumb traced it through her blouse. Emily ent weak and hot all over.

"Yes."

"Good." He drew her to him for a deep, slow kiss. Emily ung to him for support. Finally he pulled away. His voice as shaky. "I don't want another office scene. This is too nportant for that. I'm going to take you home."

Emily nodded. She was stunned and confused, but she asn't about to question her good fortune. Adam was tak- g *her* home, not Cassie, and he was kissing her and look- g at her as if he wanted to eat her up. That was all she eeded to know at the moment.

They left his office and strolled to the elevator, Adam's rm around her, pressing her tightly against his side, obli- ious to the startled glances of the people they met in the all. Adam had never openly shown his affection for her in he office before, but Emily wasn't about to question that, ither.

They rode the elevator down to the car, and he drove uickly to his condominium, ignoring speed limits and rac- g through several yellow lights along the way. But when ey stepped inside his home and he began to love her, all his urry ceased. He took his time unfastening her clothes and ulling them from her, interspersing the undressing with isses wherever he'd just removed a garment. By the time he nished Emily was limp and liquid, yet her nerves sizzled ith excitement. He kissed her, his tongue caressing her nouth. His hands roamed her body, touching her with fire, nd Emily's hands moved just as frantically over him. She nfastened his shirt and slid her hands beneath the cloth, her ingers making a path through the tangled curls of his chest

hair to the flat, masculine nipples. He sucked in his brea
when she touched him there, and his mouth widened, as
to take all of her in. Her fingernails trailed across his ski
with thumbs and forefingers she teased his nipples in
pointing hardness.

Adam groaned and shrugged out of his shirt. Emily
hands drifted lovingly over his naked torso. Adam's finge
dug into her buttocks, fitting her against the hard demar
of his pelvis. Emily arched up to him, aroused by the feel
his need. They moved against each other, skin rubbing ov
skin, delighting in the differing textures, the sensual fri
tion. Their desire fed each other's and their passion sp
raled.

He swung her into his arms and carried her into the be
room, and Emily nestled against him, feeling feminine ar
delicate and loved. He laid her down on the bed and strippe
off the rest of his clothes, his eyes touching her body as h
hands ached to. Then he went to her, and Emily opened h
arms to receive him. He lay upon her, resting his weight c
his forearms, and bent his head to feast on her breasts. I
loved her with his mouth, taking her breasts with infini
slowness and care. His mouth roamed lower. His tong
traced patterns on her sensitive skin and delved into th
shallow well of her navel. Emily moved her legs restlessl
aching for fulfillment, while his tongue teased and caress
and laved her, awakening every nerve in her body.

"Adam, please," she moaned. "Please, please love me."

He moved up and into her, his hands lifting her hips
receive his thrust. He filled her, his love hard and stror
within her. He moved, and she moved with him, boun
through their bodies to their souls. Adam buried his fac
against her neck, mumbling something she couldn't unde
stand, as he moved faster and faster. They hurtled upwar

and crashed in a shattering summit of feelings, melded together in a blinding flash.

They clung together for a long time afterward, stunned by the intensity of the experience, not wanting to let go. But finally Adam rolled his weight from Emily and cradled her against him. He ran a lazy hand up and down her side as they lay together, feeling their racing hearts slow and their breathing become easier, returning slowly, reluctantly, to normality.

"Why did you come into my office like that?" Adam asked at last, when he was again able to speak rationally.

Emily was incapable of evading him now. "Because I saw Cassie go in there. I thought—" She drew a shaky breath. "I'd heard she had left her husband, and I thought she must want you back. I knew I had lost you, and I went down to the rest room and cried. Then I thought about what I ought to say to you, how I had to set you free so you wouldn't feel guilty. And I realized that I couldn't do that. I couldn't fade back into the woodwork and give you up. I knew I had to fight for you. So I went to your office."

He smiled. "I'd say you put up a pretty good fight. That blouse was a powerful weapon." He paused. "Why did you think that if Cassie wanted me back, I'd go?"

Emily rose up on her elbow and looked at him. "You loved her; you were devastated when she left you. I knew you hadn't ever recovered from that. You still love her."

"You know, it's weird. I thought that, too. For a long, long time I wanted Cassie back. I dreamed of her returning and telling me she loved me, that she'd made a mistake. But today when she came in I looked at her, and her beauty didn't move me anymore. She told me she still loved me, and I didn't care. I didn't want her." He gazed at Emily. Her eyes shone. "I realized that you were the one I loved. The only one I wanted. Whatever I'd felt before—hurt, love, wounded masculine pride—was gone. You'd taken it away and left me filled with love." He traced her mouth with his thumb. "I love you, Emily. I love you more than anything on earth."

"Adam!" The word came out as little more than a whisper, but it was charged with wonder and joy. "Oh, Adam!"

She bent and kissed him, and he felt the faint trembling of her lips. When she raised her head, huge tears glistened in her eyes. "What about you?" Adam asked softly. "Are you going to keep me in suspense? How do you feel about me?"

"Surely you must know!" Emily returned, astounded. "I love you. I've loved you for years and years."

His eyes widened. "What?"

"I've loved you from the very beginning, since I first started working for you."

"All that time?" Emily nodded. "Through my marriage, the divorce, everything?" She nodded again, and Adam cupped his hand around the back of her neck, pulling her down for a quick, hard kiss. "Emily, Emily, when I think of what I've been missing all these years..."

She smiled and cuddled into his arm blissfully. Quietly Adam said, "I want to marry you."

"What?" Again astonishment brought Emily upright. "Adam, you must be joking!"

He lifted his eyebrows. "Why? It seems pretty logical to me. We love each other. I want to marry you. What's strange about that?"

"But you couldn't. What would your family say? Your friends?"

"They're not marrying you; I am. Besides, why should they say anything except 'congratulations'?"

"Because I'm not—" She stopped, swallowing her words—good enough, pretty enough, bright enough. Perhaps she wasn't any of those things. But Adam thought she was. Adam loved her. And she knew there was one way in which she surpassed all women. She loved him more than anyone else in the world ever could. Emily smiled. "Yes. Yes, I'll marry you."

Adam smiled back at her, and his hands framed her face. "Good. Then don't you think we should celebrate?"

Slowly his hands drew her face down to his. He kissed her, and his arms went around her. Emily released a tiny sigh of pure happiness, safe and secure in the only place she'd ever wanted to be.

You won't want to miss a single one of the heart-felt stories presented by Silhouette Special Edition; and when you take advantage of this special offer, you won't have to.

You'll also receive a FREE subscription to the Silhouette Books Newsletter as long as you remain a member. Each lively issue is filled with news on upcoming titles, interviews with your favorite authors, even their favorite recipes.

To become a home subscriber and receive your first 4 books FREE, fill out and mail the coupon today!

## *Silhouette Special Edition*®

Silhouette Books, 120 Brighton Rd., P.O. Box 5084, Clifton, NJ 07015-5084

# READERS' COMMENTS ON
# SILHOUETTE INTIMATE MOMENTS:

"About a month ago a friend loaned me my first Silhouette. I was thoroughly surprised as well as totally addicted. Last week I read a Silhouette Intimate Moments and I was even more pleased. They are the best romance series novels I have ever read. They give much more depth to the plot, characters, and the story is fundamentally realistic. They incorporate tasteful sex scenes, which is a must, especially in the 1980's. I only hope you can publish them fast enough."

S.B.*, Lees Summit, MO

"After noticing the attractive covers on the new line of Silhouette Intimate Moments, I decided to read the inside and discovered that this new line was more in the line of books that I like to read. I do want to say I enjoyed the books because they are so realistic and a lot more truthful than so many romance books today."

J.C., Onekama, MI

"I would like to compliment you on your books. I will continue to purchase all of the Silhouette Intimate Moments. They are your best line of books that I have had the pleasure of reading."

S.M., Billings, MT

*names available on request